Lon saw that the man wore a helmet, but it had no faceplate, nothing to disguise the look of naked hatred on the face. The man held his rifle in his left hand, like a shield—and his right hand held a machete. Lon swung at the arm holding the knife and moved in closer, trying to bring his rifle up to use the butt against the man's head. But they collided and went down together. Lon found himself on the bottom, his rifle out of his hands, holding onto the wrists of his assailant—who had also lost or discarded his rifle. The man still had the long knife though, and was doing everything he could to use it against Lon . . .

Ace Books by Rick Shelley

OFFICER-CADET

RICK SHELLEY

ACE BOOKS, NEW YORK

This book is an Ace original edition,
and has never been previously published.

OFFICER-CADET

An Ace Book / published by arrangement with
the author

PRINTING HISTORY
Ace edition / May 1998

The Penguin Putnam Inc. World Wide Web site address is
http://www.penguinputnam.com

Check out the ACE Science Fiction & Fantasy newsletter, and much
more at Club PPI!

ISBN: 0-441-00526-8

ACE®
Ace Books are published by The Berkley Publishing Group,
a division of Penguin Putnam Inc.,
375 Hudson Street, New York, NY 10014.
ACE and the "A" design are trademarks
belonging to Penguin Putnam, Inc.

PRINTED IN THE UNITED STATES OF AMERICA

10 9 8 7 6 5

The year is A.D. 2803. The interstellar diaspora from Earth has been in progress for nearly seven centuries. The numbers are uncertain, but at least five hundred worlds have been settled, and perhaps well over a thousand. The total human population of the galaxy could be in excess of a trillion. On Earth, the Confederation of Human Worlds still theoretically controls all of those colonies, but the reality is that it can count on its orders being obeyed only as far as the most distant permanent outpost within Earth's system, on Titan. Beyond Saturn, there are two primary interstellar political groupings, the Confederation of Human Worlds (broken away from the organization on Earth with the same name, with its capital on the world known as Union) and the Second Commonwealth, centered on Buckingham. Neither of those political unions is as large or as powerful as they will be in another two centuries, when their diametrically opposed interests finally bring them to the point of war. In the meantime, humans who need military assistance, and do not want the domination of either Confederation or Commonwealth, have only a handful of options. Those who can afford it turn to mercenaries. And the largest source of those is on the world of Dirigent. . . .

Prologue

The series of sonic booms came as no surprise. Lieutenant Arlan Taiters scarcely blinked. Mentally, he counted the snap-roar reports of attack shuttles coming in hot. Six: Three companies were coming in at once. One lander had come in earlier, more sedately, with the dead and wounded—too many of each. It was always too many, but it could have been worse. The Belatrong contract had been short, if bloodier than anticipated. At least that was the early scuttlebutt on base. The rumors had started floating through the regiments as soon as the first messages had arrived from the returning ship when it broke out of Q-space entering the Dirigent system three days earlier.

Arlan stared out the lone window of his tiny office. He stood so close to the window that his shadow made the office seem dark. Through unconscious habit, he stood at a rigid parade rest—legs slightly spread, hands clasped behind his back. He found that as comfortable a stance as any. Only his green eyes moved. He had glanced upward briefly during the thunder of returning attack landers, even though he had known that he would not be able to see them, then returned to his casual survey of the regimental area. The shadows outside were starting to creep onto the parade ground.

The shadows inside the office—Taiters rarely turned on an inside light during daylight hours—made the room look even starker than it was. Nothing suggested that Taiters had occupied the office for three years, since he had won his commission. There was little to suggest that *anyone* ever used the room. The small desk and straight chair had become antiques through the simple expedient of surviving in place. They had been inexpensive but functional to start with and had gained no value by virtue of age. They remained serviceable decades after purchase. The complink was nearly as old. The room held no other furnishings or decorations. Arlan did not use the office much. It simply gave him a place to work on the reports that he had to complete each week, a place to talk to his men privately. And it provided a modest extension to his living quarters— an adjoining room that was scarcely larger than the office.

When the knock came at the hall door, Arlan pivoted toward it and said, "Enter."

The soldier came in, shut the door behind him, and snapped to attention. He saluted and said, "Cadet Lon Nolan reporting as ordered, sir."

Arlan straightened up to attention and returned the salute. Although Taiters had spent most of the day training with his two platoons, his camouflage battledress appeared fresh. "At ease, Cadet," he said. Both men relaxed—slightly.

"We don't have nearly as much time for this as I would have liked," Taiters said. "Regimental Honors Parade will be called in ten minutes or less." He stared at the new apprentice officer, evaluating. Lon Nolan was two inches taller than the lieutenant but weighed about the same. Nolan looked considerably younger than the twenty-two years his dossier showed. He looked as if he had not yet completely matured physically. *An illusion,* Taiters reminded himself. *They always look too damn young.*

"For now, I just want to make absolutely certain that you know your place in the organization, Cadet. You are not in line of command. You do not outrank anyone. Bottom of the heap. No man commands other men in the Corps until he has been in combat himself. It doesn't matter how many fancy military academies he has *almost* graduated from, or how long he has worn the uniform of the Dirigent

Mercenary Corps.'' The lieutenant held a small metal device up in front of Lon, a lieutenant's dress uniform insignia—diamond-shaped, of gold, with a red enamel diamond in the center. ''These have to be earned. Is that clear?''

''Yes, sir,'' Lon replied crisply. His eyes did not waver. The same message had been drilled into him over and over since his arrival on Dirigent. He thought that it was a good policy—though it would never have been practical back on Earth.

''Any questions, Cadet?''

''Just one, sir.'' *For now,* Lon thought. ''How soon can I expect combat?''

Arlan allowed himself a slow blink. The question was the . . . anticipated one. ''I'm not on the Council of Regiments, Cadet. I doubt that it will be very long, though. We've been on the ground quite a while without a paying contract.'' He did not elaborate beyond that, about the expectations of the Corps, that the ideal the Council of Regiments strove for was to have eight of the fourteen regiments occupied on paying contracts at any one time while three recuperated and trained and three handled Dirigent's planetary defense. The ideal was rarely realized. At present not quite half of the Corps' men were on contract.

''Thank you, sir,'' Lon said.

''Administratively, you are assigned to the second squad of third platoon,'' Taiters said. He did not bother to add the rest: A Company, Second Battalion, Seventh Regiment, or—in the more common military shorthand—A-2-7. ''That is Corporal Girana's squad. You'd better haul your duffel up to the barracks, find Girana, and get yourself squared away in a hurry, Cadet. You may have less than five minutes before parade.''

''Yes, sir.'' Lon stiffened to attention again, saluted, and left as soon as the lieutenant returned the salute.

''Too damned young,'' Arlan muttered after he heard Lon Nolan's boots hurrying along the corridor toward the stairs that led upstairs to third platoon's squad bays. He returned to the window and stared outside again. *Too young, and too eager.* Taiters was a decade older than the cadet. He had been in the Seventh Regiment of the Dirigent Mercenary Corps—DMC—for all of that decade and more. He was a native Dirigenter. His father and both grandfathers—and most of the men in his family for the past five generations—had been in the Corps, most of them in the Seventh Regiment. There had never been any doubt that Arlan would enlist as soon as he turned eighteen. It was in his blood, and in his upbringing. The commission *had* been something of a surprise when it was offered.

The two-toned parade call sounded over speakers that ringed the drill field. "Stand to for Regimental Honors Parade," came next. Arlan took a deep breath and turned away from the window. He did not run for the hall door. Instead, he walked, almost casually, to his room next door for a quick drink of water. Then he got his fatigue cap and adjusted it carefully as he checked his appearance in the mirror. By the time he got outside, most of the men of his two platoons were already in place—or hurrying to get there—ready for the command to "Fall in."

It was an ancient ritual, centuries if not millennia old, differing only in details from one army to the next, or from generation to generation. The enlisted men hurried to their positions in ranks. The corporals and sergeants made sure that their men were present and that the formation was acceptable. By that time the platoon leaders and company commanders would be stepping into position in front of their units, ready to receive the manning reports of their subordinates, and then to do about-faces to report to their superiors. Arlan could rarely escape recalling an observation that his father had made many years before. "It's the military ballet, boy." Arlan had never seen ballet (nor had his father—entertainments on Dirigent were rarely so lofty). But the phrase had left an impression.

Taiters moved to his accustomed spot in front of the third and fourth platoons of A-2-7. Sergeant Ivar Dendrow did an about-face, saluted, and reported, "Third platoon all present, sir." Arlan returned the salute. Sergeant Weil Jorgen snapped to and reported, "Fourth platoon all present or accounted for, sir." Fourth had one man in hospital. Again, Arlan returned the salute and did his own about-face. To his left, Lieutenant Carl Hoper was reporting on the first and second platoons. As soon as Hoper had finished, Taiters saluted and called out his own report: "Third and fourth platoons all present or accounted for, sir." Captain Matt Orlis returned Arlan's salute and turned to report to the battalion commander, who reported to the regimental commander, who reported to the General—the head of the Council of Regiments. Around the vast parade field, similar formations were being held by each of the regiments that had men on base.

The Corps was put at parade rest. The troops had a ten-minute wait before the buses carrying the returning soldiers came into view. The Corps was called to attention again. While the buses drove across the center of the field, between the ranks of the waiting regiments, the colors of each regiment were dipped in salute, in turn. The officers held hand salutes. The men in ranks stood at rigid attention.

The buses moved in their own formation. The lead vehicle was well ahead of the others, strictly alone, traveling at seven miles per hour. Regimental colors flew from either fender. Crossed white and black pennants were attached to either side of the vehicle. Every man watching—save for those few who were too new to the Corps to know what it signified—stared, sharing the same thought. *This is how I'll come home for the last time if I'm killed in battle.* The dead of the DMC always came home first—if it was possible to bring them home at all.

Once the lead bus cleared the field, it sped away. The rest increased their pace as they passed in review. After the last was gone, the regiments were dismissed. The returning warriors had been properly honored for a victory—a fulfilled contract.

1

"Hey, Nolan! Where do you think you're going?'' Corporal Tebba Girana shouted as Lon started away from the dismissed honors formation.

"Back to the barracks, Corporal. I didn't have time to get all of my gear squared away."

"Forget it for now. That'll wait. The mess hall is this way." Tebba pointed. Girana was a little below average height for Dirigent (five feet, eleven inches for men) but built stockily. Solidly muscled, he was a veteran of more than fifteen years in the Corps. He pushed himself harder than he pushed any of his men, and he kept himself as fit as he had been when he finished recruit training when he was eighteen years old. There was no room in the DMC for flabby soldiers—not even officers, let alone noncoms. If a man could no longer pass muster, he was gone. Even the regimental commanders had to meet physical training standards each year.

"I don't mind missing a meal, Corporal," Lon said. "I'm really not all that hungry."

"Well, *I* mind. The lieutenant says I gotta get you up to speed in a hurry. We might get a contract almost anytime. And missing meals when you don't have to is a bad habit to get into. There'll be times enough in the field when rations are short. Body's gotta have fuel to work right."

Nolan had been under military discipline too long, on Earth and Dirigent, to argue any longer. He nodded and walked with Girana toward the mess hall. Automatically,

Lon fell in step with the corporal. After more than three years at The Springs, the military academy of the North American Union, and two months of recruit training on Dirigent, Lon could scarcely walk anywhere with anyone *without* subconsciously walking in step.

More than three years, almost four, Lon thought. It was still hard to accept the sudden and unexpected change in his life. He had been less than eight months from graduation at The Springs, and his commission in the NAU Army. Ranked third in his class at the beginning of his senior year and with a spotless disciplinary record, he had looked forward to rapid promotion and a good career. And then the bottom had fallen out.

"It's a good life here, most of the time," Girana said, and Lon realized that he had missed whatever the corporal had said before that. "An honorable life for a man."

"I never wanted to be anything but a soldier," Lon said, hoping that it would sound as if he had been following what Girana had been saying. *I never wanted to be anything but a soldier.* That was the problem. That was why the bottom had felt as if it had been yanked out from under him at The Springs.

"I don't imagine you'd have faced the sort of operations we do," Girana said. "Earth is so damned crowded. I doubt that the total population of all the worlds I've been on add up to a third of the people who live on Earth. Of course, I've only been on a small fraction of the worlds that people live on."

"Does anyone even know how many planets have been settled?" Lon asked. "Back home—back on Earth, I mean—there'd be a different number anywhere you looked."

Girana grinned. "I'd guess that Corps Intelligence has a pretty good count on the number of worlds. That's their pidgin, after all. You never know where you might find a contract. There must be more than a thousand settled worlds. Maybe half as many space habitats. Now, *those* are hairy for a foot soldier.''

"I can imagine," Lon said. It was something he had never considered. He started to think about the possibilities, but Girana kept talking.

"Like fighting with your hands tied behind your back. You can't use half your weapons because you might breach hull integrity. Zero gravity—or, at best, partial gravity from spin—I don't think any of the deepers bother with anything near full gravity. Sure not on the few habitats I've been to.''

"I think Over-Galapagos keeps its outer levels at seventy percent, but I know what you mean," Lon said. "I guess if they wanted full gravity, they'd have stayed on the dirt, like us.''

"Yeah, something like that," Girana agreed. "They're a weird lot, the deepers, the few I've come across.''

"I spent eleven days at Over-Galapagos on the way here. That was the first permanent deeper structure over Earth, out at geo-stationary. Something like twenty-five thousand people live there permanently, and there are always a few hundred temporaries—or so I was told. I had to wait to change transport coming here. Eat, sleep, and exercise so your bones don't soften up, and all the other stuff. Most of the folks don't live out where they'd have seventy percent gravity. There's not much time for anything else. I don't know how they get anything done.''

"They don't, not much," Girana said with the unquestioning confidence of a man who knew almost nothing about it. "The deepers are a dead end. Freaks. Another fifty years, most of those habs will be deserted. It's just not natural for people to live out in space like that.''

Maybe, but I doubt it, Lon thought. He would not openly disagree with the corporal, not within thirty minutes after joining his squad. There were millions of people living in space habitats. Some of the habs had been in constant use for nearly five centuries. It was hard to write their inhabitants off as freaks on a dead end.

The first and second battalions of Seventh Regiment shared a mess hall, but each company had its own dining room. They were on two floors, ranged around the central core that allowed Food Services access to each of them. Girana led Lon up to the second floor and through a door marked A-2-7.

"We eat good in garrison," Girana said as they moved toward the cafeteria-style serving line. "Civilian cooks, good chow, and plenty of it. It makes up for the lean times."

"You talk like nobody ever eats on a campaign," Lon said.

"Contract, not campaign," Tebba corrected absently. "Naw, it's not that so much. Just, well, sometimes it's hard to get your fill in the field. Battle rations may provide all the stuff that a body needs, but it don't always fill you up right. And there's times when even the BR packets don't get around on time."

The serving trays were large, and Girana took liberal portions of just about everything as he moved along the line—and the available choices were quite broad. Nolan took less, but more than he had expected. The aromas were enticing enough to waken his appetite. *I guess I'm hungrier than I thought,* he decided with a thin smile. The drinks carousel had everything but alcoholic beverages.

Nearly half of the men in the company had reached the dining hall ahead of Girana and Nolan. There was already considerable noise—people talking as they settled in at their places and started to eat. But the noise never became overwhelming. Acoustical ceiling panels kept the sound level bearable. The dining halls at The Springs had never been so relaxed. There, it was all sit at attention on the edge of your seat. Don't speak unless you're spoken to by a superior, and *then* keep your response down to the fewest

syllables possible—"Yes, sir," and "No, sir," were preferred. Eat by the numbers. Finish and get out. The mess
hall of the training battalion on Dirigent had been less for-
mal, but the training had been so long and arduous that few
of the recruits had retained energy for talk when they came
in from the field at the end of each day. There had been
times when just staying awake through the meal had been
an almost insurmountable challenge.

I like this place, Lon told himself before he got to the
table or took his first bite of supper. The colors were warm,
the atmosphere friendly. Between the serving line and the
table, Girana stopped a half dozen times to return greetings
or to say something to someone at one of the other tables.
Lon found himself more relaxed than he had been in ages.
It felt good.

The men of second squad had reached their table more
or less together. Including Girana, there were eleven regular
members of the squad. They were one man short of full
manning. Until Lon received his commission, he would
make up the difference. Girana seated the cadet next to him
at one end of the long table and introduced the new man
to the rest of the squad. Lon concentrated on the names and
the faces that went with them. Remembering names had
never come easily for him. These were men he would go
into combat with, at least once. And, unless things went
terribly wrong, Lon might command these same men someday. He had to know them.

Janno Belzer had curly black hair and eyes, and an olive
complexion. He was tall and thin. Dean Ericks was blond,
with light brown eyes and the sort of pallor common to
people who never got out in the sun. He seemed to be
almost exactly Lon's size and build. Phip Steesen was
shorter, with a receding hairline; the hair, what was left,
was an indeterminate brown. Gen Radnor was big and
beefy, dark hair, bushy eyebrows, and sunken dark eyes.
He seemed to be the most reticent of the men in the squad.
Lance Corporal Dav Grott was the assistant squad leader.

He looked older than his thirty-two years, as if he had lived a particularly hard life. Frank Raiz was the youngest member of the squad—excluding Lon—at twenty-three. He kept his scalp shaved. It gave him a fierce look. Raphael Macken was the kind of man who could escape notice in a group of three. Tod Schpelt was distinguished by an accent different from the rest, despite the fact that his family had been on Dirigent for three generations—still newcomers. Harvey Fehr concentrated on his eating. Lon did not hear him speak at all during that meal. Balt Hoper was a distant cousin of Lieutenant Carl Hoper, platoon leader for the company's first and second platoons.

The first real question, after all of the greetings and exchanges of names, was, "Where are you from?" Lon's accent did place him as an off-worlder.

"Earth," Lon said, without really thinking about it. He was cutting into his roast. The sudden silence that greeted his announcement made him look up. He scanned the faces that were staring at him—everyone but Girana and Fehr.

"Did I say something wrong?" Lon asked.

A couple of heads shook. A couple of mumbled negatives were voiced. "You caught us off guard," Janno Belzer said. "I don't think I've ever met anyone who came right from Earth."

"You pulled a fast one on us, Tebba," Dean Ericks accused, pointing his fork at the corporal. "You shoulda warned us."

Girana grinned. "What, and spoil the fun? And you can bet you've met guys from Earth before. There must be sixty or seventy in the Corps, maybe more. There's always some."

"Hey, a couple of million people a year go outsystem from Earth. They've got to be around *somewhere*," Lon said.

"Maybe they lie about where they're from," Phip Steesen suggested. That drew a laugh from most of his squadmates.

"Could be," Lon said, falling into the bantering spirit more easily than he would have guessed possible. "They probably don't want to hurt any colonials' feelings."

"I hear they's so many folks on Earth now that they gotta sleep in shifts, that there ain't enough room for them all to lay down at once," Dean said.

"Naw, the problem is they spend so much time in the sack that they make more people than they know what to do with," Phip said before Lon could respond.

Supper went on at length. Now and then someone would get up to go back through the serving line. Someone else would make a run to the drinks carousel with a tray to bring back refills for anyone who wanted them. Lon continued to do more listening than talking, but he did answer questions when they came his way. Janno, Dean, and Phip did most of the talking for the veterans in the squad. Lon's longest contribution came when one of them asked why he had come to Dirigent.

"Now, that's the kind of question you don't have to answer, Nolan," Girana said, scowling down the table at the person who had asked it. "Every man's past is his own."

"I don't mind." Lon shrugged. "It's probably better that I do talk about it. I haven't had much chance. Sometimes I'm not sure that I really . . . comprehend everything about it." After that, he had the full attention of everyone at the table. Even Fehr looked up from his eating.

"Since I was little, I never wanted to be anything other than a soldier," Lon said. "Now, it was never just a kid thing with toy soldiers and playing war. Even when I was only, oh, six or seven, that's what I wanted to be. The older I got, the more set I was. I wanted to be a soldier. When I was in my junior year of high school, I took the preliminaries for competitive appointment to The Springs—the North American Military Academy—passed, and went on to the second round of testing." He paused long enough to take a last bite of his dessert and to wash it down with a long sip of coffee.

"I won the appointment, went to The Springs, and did fairly well. By the start of my final year, I was . . . near enough the top to look forward to a good career in the NAU Army." There was no point in bragging that he had been ranked third. "Then the commandant called me into his office." Lon paused for a long time then, but no one said anything. He was remembering that morning when his carefully planned future had been taken away from him. In his mind, he relived the interview with the commandant, hardly aware that he was describing the events to his new squadmates at the same time.

"Cadet Nolan reporting as ordered, sir." Lon had been nervous about the summons to the commandant's office, but he could not think of anything he might have done that would call for disciplinary action, even though he did not know of anyone who had ever been called in for anything else. In the few minutes he had been given to prepare himself, Lon had thought back over everything he had done recently, and he could conceive of no reason why he might be called to account.

Commandant Banks returned Nolan's salute. "Sit down," he said, gesturing to a chair near the corner of his desk. That invitation was more of a shock to Lon than the summons had been. He sat on the edge of the seat, at attention, the way he had always been forced to sit as a plebe. The commandant swiveled his own chair until he was facing Lon.

"Relax. You're not on the carpet," Banks said, correctly gauging Lon's worries. "Far from it. You have one of the most nearly spotless records I've seen in my years at The Springs. In a way, that makes what I have to say even more difficult."

"Sir?"

"I have received a directive from the Secretary of Defense," Banks said. "The curriculum for the spring semester will be drastically changed for this year's first classmen, concentrating on riot control and criminal justice topics. And the top one hundred and fifty members of your graduating class will be transferred to the Department of Justice for commissioning in the NAU Federal Police. No exceptions will be permitted."

Lon did not realize that he had fallen silent, lost in his memories, until Phip asked, "So what'd you do, resign?"

Slowly, Lon shook his head as he looked around the table at his new comrades. "I couldn't. I didn't have acceptable grounds. And, in the time I had left, I couldn't lower my grade average enough to get below the top one hundred and fifty unless I simply stopped doing my classwork and intentionally failed tests, and that would have opened me up to disciplinary action for willful misconduct. When the commandant hit me with the news about being sent to be a federal cop . . . well, I really can't describe all of the things that went through my head, all at once, mixed together in a crazy jumble. The only way out that I could see was to do something really desperate—and incredibly stupid. But the commandant was a couple of steps ahead of me."

"*He* sprung you?" Janno asked.

"In a way," Lon said, nodding. "He took a big risk."

"Look at me, Nolan." Lon had blinked and looked up. He had not even noticed that he had let his gaze, his head, drop. The news was simply too devastating to be true.

"Yes, sir."

"I've got a good notion how this hits you. It sticks in my craw as well. We're soldiers, though, you and I, and soldiers take orders, even when they don't like them." A grim smile fixed itself on the commandant's face. "My job here has been to turn out soldiers, not combat-ready police." He glanced toward the office door, then leaned closer to Lon.

"What I have to say to you isn't to go any farther. You're not to repeat it outside of this room. Is that understood?"

"Yes, sir." Lon felt puzzlement return, but all he could do was sit and wait for the commandant to continue.

"As I said, I've got a damn good idea how this hits you. I've been stewing over this directive since I received it four days ago and found that there is no give to it. Now, there is absolutely no way that I can get you a commission in the NAU Army, or in any other army . . . on this planet." When Banks paused, Nolan raised his head a little more.

"You do want to be a soldier, rather than a cop, don't you?"

"Yes, sir. I've never wanted to be anything else."

"That's what I thought. Now, I'm going to give you a name and a complink code. Memorize them. Don't write them down. Things may get rough for you here for a while, Nolan, but stick it out. Then, when the time comes—and you'll know when that is—give that code a call and take it from there."

Lon blinked again, several times, and looked around at his new squadmates. "The complink number was for a DMC recruiter who was operating, illegally, on Earth."

"Yeah, but what happened?" Phip asked.

Lon grinned, but there was pain behind it. "Thirty-two of the top one hundred and fifty members of my class were dismissed from the academy for 'conduct unbecoming.' The commandant rigged a shakedown inspection and we were all caught with contraband. He gave us all the maximum penalty permitted—expulsion from the academy with prejudice—and then he resigned his own commission the same day. And here I am."

"Here you are," Corporal Girana said. "And it's time

to get back to the barracks, Nolan. We've got to draw your equipment and start checking you out on everything. You go right into training with the platoon, first thing tomorrow morning, so we've got to get you ready tonight.''

2

"I wish I could tell you that we have up-to-date files on every planet where we might be called upon to fight," Lieutenant Taiters told Lon. "But I can't. Corps Intelligence does what it can, but there are simply too many worlds, and conditions change too rapidly. We can hardly hope to know the *names* of all of the worlds that have been settled, and any information we might have on planetary affairs or population data could be hopelessly obsolete when we need it. There are times when all we have is what the contract officer can glean from the client, and that isn't always, shall we say, completely accurate."

Alpha Company had been split up for the day, with the men assigned to work details around base—one of the routine hazards of garrison duty. Lon was exempt from fatigue duty, but that did not give him time off. There were always lessons to be learned, equipment and procedures to be mastered. Usually Arlan Taiters was his tutor, but occasionally Captain Orlis, the company commander, took over. This particular afternoon, nearly a month after Nolan's assignment to A-2-7, Lon and the lieutenant were in one of the offices at regimental headquarters, using a desktop complink with a large monitor screen.

"The files are kept updated, as possible," Taiters said. He had already shown Nolan how to log on and get through the indexing system of the database. "Geographical features are least likely to change—over the time scales we're concerned with. Once we have reliable physical survey data on a planet, we can count on knowing *something* about the terrain and climate if we have to go in. But that's about it. The social and political data change too quickly. The smaller the population, the faster it tends to change. And even though most colonies tend to go through the same basic stages, there are exceptions, and even when there aren't radical departures, colonies take different amounts of time to pass from stage to stage.''

''Are you saying that this is all wasted effort?'' Lon asked.

Arlan shook his head. ''No, of course not. The point is that you can never take it for granted that anything in the files will be accurate when we get to a world on contract. There are serious limits. We gather all of the information we can get, and put a lot of effort into analyzing it. And when someone approaches the Council of Regiments about hiring troops, we can usually get considerable information about the zone of operations. But that is not always *accurate* information. There are times when the people who hire us prefer that we not know certain facts that might affect whether or not we accept a contract, or information we might find, ah, too useful. The database is a useful tool, but it can never be the *only* tool.''

''Do we run our own surveys first, before committing troops?''

''When possible. Too often there are time pressures that preclude it.'' Arlan logged out of the database. ''Enough of this for one day. It's starting to fog my brain.'' He got up from the desk. Lon stood just as quickly. ''Let's go burn some calories.''

''Yes, sir.'' There were times when Lon would have preferred accompanying the other men of his squad on their work details. Sweating at physical labor was a relief from skull sweating.

There was a large, fully equipped gymnasium in the basement of regimental headquarters. There was also a swimming pool in an adjacent room. The facility was maintained for officers and noncoms who escaped some of the physical exertions of their charges. Lon had even seen Colonel Gaffney, the regimental commander, sweating away at the machines. And, since Lon was exempt from work details, he was allowed—encouraged—to use the gym as often as he wanted to as well.

"How much time do we have?" Lon asked the lieutenant as they changed to shorts and sneakers in the locker room.

"*You* have all the time you want. Just leave yourself time to get cleaned up before supper," Arlan said. "I'll have to leave at 1600, though. Battalion staff meeting."

They split up when they entered the gym. Taiters headed directly for the punching bags. At one time he had been Corps champion for his weight division. Lon started out with a few stretching exercises to loosen up and then started running the track that marked the perimeter of the gym. Lon had been a distance runner in high school and at The Springs. He had won a good share of the races he had entered, and had rarely placed farther back than third—but he had never quite managed to reach record time, no matter how hard he pushed himself.

He still pushed himself, but his times had started to decline. While the records back on Earth were improving, he was getting worse, lagging farther behind, if not by much. But he did not give up. He would not.

One really good run, he told himself as he started the stopwatch on his wrist. *It doesn't matter if anyone else knows. I just need one really good run to satisfy myself.* Although there were a dozen others using the gym, Lon had the track to himself. When other exercisers came into or left the gym, they waited to cross the track until he was clear. A runner always had the right-of-way. Lon stretched into his best form, breathing deeply and focusing as far out in front as he could, concentrating, narrowing his universe. The run was all there was, the only thing that mattered. It was a short track. Seven laps equaled one mile. Distances were marked along the wall and on the floor. Lon kept the count of laps without conscious thought.

He looked at his watch just as he crossed the mile marker—before he started to slow down. "Damn," he muttered. He had not even broken four minutes. *Way too slow.* He put his hands on his hips as he slowed to a trot for a final half lap. He put in five minutes on the rings to exercise his arms and upper body, then moved to a machine that allowed him to alternate weight work with his arms and legs. By the time he got up from that apparatus, his arms and legs were trembling. He was covered in sweat, and about ready to collapse for a long rest.

But he did not stop. He forced himself through several minutes of light work to cool off, then headed for the swimming pool. Stopping just long enough to strip off his shoes and socks, he dove into the pool, welcoming the shock of cool water. He took fifteen minutes for ten laps of the pool, resting for a few seconds after each lap, not pushing himself to his limits in the water. Then he flipped over onto his back and floated for a few minutes, kicking gently through wide circles around the center of the pool. He stayed in the water until he felt as if he were nearly relaxed enough to fall asleep where he was. Then he paddled lazily to the edge and got out. He glanced at his watch. It was nearly 1630 hours.

"Still plenty of time before supper," Lon muttered. Everyone seemed to be overly anxious that he not miss meals, and that puzzled him. He was not underweight, and certainly not malnourished or anemic. He took a towel from a rack, dried off, then picked up his shoes and socks and headed for the locker room. He took a shower, first so hot that it turned his skin pink, then icy cold, raising gooseflesh. By the time he was ready to leave the gymnasium, it was time to head for the mess hall.

Dirigent City was adjacent to the main base of the DMC. The city and the base had grown together over the past five centuries. For most of that time the commander of the Dirigent Mercenary Corps, the General (there was only one general at a time in the DMC, the head of the Council of Regiments, elected by that council from its own members), had also been—*ex officio*—head of the planetary government. Together, the base and the city accounted for two thirds of the world's population. Most of the rest could be found within a two-hundred-mile radius. That was an unusual concentration for a world that had been settled as long as Dirigent—more than six centuries—but Dirigent was an unusual world, still almost entirely dependent on a single industry. Most colony worlds became more diversified within three or four generations of their founding.

Although Dirigent City was, overwhelmingly, an army town, there was one important distinction from army towns on other worlds. The civilian area immediately bordering the main gate was not given over to businesses designed to service soldiers and separate them from their pay. The blocks nearest the main gate, and along the route between it and the spaceport across town, were maintained to impress off-world visitors—especially potential clients. Government agencies and offices for civilian professionals were concentrated along the route that diplomats were most likely to travel. There were also factories visible from that route—at a distance, mostly, away from densely populated neighborhoods—factories that produced the weapons of war, and the supplies that soldiers needed. Dirigent exported munitions as well as men.

The off-duty haunts of the soldiers were hidden behind the public facade, on side streets and in neighborhoods away from the showy face of the city. The nearest were close enough for a thirsty soldier to reach without too great an effort, but the fancier watering holes were farther off, along with the other establishments that dedicated themselves to the wants and needs of the soldiers—particularly the unmarried soldiers, who comprised more than 60 percent of the DMC. There were always taxis available near the gates of ''The Base'' to take soldiers where they wanted to go, and two bus routes had stops across the street from the main gate . . . for the budget-conscious.

After a quick supper, Lon Nolan left base, alone. Most of the squad had headed for town and their favorite places an hour or more before. No one was telling *them* not to skip meals. Lon was in civilian clothes. Off-base, few men of the DMC wore uniforms unless they were on duty or on thirty-minute-recall alert status—part of the planetary defensive contingent.

Despite his earlier efforts in the gym, Lon walked, passing the bus stop and cab stand without a glance. He did not plan to go too far. It was only about two thirds of a mile to the bar where he expected to find several members of the squad. It was where they usually went—at least for the first part of an evening on the town.

It was close to sunset. Streetlights had already come on. There were plenty of people out, walking or riding. Three blocks from the main gate, Lon turned onto a side street. Past the first few doors on either side, this was where the military were welcomed. There were bars, restaurants, pawnshops, gaming parlors, and other *entertainments* available behind respectable facades. The city council was extremely obliging to its military contingent. It was not only that they provided a large part of the commercial life of the city, there also was not a member of the council who did not have several relatives in the DMC. Destructive drugs and physical mayhem were about the only human vices that could not be openly practiced. Crime was low in Dirigent City—on the entire planet. Military discipline was severe. Infractions were treated with draconian punishments.

The neon signs grew larger and more ornate the farther from the main streets they were. The sounds of music were louder, coming out of almost every opening door.

Lon found the place he wanted, the Purple Harridan. Despite the name, the garish decoration, and loud music, the

Purple Harridan was usually relatively sedate. The public bar was where most of the commotion was. But there were other rooms, behind and above, and most of those were more subdued.

The noise always stopped Nolan. The music was raucous and loud, grating to him. But the lighting of the public bar was worse. Purple lights, half of them strobing, fell on the purple and red that were the main colors. One small white light also strobed, erratically, making Lon blink every time it came on.

He did not see any of the men of his squad in the public bar. That did not surprise him. Most of them were old enough to prefer more sedate surroundings. As soon as Lon's eyes adjusted to the lighting, he moved toward the arch that led to the next room, and to the stairs and lift tube that led upstairs. Phip and the others might be anywhere, but Lon guessed that since they had come out without eating at the mess hall, they would be in the salon on the second floor, the restaurant.

Lon took the stairs. As he climbed, the noise from below started to fade, absorbed by walls and ceiling, baffled by the turns. Even though there were no closed doors between the various public rooms of the Purple Harridan, each seemed to be acoustically isolated. Lon had asked about that after his first visit. Tebba Girana had given him the answer. "It's the same technology we use to make life bearable for our tankers and artillerymen, on a different scale. Sound-deadening is important, and the military isn't the only place it can be used." "It's not top secret?" Lon had asked. Girana had shook his head. "Not for the last fifty years, I guess. We even license factories on a few other planets to make it, take a royalty."

Phip, Dean, and Janno were sitting at a table near the bar. Although this room was called the restaurant of the Purple Harridan, it was not strictly for diners, and the same food was available in all of the rooms. The "restaurant" *was* nearest the kitchen and most likely owed its name to that fact.

Lon got a beer at the bar before he headed to the table. Phip Steesen pushed out a chair for him.

"Thought maybe you weren't going to make it out," Phip said. His eyes showed that he had already done some serious drinking. He spoke slowly, taking great care with his enunciation.

"I ate in the mess hall. It saves more money for this." Lon raised his beer. He knew that it was a safe excuse, one that would prevent any jokes about him being cheap.

"Tebba said you was tied up with the lieutenant," Dean said. "Sometimes he don't know when quitting time comes around."

Lon grinned and shook his head. "He had a staff meeting at four o'clock." Off-duty, the enlisted men of the Corps made a point of not using military time.

"You hear anything useful, like when we might pick up a contract?" Dean asked.

"You guys will probably hear before I do." That was a matter of some concern to the men. Pay on contract was higher than pay in garrison, and the battalion had been at home far too long for most of them.

"There's been times, since I've been in the Corps, that they had to turn down contracts because we were all too busy," Phip said. He shook his head, then took a long drink of beer. "Now, nothing. We were ready to ship out six months ago, had our turn at refitting and training, our time on planetary defense detail. Now we're back at training, and pulling work details all over the place, just waiting."

"We are next in line, any contract calling for a battalion or more," Janno said. Next to his two comrades, he sounded positively sober. He did not work at getting intoxicated, the way the others, especially Phip, did. "Seventh is next regiment out, and within the Seventh, we're the first battalion due."

"Way our luck is running, won't be nothing but con-

tracts for a company or less coming in till next spring,"
Phip said. "We're way down on the company list, four or
five ahead of us."

Lon sipped at his beer, intending to make each one last.
The way the Corps scheduled who was sent on a contract
was fairly simple. Rosters were maintained for regiments,
battalions, and companies. The unit of the proper size that
had been longest in garrison went out. Choosing units when
part of the first-up outfit had been out recently got more
complicated, but the idea was to be as fair as possible in
the allocation of work. The DMC did accept contracts of
any size, down to sending no more than a squad out. On
rarer occasions a single officer might be dispatched to conduct an evaluation of a client's own military capabilities—
or problems—but that was usually just in hope of landing
a more substantive contract later.

"There's got to be work not too far off," Lon suggested.
*It's important to me too, and not just because the pay is
better on contract.* He needed combat to get his commission, his lieutenant's pips.

"Right now, I'd even settle for a safari," Phip said.

"Safari?" Lon asked.

Phip just nodded, more or less into his beer. Janno took
over. "Once in a while, colonists on a new planet have
serious troubles with native predators, so serious that they
can't handle it themselves. Either they're losing people or
they're losing livestock. They need soldiers to come in and
thin out the offending predators, or drive them away from
the settled area."

"Problem is," Dean said, almost dripping beer from his
mouth in his hurry to speak, "new colonies don't often
have the money or trade goods to hire enough soldiers to
do the job right. And sometimes they don't know enough
about the critters they want killed to make the job as safe
as it should be."

"Even if they scrape up enough to pay for a platoon or
so, they don't have enough to offer bonuses," Dean said.

"What's the biggest contract you guys have been on?" Lon asked. "The most men."

The three of them looked around at each other. "Two regiments," Janno said. "That was almost a real war like they used to have back on Earth. The opposition even had a couple of old skybolts, fighters."

"That was a hairy bastard," Phip said. Then he drained his glass and raised it, gesturing for the waitress to bring a refill. "Hairy bastard," he repeated, muttering this time. "We lost four men in the platoon that time."

Dean and Janno both drained their glasses then. Lon did the same. It seemed to be expected.

Two hours later the four men were out the street, heading for another bar that Phip insisted that they visit, the Dragon Lady. Janno and Lon held the outside. They were still walking straight. They worked to contain the weaving of Phip and Dean. Those two were far gone in the booze. "Weekend," Phip had explained before he ceased to be coherent. "Two days, no work."

Lon had finished four beers in the Purple Harridan. He suspected that Janno had not had many more, even though he had been out longer. Lon had not asked where the rest of the squad might be. Although nothing had ever been said, he suspected that the rest of them were more . . . choosy about their drinking companions. Lon was a cadet, an apprentice officer; someday he might be commanding them, might send one or more of them to his death. At his most suspicious, Lon sometimes suspected that these three included him only because Corporal Girana or Sergeant Dendrow had asked them to take care of him and see that he did not get into trouble on his own. But until proven wrong, he chose to act as if they included him for other reasons.

Phip started singing an impossibly obscene song about Harko Bain—supposedly Dirigent's first mercenary, back before the creation of the DMC, when young Dirigenter men sometimes went off-world to join mercenary forces. The song seemed to have an infinite number of verses, about equally divided between Bain's military and sexual prowess . . . both Herculean according to the lyrics. The refrain was the mildest:

> *He fought a thousand battles*
> *On five hundred different worlds,*
> *And gave ten thousand bastards*
> *To as many willing girls.*

Now and then, Dean would join in, but the two men's voices did not harmonize well, and when they started trying to outdo each other, Janno shushed both of them. Too grand a show of public intoxication could bring trouble down.

Lon paid little attention to the singing, but smiled each time the refrain came up. He had looked up Harko Bain in the library. Little was known about the real man except for his birth and death dates, and his children on Dirigent—two sons and a daughter. Other than that, there was just the comment, "Supposedly one of the first Dirigenter mercenaries." At the time that Harko had lived, there had not been five hundred settled worlds in the galaxy. The number had been closer to two hundred. But he had left a rousing legend.

The Dragon Lady was a smaller place than the Purple Harridan, but tried to crowd as many customers into its main bar. There was scarcely room to move between tables, and the bar was only visible if you were leaning against it. Customers were three and four deep in front of it. Lon and his companions wedged in along one wall, crowded together at the edge of the traffic flow.

"I know why you wanted to come in here," Lon shouted close to Phip's head—to be heard over the commotion of the people and the loud music. "There's enough guys in here that you couldn't fall down if you wanted to."

Phip gave Lon a broad, uncomprehending grin. He had

heard only part of what Lon had said, and understood none of it.

Janno hooked an almost naked waitress—she wore nothing but a tiny apron around her waist with two pockets in it, one for tips, the other for her order pad—by grabbing her around the waist and pulling her toward him. He put his mouth right up against her ear to order beers for the four of them.

Lon raised an eyebrow. Janno seemed to be taking an awfully long time to say, "Four beers."

The waitress giggled as she freed herself from Janno's grasp and headed toward the end of the bar reserved for waitresses. Lon expected a long wait, but she was back in only a couple of minutes. After the beers had been distributed and paid for—Janno paid for all of them, it was his turn—he grabbed the waitress again to whisper something else in her ear. She giggled and nodded, and when she left the group this time, Janno was still attached to her waist.

"What's that all . . ." Lon started to ask, but then he shut up as it penetrated. Liquor was not the only thing for sale in the Dragon Lady. He watched as Janno and the waitress went toward a narrow stairway at the back of the room and went up. *Okay, now I know what it was about,* Lon thought, smiling to himself. The waitress had not been bad-looking. Nor were the other ones that he could see, and all of them were dressed the same way.

When Janno returned a half hour later, he seemed to be whistling, but Lon could not hear anything over the general din of the Dragon Lady.

"That was a nasty trick, leaving me with these drunks while you get laid," Lon accused, fighting to keep from laughing.

"Hey, I bought the drinks first. Anyway, it's your turn, if you want it," Janno said, grinning. "That's the only reason I let Phip talk us into coming here. Some of the best girls in town."

"I thought you were engaged."

"I am. That was her."

For a second, Lon felt stunned. He was not certain that Janno was joking with him. Then he decided that Belzer was on the level. "Are you serious?" Lon asked.

Janno nodded happily. "She makes five times the money I do, maybe more, and she knows every way in the universe of making me happy in bed—and everywhere else as well. We'll have a hell of a time when we get married."

When the four of them finally left the Dragon Lady, Phip and Dean were out in front, occasionally steered in the right direction by Lon or Janno.

"You looked shocked before," Janno said after they had walked about six blocks. "About Mary, my fiancée."

"Startled, perhaps," Lon said. "You caught me by surprise."

"Because I plan to marry a whore?"

Lon hesitated before he admitted, "Well, yes. But, remember, there's still a lot I don't know about Dirigent."

"There's really no difference at all between Mary and us, Lon," Janno said very softly. "We all make our living selling our bodies. Her profession is just as honorable as ours."

Not on Earth, it wouldn't be, Lon thought, but what he said was, "I've still got a lot to learn, Janno."

"That's why I told you," he replied. "Saves embarrassing situations later. I mean, if you had gone off with Mary and then found out later that she's my fiancée, you might have had trouble coping. This way you'll know, and, no, it doesn't matter. I recommend her to all my friends. I'm proud of her. She's damned good at what she does."

3

There were fresh rumors every day. New contracts were in the offing. Whenever soldiers got together with nothing more important to occupy their minds, the rumors flowed. It was not just privates who relished the unfounded gossip. Lon heard the same thing, less often and in more subdued form, from noncoms and even between Lieutenant Taiters and Captain Orlis. Everyone was anxious to be heading out on a paying contract. The only protocol seemed to be that the gossiping was done only with one's peers. Lon, because of his peculiar status as a cadet, heard it on every level.

But for the next three weeks, each rumor proved baseless. There were no new contracts, and only two diplomats had arrived to conduct preliminary talks about the possibility of future employment for men of the DMC. Then . . .

Lead Sergeant Jim Ziegler, the top enlisted man in Alpha Company, came into the mess hall while the men were at supper.

"Listen up, I've got an announcement," he said. "As of this minute, A Company is off-duty. You've got two days free. No training, no fatigue details, no duty until reveille Friday."

The cheers were almost deafening. Some of the men used silverware to beat against their serving trays several times.

"All that for two days off?" Lon asked when the tumult started to fade.

"You don't understand!" Phip said, excited. "It means

we're going out. We've got a contract. We're finally going to get a chance to make some contract pay."

During the two and a half days of freedom, Lon was spared even from tutelage. Captain Orlis and Lieutenant Taiters were gone the entire time. The company was under the command of Lieutenant Hoper, and even he was rarely in evidence. All of the married noncoms were gone as well. And many of the privates showed up only for sleep and food.

"Aren't we going to learn anything about the contract?" Lon asked Corporal Girana before Tebba left.

"Time enough for that Friday, or on the trip out," Girana said. "Don't worry about it. Make good use of your free time. No telling how long we'll be gone. With any luck, it might be next spring before we get back." Summer was not quite over.

Lon was the only member of his squad who remained in the barracks that first evening of freedom. Phip and Janno had come to tell him they were off and to suggest that he come along. "No, you guys go ahead," he had said. "I may track you down later."

"Sooner or later we'll get to the Dragon Lady," Janno had added with a grin. "Come over there if you want. Give you a chance to meet Mary proper."

"I may not catch up with you tonight," Lon said, not certain what Janno meant by "meet Mary proper." Dirigenters might look at it differently, but he was not yet ready to have sex with a friend's fiancée, even with his blessing.

Lon ate in the mess hall, which was almost completely deserted. Of the entire company, fewer than thirty men— barely more than half a platoon—came in for supper. Sitting alone, Lon took more time than usual with his meal while he tried to decide what he would do with the evening and with his free time. After supper he went back to his barracks cubicle.

I could still go out, he told himself. *I don't* have *to go to the Dragon Lady.* But he still might run into Janno, Dean, and Phip, and if he did, they would insist on dragging him along for the rest of the evening.

He spent a half hour working on a letter home. *I guess I'll send it out before we ship out,* he decided. He had been writing on the same message chip since his arrival on Dirigent. The chip was not yet full, but . . . the time to send it seemed to be before heading out for combat. Mail was not particularly fast. It could not go by radio, since that was limited by the speed of light. A message home from Dirigent would not arrive for decades. Electronic data chips, physically mailed, were the only practical means of personal interstellar communication. It was expensive, especially when they had to be routed indirectly (there was no direct service between Earth and Dirigent), which was why Lon had decided early on to send one only when he had a chip filled. His parents had not heard from him since his layover at Over-Galapagos. And he had not heard from them.

After he had said everything he could think of to say in the letter, Lon read for a while, then went to bed early. And in the night he dreamed—of combat . . . and fear.

Like most of the worlds that had been settled by humans, Dirigent retained as much of the old as possible in reckoning time. The year was divided into the same days, weeks, and months, with the same names. But the year and the day were not precisely the same as on Earth. The day was seventeen minutes longer; to compensate, the Dirigentan "minute" and "second" were fractionally longer than their terran progenitors. There were only 363 and a fraction days in the Dirigentan year; so its twelve months each had thirty days, with a three-day (four in the leap year that came every six years) intercalary New Year holiday to make up the difference. But Dirigent only used that calendar for its own reckoning. It also kept track of the "standard" time and calendar common to most human worlds. Those all needed some common system to avoid hopeless confusion.

The men of second battalion started to drift back in late Thursday evening, broke, exhausted, and—for the most part—quiet after the end of their unexpected holiday. "We can't spend money in the field," Phip had said earlier that day when Lon ran into his buddies in town. "And we'll have pay coming when we get home, so there's no reason not to blow it now." *Besides, there's always a chance of not coming back,* Phip had thought. *I'd hate to die knowing I hadn't spent all of my money, hadn't drunk every beer I could afford.*

No one went to sleep drunk that night. Those who came in inebriated took killjoy pills to sober up and prevent hangovers. If they were too far gone to think of it themselves, every man had buddies to make sure.

Lon had posted his letter chip home that morning. That evening, when the barracks started to settle down, he started another letter home. This one would not go out until he returned to Dirigent . . . or until it was clear that he would not be coming back. He would take it along on the ship, work on it when he could, when he thought of something else to say to his parents or to the few other people who might want to hear from him.

"The other guys in the squad are all veterans. They've been through this before, some a dozen times or more. They go out, drink, relax, and then come in and sleep—peacefully to all outward appearances. But this is new to me. I'm sober and . . . not at all certain that I'll be able to sleep at all tonight, or during the couple of weeks it will take us to get wherever we're going." He spoke softly to his complink, knowing that it would pick up a whisper, wanting to avoid disturbing any of the others nearby—and wanting to avoid being overheard.

But the time came when he ran out of things to say. He turned off the complink but continued to sit in front of it, staring, trying to avoid the uncertainties that surrounded him.

It's too soon to start worrying. I start now, by the time we get wherever we're going, I'll be a vegetable, or a raving lunatic. The trip out would take between fourteen and sixteen days. Any interstellar transit took that long, even between neighboring star systems. A ship would travel five days in normal space before making its first of three Q-space jumps, and there would be three more days in normal space after each jump, sometimes five after the last.

You don't even know what the contract is yet, he reminded himself. *It might not be all that dangerous. It could be training, or a safari, or . . . anything else.* He frowned, then got to his feet. There was not much room to pace in his cubicle, little more than the length of his bed, but he used all of that. *If it's not combat, it doesn't count for getting me my pips. It takes* combat *to get a commission.*

Eventually, he slept.

Not one man in the battalion missed reveille Friday morning. The manning reports were made. Lieutenant Colonel Medwin Flowers, the battalion commander, accepted them, then turned the men over to their company commanders.

"Orders for the day," Captain Orlis told A Company. "Spend the morning at equipment maintenance. Get yourselves ready to leave. Immediately after lunch, we'll have a contract briefing." Before he dismissed the company, Orlis said, "Nolan, my office at 0800."

Such summonses were not unusual, but Lon suspected that this one was different. So did the men in his squad.

"Looks like you're going to get the lowdown before we do," Dean Ericks said at breakfast.

Lon shrugged. *As long as the captain doesn't tell me that I'm staying behind, that he doesn't think I'm ready for combat.* "Maybe he just wants to make sure that I haven't wasted the last two days the way the rest of you did," he said, trying to sound unconcerned.

"We haven't wasted anything," Phip said. "We've done it all, gone the whole route and back again."

"Done it all, spent it all," Janno contributed.

The mood in the mess hall was light that morning. Nearly everyone seemed genuinely excited at the prospect of contract pay. For the veterans, it was too soon to worry about what the contract might entail. Once they knew what the job was, and once they were on the ship heading out, there would be time enough for worry—if it was appropriate. Until then, they would console themselves with thoughts of having their extra pay waiting when they got home.

Lon ate steadily but slowly. He had little appetite. He had not slept well, and he was still worried. *One way or the other, it'll be good to have the first time over,* he told himself, but it did not stop the nervous twisting in his stomach.

He was spared too much attention from his squadmates. They were all so excited that they did not notice that he had withdrawn from the conversation. And, as soon as he could without drawing attention, Lon left. It was not nearly time for him to report to the captain, but he wanted time to himself.

It was still ten minutes before eight o'clock when Lon went to the orderly room. Lead Sergeant Jim Ziegler was there already. "Captain's waiting," Ziegler said. "He said to send you right in as soon as you got here."

In the commander's office, Lon did not have a chance to salute and report formally.

"Skip the ritual, Nolan. Sit down, here." Orlis pointed at the chair next to his desk. Lon sat. "Nervous?" The captain leaned back, staring directly at the cadet.

"Yes, sir, you could say that," Lon admitted.

Orlis smiled. "I know that nothing I say will stop that, but I can at least tell you not to worry about worrying. Waiting for the first time is difficult for everyone. You know it's coming—not as an abstraction but as a concrete thing finally—and you're not sure what to expect, how all of your training will measure up to the real thing. Something like that?''

Lon nodded. ''I worry more about fouling up, doing something stupid, and getting people hurt or killed. That doesn't give me a lot of time to worry about what might happen to me.''

''Well, at least you're worrying about the right things. But we've been doing this for a long time. We're not just going to turn you loose to fend for yourself. That's why we have the apprenticeship program. We don't like to waste anything in the Corps, especially men. You have a lot of training behind you, on Earth and here. The Corps has an investment in you, hopefully a long-term capital investment. You do as you're told and stick close to Girana, or whichever of the veterans you're with, and you should do fine.''

''I hope so, sir,'' Lon said.

Orlis nodded. ''Now, I didn't call you in just for a pep talk. We could have done that anytime during the next couple of weeks—and we probably will. The reason I wanted you here is that Colonel Flowers specifically said that you were to be included in the officers' call this morning.''

''The contract briefing?''

Orlis nodded.

Lon finally smiled. ''One of the guys in the squad guessed that when you told me to report, said that I'd find out what was going on before the rest of them did.''

''And the minute you get back, they're all likely to grill you about it.''

''I expect so, sir. Is it all secret, or can I tell them?''

''I doubt that you'll get much chance. The briefing is likely to take all morning. The colonel might even have the mess hall send our lunch over to battalion headquarters so we can continue right through it.'' He grinned. ''Even if it doesn't run that long, I'll see to it that you don't have to worry about questioning long enough for it to be a problem. Not that it's secret or anything—the men will find out right after lunch, or as soon as the briefing is over—it's just that I don't like to have anyone stealing my thunder."

"Yes, sir. Do you know where we're going now, sir?"

"Norbank is the name of the world, and that's all I know, except that it's a one-battalion contract. Colonel Flowers likes to keep his thunder too. We'll find out soon enough." He glanced at the clock. "Lieutenants Hoper and Taiters should be here in a minute, and then we'll all head over to battalion HQ together. The officers' call is scheduled for 0830."

The scheduled start for the conference might have been 0830, but every officer except the battalion commander and his executive officer was seated around the U-shaped table in the headquarters conference hall ten minutes early. There were drinks available, juice, coffee, tea, and water. Captain Orlis poured orange juice for himself. His two platoon leaders took coffee. Lon also took coffee. They talked softly. A half dozen complink monitors were on the table, on but showing only blank screens. On the wall behind the top of the U, a six-by-eight-foot wall monitor likewise waited, on but blank.

Precisely at 0830 hours, the door next to the wall monitor opened. Lieutenant Colonel Medwin Flowers came in with Major Hiram Black, his executive officer, and Battalion Lead Sergeant Zal Osier close behind. No one yelled, "Attention!"—not for an officers' contract briefing. Flowers went right to his position, a podium set to one side of the wall monitor. Major Black sat at one end of the U, near Flowers. Lead Sergeant Osier went to the other end of the room, to handle the complink program that was part of the briefing.

"You all know the basic fact that we have a contract on the world of Norbank," Colonel Flowers said, giving Osier time to get in position and key in the first video command. A global view of Norbank appeared on all of the monitors, a view from space, over the equator, showing the planet rotating, speeded up enough to show a complete rotation in a minute, then slowing down and finally coming to a stop over the region of interest.

"The colony on Norbank has been there for just under a century," Flowers continued. "The total human population is approximately two hundred thousand. Slightly less, actually, according to the information we have been given. The colony is still fairly basic, barely into second stage." Roughly, colonies were categorized through four stages. Stage one was the early, primitive "first settlers" time, with colonists concerned with carving out homes and farms for themselves and surviving, then getting the basics of a local infrastructure in place. Stage two would see the beginning of cottage-scale industry, with colonists beginning to find things they could use in trade with other worlds, but still in need of more from outside than they could match in trade. Stage three saw growth and economic independence, larger factories, and more trade, the beginnings of urbanization. Stage four was the final, developed product, with the move from rural to urban centers accomplished. The classification was, however, vague and largely subjective.

"Our contract is to put down a rebellion and to train a militia to keep the peace in the future. The rebels are from a second wave of colonists who arrived a generation after the initial settlers. The two groups have, according to our liaison with the planetary government, remained separate, and have, ah, gone their separate ways. The dissident group comprises about thirty percent of the total population, but the faction actively fighting the government is much smaller. Again, according to the information given to us by the contracting negotiator. These rebels are attempting to overthrow the majority government to impose their own ideas on the entire population."

Flowers paused and looked around the table at his officers, his gaze moving up one leg of the U, around the end, and back up the other side. "I don't have to tell you that all of this information is tentative, based solely on what the contracting party has been willing to share.

"The number of open combatants is supposedly under five hundred on the rebel side, and about the same number for the government, despite the greater population base the government can count on. The government's soldiers are all volunteers. None of them are trained soldiers, though, on either side. If the information is anywhere near correct, we will have approximately a two-to-one advantage over the rebels without taking into account the loyalist forces on the ground, about three-to-one if we take them into account. But the rebels are almost certainly more highly motivated. That is usual in such cases. If they were not, they would be unable to mount a creditable threat. And even though the actual rebel combatants may number fewer than five hundred, they will probably have thousands of sympathizers willing to offer more or less help. And our arrival might help their recruiting.

"The government does fear that it will not be able to put this rebellion down on its own, or they would not be contracting for our services. And, by the way, the contract allows one month to put down the rebellion and another two months to train the militia that the government intends to raise to prevent a recurrence of the situation. In addition to our services, they are also purchasing infantry weapons to supply a thousand men. The weapons and ammunition are not to be delivered on-planet until such time as the military situation is stable enough that there is no fear of those weapons falling into the wrong hands."

The map projection had moved into a view of an area about a thousand miles square by this point. On the large wall monitor, the general topography was apparent, but the view still did not show human structures.

"As is customary, the initial colonists picked the site for their settlement based on climate and available resources," Flowers continued. "Although the survey they had available covered only three months of the local year, they lucked out. They have temperate to subtropical conditions, with the worst of the summer heat alleviated by prevailing south-westerly winds off of a stretch of ocean unbroken by major landmasses for fifty-five hundred miles. The autumn and winter, of more interest to us, are mild, with the wet season due to begin about six weeks or two months after our arrival. That means," Flowers said, looking up from his notes, "that if we conclude the first part of our contract on schedule, putting down the rebellion, we shouldn't have to worry overly about foul weather affecting operations. Rain is of less concern when we are in the training stage." He returned to his notes. Lead Sergeant Osier narrowed the limits on the map projection again. According to the scale at the bottom, the view was now down to a section about two hundred miles by three hundred.

"There are two main centers of habitation, corresponding to the two waves of settlement. The second group, the one that is rebelling, chose an area about one hundred and forty miles from the first, farther upstream, along what the Nor-bankers call First River." He used a pointer to indicate the river on a small complink monitor built into his lectern. An arrow showed it on the rest of the monitors. The scale of the map closed in more. "The respective towns are here and here," Flowers said, again using the pointer, "Norbank City and Fremont." Around the towns, Lon and the other officers could see the patterns of farming, but not yet build-ings.

"The country between the two areas is hilly and heavily forested, with a number of major tributaries entering First River. Both settlements are located primarily on the north bank of First River, although both have spread to the op-posite bank. There is a single bridge at each town, of ques-tionable strength, I might add, built by amateurs of locally available materials."

Flowers had a rapt audience. None of the officers both-ered to make notes. They would have recordings and tran-scripts available on their complinks. What they were concerned with now was listening, concentrating fully on that, without the distraction of trying to copy anything. Flowers went on to show the two primary settlements, describe the condition of the colony, and then talked about some of the major flora and fauna that they might have to contend with. He talked steadily for more than three hours, pausing only for an occasional sip of water.

"The latest information we have, now twenty-three days old," he said then, "is that the rebels appeared to be staging for an attack on the capital. Our plan, subject to revision once we see for ourselves what the conditions are, is to land at the capital and move out to engage the rebels, preferably at some distance from Norbank City. One last note for now. Norbank was the name of one of the founding families. The current head of the planetary government is named Norbank, as is the contracting official." Flowers glanced at his watch then.

"At 1300 hours, you will brief your men on the contract. At 1500 hours, the battalion will fall out, ready for movement. Duffel bags and field packs should be stacked, ready for transport prior to that time. Buses and trucks will be waiting to take us to the port. The ship is scheduled to head outsystem at 1815. Questions?"

No one spoke up. The questions could come later, aboard ship.

4

***Combat.* The word** became fixed in Lon's mind. He could not shake it loose. Captain Orlis kept Lon with him through lunch, as promised. They ate in the Officers' Club, away from Lon's squad and any temptation he might have to leak information about the contract. The two lieutenants were at the table as well, and the talk among the three officers was all about the contract. From time to time, Orlis or Taiters made an effort to include Nolan in the conversation, but Lon kept his contributions short and noncommittal. He was more concerned with the word—a snare drum beating itself to death inside his head. *Combat.*

That is *what it's all about,* Lon told himself. *I came here to be a soldier.* But that did not quiet his nerves.

"Nolan."

Lon blinked several times and looked to his left. Captain Orlis was staring at him. "Yes, sir?"

"At least lose the look of panic," Orlis said. "You look as if you're waiting for the hangman. I know you're nervous. But you've got to keep it inside. You're going to be an officer, if you make the grade. And part of being an officer is maintaining the front. You let men under your command see that you're afraid, and you'll have good reason to be. They'll pick up your fear and lose half their effectiveness. We can't have that."

"I know that, sir." The lieutenants were also staring at Lon. "Maybe it's just having too much time to think. I'm okay when I'm with the squad. Really, I am. I don't feel like the odd duck in the pond then, if you know what I mean.''

The captain's serious look gave way to a grin. ''I'm not sure about the way you put that, but, yes, I understand. Still, the point remains. You should do fine, Nolan. You've got the talent. You've had the training—more than most apprentice officers we see. But if there's one thing I've noticed, it's that you wear your thoughts on your face. The men pick up on things like that. They watch us, take their cues from us. If we project confidence, they'll be confident, and twice as strong. If we project weakness . . .'' He shook his head. ''That can be a slow wound. Maybe I should have sent you 'round to the base theater group, gotten you some acting experience.''

''I tried that, sir, at The Springs. The director said I had a wooden face, couldn't get the proper emotions to show, couldn't get the words to sound convincing. I worked on it, hard, and was all set to try again when . . . well, you know what happened.''

''Keep working on it,'' Orlis said. ''Besides, this shouldn't be too rough. We'll have the numbers, the equipment, and the training. We're professionals up against amateurs. If the odds were the other way around, I still wouldn't be too worried.''

''I'll try to remember that, sir,'' Lon said, so earnestly that all three of the officers at the table with him started laughing. That helped. Lon managed a smile of his own.

I'll be okay after the first time, Lon told himself. *Baptism of fire. That's the hurdle. After that, I'll know.*

Captain Orlis kept Nolan with him until the order to fall in was given. Then Lon had to run to take his place with the rest of his squad. They were all at attention. No one could ask questions. He could not answer. Even after the ''At ease'' order was given, there was no talking in ranks. The platoons were moved into a semicircle, the men close together.

"Sit down and relax. Here's what you've been waiting for," Captain Orlis said. The briefing he gave the men lasted just ten minutes and covered only the highlights: the world, the basics of the contract, the anticipated opposition. There would be time on the ship for detailed information, after the platoon sergeants and squad leaders had been filled in. It would be the noncoms who drilled their men on the necessary data.

"Get your gear together and have your duffel bags and field packs stacked in front of the barracks by 1430 hours," Orlis said then. "We'll form up for movement just before 1500 hours. Supper will be aboard ship."

He dismissed the company. Lead Sergeant Ziegler got up and started shouting orders. "Platoon sergeants and squad leaders, see to your men. Make sure nobody forgets anything. Make sure everything's out and ready to go on time. Move it, men, at the double. We're on contract now!"

"You didn't come back to let us know what was going on," Phip said to Lon. "You *did* find out this morning, didn't you?"

"The captain didn't give me a chance," Lon said. "He told me that he doesn't like for anyone to steal his thunder."

There was a bus for each platoon. That crowded the line platoons and gave extra room to the smaller headquarters and service detachments. The vehicles moved out in convoy, with Colonel Flowers in the first bus.

"Here's where we put on a parade for the civilians," Janno said, leaning across the aisle to poke Lon in the arm.

"What do you mean?" Lon asked.

"We've got a good landing strip right here on base, enough to handle the shuttles to take us up to the ship, but that's not where we'll go. We'll make the trip all the way across town, hold up traffic along the way, so the civilians will know that we're going out on contract," Janno said.

"Let 'em know that we're going to have money when

we come back," Phip added. He was sitting next to Lon, by the window. "It's always like this."

"What about coming home?" Lon asked.

Janno's voice lost the joking edge it had held before. "That depends on how we do. We fulfill the contract, win, and we come back the same way. We botch the job and they sneak us home via the base strip."

"The casualties come in that way, regardless," Dean said. "The wounded, those who still need treatment after the trip, are closer to the base hospital then. The dead . . ." He shrugged then and turned away. There was no need to finish.

The dead and wounded, Lon thought. There would not be many wounded still needing treatment after two weeks. Medical trauma tubes, with their molecular repair systems, could treat all but the most serious wounds or injuries in hours. Traumatic amputation and the most severe spinal cord injuries were those most likely to keep men invalided for any length of time. It could take several months to regrow an arm or leg and rehabilitate the injured man.

"I don't like the idea of sneaking in the back way," Lon said, forcing a smile, determined not to get caught in morose thoughts. "We'll just have to make sure that we do the job right. That's what they pay us for, isn't it?"

A few minutes later, while the convoy was in town, he had another thought. "If they really wanted to do this parade business right," he said, looking around at the others in his squad, "they'd take us past the Purple Harridan and the Dragon Lady, places like that, give us a *real* incentive. That'd be better than taking us past the government offices and department stores, wouldn't it?"

That earned a laugh from several people, and not just the three who usually socialized with him. "Write it up and drop it in the suggestion box when we get home," Phip suggested. "Hell, maybe we should *all* write that one up."

Lon had seen this route before, when he arrived on Dirigent. He had looked out the window of the taxi then, trying to see everything at once. Dirigent was the first colony world that he had ever been on. Everything had been new, exciting, and seeing it for the first time had taken his mind off of his memories, the way things had ended at The Springs. He had spent a lot of the voyage out, and the stopovers along the way, brooding on that.

I've still got a lot of "firsts" ahead of me, Lon told himself with utter determination. *Look forward to them. Most of them are going to be good.*

When he caught himself humming *"The Ballad of Harko Bain,"* Lon smiled. *I guess I'm going to be all right after all,* he decided.

The transport they would be riding to Norbank was too large ever to land on a planetary surface. The men of the second battalion of the Seventh rode up to it in shuttles, the same attack shuttles they would use when they got to their destination. The *Long Snake* carried just enough landers to surface the complement of troops it could carry, one battalion at full strength. Lon recalled seeing, at a considerable distance, one of the DMC transports when his own ship arrived over Dirigent. Even under the magnification of the complink in his stateroom, the transport had appeared small. But it was large enough to carry a thousand fully equipped troops and everything they might need for a month in the field, complete with attack shuttles, transport shuttles, and its own crew. A second ship, a smaller transport, would be going to Norbank as well, carrying extra supplies for the troops, and the weapons and ammunition that were being sold to the Norbank government.

It took two shuttles to carry a full company of DMC troops. The luggage and trade goods had already gone up to the ship, carried by transport shuttles.

"Get to your seats and strap in," Lieutenant Taiters said as the men of third and fourth platoons filed into their shuttle. "We'll be taking off in just a couple of minutes and I don't want any floaters. Secure all gear."

Noncoms made the final checks before they took their own seats and strapped in. A shuttle was not equipped with artificial gravity. A Nilssen generator would have doubled the size and more than doubled the mass of an attack shuttle. Only ships carried Nilssens—which also provided the field distortion that permitted the ships to transit Q-space for interstellar jumps.

"Hurry up and wait," Phip said under his breath after several minutes had passed with no indication that the shuttle was about to take off. The engines had not been started. Once they were, it might be another five minutes before the lander started moving toward the runway for its short takeoff run.

"You got somewhere else to go?" Janno asked.

"We could be aboard ship, eating, and ready for a long sleep," Phip said. "Why make us wait here, where it's least comfortable, packed in like cardulas in oil?" Cardulas were a plump delicacy on Dirigent, legless rodents with a tangy flavor.

Company A's third and fourth platoons had not been strapped in for ten minutes before the shuttle started to taxi away from the line. The shuttles took off four at a time, ten-second intervals between them, then a minute before the next group started. That would space out their arrivals at *Long Snake,* which could dock only four landers at a time.

As soon as the landing gear were off the ground, the shuttle tilted back at a fifty-degree angle and the throttles were cycled forward to maximum, subjecting everyone aboard to more than four g's of force. Then the lander banked left, carrying them toward the ocean and away from the settled areas of Dirigent.

"This lasts about three minutes," Janno said through clenched teeth, turning his head fractionally toward Lon. "When the engines cut out, we drift the rest of the way, until it's time to maneuver for docking. Me, I prefer acceleration to zero gravity. At least you still know which way is down.''

Lon did not bother to answer. Even a grin was out of the question. *It's a hell of a choice,* he thought, *weighing eight hundred pounds or nothing at all.* Then the weight was taken away and he felt himself rebounding against his safety harness. His arms did not move, though. He was gripping the armrests of his seat too tightly.

''I don't much care for either,'' he said then.

''This is nothing,'' Janno said. ''Just wait for the first time we make a really hot combat landing, with the pilot pushing the throttle wide open going in.''

''Gee, thanks,'' Lon replied, making it sound as sarcastic as he could. ''Just what I needed, something else to look forward to.'' When Janno laughed, Lon joined him, but it was an effort. The first three times that Lon had experienced zero gravity, he had been nauseous, and once he had vomited. There was no nausea this time, though. Lon waited for it, then decided that his stomach was finally used to the loss of gravity. He breathed out softly. *That* was a relief, one less thing to worry about.

Several video monitors were spaced around the troop compartment of the shuttle. Going in for an attack landing, they would display views of the terrain, give the soldiers some indication of what they were about to face. A few minutes after the shuttle left the atmosphere and its engines went idle, the screens came alive.

''This must be for your benefit,'' Janno suggested, elbowing Lon softly. ''We've all seen this before.''

''What do you mean?''

''Just watch,'' Janno said. ''You're going to get to see us come in to dock.''

Nolan watched. At first there was nothing to tell him that it was not simply an ''empty'' space shot, with stars or planets only distant points of light. Then he noticed one of the other shuttles, off to the right, almost out of frame. A few minutes later, he saw that one of the spots of light in the center of the screen was not moving the way it would if it were a star or planet. It seemed to remain stationary. And it grew.

That's the ship, he realized. It was still far enough away that it was no more than a point, but it grew quickly. Then there were two sorts of light. Besides the dim reflection of sunlight—dim because the exterior was designed to minimize any electromagnetic signature—there were lights glowing within the ship, in open docking bays.

Details became visible. Lon could see the three capsule-shaped main hull sections in line, within a framework of supporting girders; two of the three outrigger pods that held the Nilssen generators that powered the ship through Q-space and provided artificial gravity in normal space; the cone-shaped nozzles of the rockets; the bulges of weapons turrets, their rocket launchers and beam cannon not yet discernible. At first there was no way to gauge scale. *Long Snake* was merely an object of indeterminate size at an indeterminable distance. Even the outline of the ship was difficult to focus on. The matte-black coloring and angled surfaces made it difficult to find the edges except where one was backlit by a partially occulted star.

Lon's memory could supply the numbers, but they were only abstractions without solid visual references. Overall, *Long Snake* was twenty thousand feet long. The main hull sections were ellipsoidal, eleven hundred feet thick and fourteen hundred feet long. The hull ranged between thirty and forty feet in thickness, dense sandwiched layers of various materials that could provide full protection for its crew and passengers against the most intense cosmic radiation—and absorb considerable battle damage as well.

It was not the largest ship in space. Lon had seen ships a third larger than *Long Snake* during his layover at Over-Galapagos. He had gone to an observation pod to look at them, standing off two miles from the station and still hiding a considerable portion of the view of Earth below.

"Stand by for maneuvering," the shuttle pilot announced. *Long Snake* had already expanded to cover most of the monitor screen. More details were visible. Lon felt the pull as the shuttle worked to match speed with the ship.

"It won't be long now," Dean said. "This part always goes faster than you'd think."

Lon did not answer. He just stared at the monitor, fascinated. The pilot of the civilian shuttle that had taken him to Over-Galapagos had done the same thing, let her passengers watch the approach. But the geostationary habitat was so much larger than *Long Snake,* large enough to hold twenty-five thousand residents in comfort, along with everything a community of that size needed—stores, schools, churches, factories, warehouses.

There were several short bursts from the shuttle's maneuvering rockets, then nothing. They were on-line, and at the proper speed. The lighted landing bay filled the monitor. The shuttle was parallel to the ship, moving in at a gentle angle. At the last instant, there would be one more short thrust from the maneuvering rockets, enough to kill the shuttle's momentum completely just as it came to rest inside the hangar, where shipboard grapples would latch on and anchor it.

Lon waited for some feeling of impact, but the docking went smoothly. It was not until the grapples took hold of the shuttle that he felt anything, and then it was more the pull of the ship's artificial gravity than any motion of the shuttle's. By that time the pilot had switched off the monitors.

"We're here," Phip announced unnecessarily. He hit the release on his safety harness. None of the others in the squad did. They had not been given the order.

"How long does it take to close the hatch and cycle air into the hangar so we can get out?" Lon asked.

"In a hurry to go somewhere?" Phip asked.

"Just curious. This is my first time, remember?"

"The process only takes about three minutes," Janno said. "That doesn't mean we'll get the order to move that soon. We may sit here until the entire battalion's aboard, just in case there are problems with one of the later shuttles.''

''What sort of problems?'' Lon asked.

''He means in case a shuttle pilot botches docking and smashes into the ship with enough force to knock us all on our butts,'' Phip said.

''That happen often?'' Lon could not do the math in his head, but he suspected that it would take a lot of speed for a shuttle to have any noticeable effect on a ship the size of *Long Snake.*

''Once is all it takes,'' Phip said, almost cheerfully.

Eight minutes passed before the order came to unfasten safety harnesses and get ready to board the ship. The click of buckles being released came as one sound. Lon stood, carefully, even though the artificial gravity was more than 90 percent of Dirigent's surface gravity.

''Nolan, stick damn close to the squad,'' Corporal Girana said, moving out into the aisle. ''I don't want you getting lost between here and our compartment.'' Lon nodded. He had planned on sticking with his squadmates.

''Okay, people,'' Lieutenant Taiters said from next to one of the two exits. ''Let's move out, sharply. The sooner we get out of the way of traffic, the better.''

5

"Thirty seconds to Q-space insertion.'' The announcement blared over every speaker in *Long Snake*. There had been frequent reminders during the past two hours. Every piece of loose gear had been secured. Lon was in his bunk in third platoon's barracks bay. He checked the straps across his chest and waist, to make sure they had not come loose in the minute since he had last checked them.

This would be the final Q-space transit of the voyage to Norbank. The battalion had been en route for eleven and a half days. *Just routine,* Lon told himself as he mentally counted down the seconds. Powerful as they were, *Long Snake*'s Nilssen generators were not able to perform both of their functions at once. For the duration of the Q-space transit, the ship would be without its artificial gravity.

''Ten seconds to Q-space insertion.'' The synthetic voice counted those seconds down, finishing with, ''Q-space insertion.'' There was a shudder as the Nilssens cycled up to full power, creating the field distortion that wrapped a bubble universe around the ship.

Long Snake vibrated noticeably. Lon's head ached dully. His stomach felt queasy. Those were normal sensations, always accompanying the full stressing of Nilssens through Q-space. They would last until the transit ended, then fade over a period of two or three minutes after the Nilssens started propagating artificial gravity again.

It had not been an idle voyage for the second battalion

of Seventh Regiment. Except for the hiatuses of the Q-space transits, the men had spent their days training, maintaining their physical conditioning, and studying the preliminary assault plan for Norbank. They knew where each company would land, what they would be called upon to do in the first minutes and hours after landfall . . . *if* the situation had not changed materially.

"Don't count too much on any of this remaining valid," Sergeant Dendrow had told the platoon after their first complete operational briefing. "It would be nice, but all of the information it's built on will be more than a month old before we land. We'll get new data, we hope, when we come out of Q-space after our final jump. We'll be in Norbank's system then, close enough for direct communication with the government."

Inside its Q-space envelope, *Long Snake* realigned itself, stressing the proper point on the bubble for just the proper time to come out at the right place. The equations that defined Q-space and were behind the operation of the Nilssens treated the "normal" universe as a point mass. The speed-of-light limit was never violated. The stay in Q-space was almost four minutes, near the longest the delicate maneuvering ever took. And once more there was a countdown over the speakers. The ship emerged from Q-space. The vibrations ended. The Nilssens started to cycle up the gravity, taking forty-five seconds to get it to shipboard normal.

"Okay, you can get out of your racks now," Corporal Girana said. "Down's where your feet go again."

"How long do you think it'll be before we know whether or not the plans remain the same?" Lon asked his squadmates as they unbuckled the straps that had secured them to their beds.

"Hard telling," Janno said. "We've got three days or more, depending on how close to Norbank we came out. I imagine they're already opening contact with the government—if the government's still around. If the rebels have knocked them out, it's anybody's guess."

"Don't even *think* about something like that," Phip said. "If the contracting government's out, we'll either turn around and go home, or try to find a place to land so we can put them back in. Either way, it'd be a royal pain in the ass. We go home, it's no contract pay and wasted time. We go in, then we've got to start from scratch, with no local support to count on."

"What if the rebellion's already over?" Lon asked. "What if the government managed to put it down without us?"

"At least we'd have our training set to look forward to," Dean said. "Making proper soldiers out of the Norbankers."

"And that won't be easy if they've won their war without us," Phip said. "They'll be right cocky bastards, thinking they know it all already. Make our job twice as hard. Three times."

It was eighteen hours later before they learned anything more. Ship's time had been synchronized with time in Norbank's settled area. The men of the battalion had had a short "night." Immediately after breakfast the next morning, there was an officers' call. Once more, Lon was included in that briefing.

"Throw out the plans we've been working on" was the way that Lieutenant Colonel Flowers opened the session. He shrugged. "We knew that was likely to happen. The situation on the ground has changed considerably. The rebel army has managed to besiege the capital. Their numbers are now estimated to be near our own, according to the latest information from the surface. That means they probably actually outnumber us, at least slightly.

"We have renegotiated the contract to reflect the changed circumstances, the fact that we will have to break the siege before we proceed to the rest of the mission. Of particular importance is the fact that the rebels control the only improved spaceport on Norbank, and the area of the capital still controlled by government forces is not large enough to let us set down peacefully inside the capital. We'll be in range of the rebels—and, yes, they do have antiair rockets, or we have to assume that they do. There are two ways we could go on this. We could make a fighting landing, put down right where we need to be to make an . . . impression, or we can put down farther back, away from the front lines, and move in to make our attack.

"The government wants us to hit directly, on the way in, as the fastest way to hurt the rebels and end the siege. I vetoed that. It might be too costly in casualties. We'll try to find a landing zone close enough to get us into action quickly, but without risking losing shuttles and men before we're in position to defend ourselves." Flowers paused and looked around.

"It does look as if we're going to earn our pay on this contract."

There were detailed charts now, photographs and maps that had been compiled from them. Every commissioned and noncommissioned officer had a mapboard, a specialized complink node that could display any of the computer cartography with various enhancements and overlays. The computers in *Long Snake*'s Combat Information Center served the network of mapboards. As long as the ship remained in normal space over Norbank, with the area of operations in line of sight, the charts could be updated continuously to show the movement of troops, friendly and hostile. Rebel positions were plotted slowly as the ship approached the world, based on direct sensor information and on news relayed from the capital.

"Right up to the last minute, all of the details about our landing will remain tentative," Lieutenant Taiters told his two platoons twenty-four hours before the scheduled deployment. "The only thing we can count on is that we're going in." He shrugged. "Our landing will *probably* be on the north side of First River. That's where the majority of both armies are, and since the rebels have destroyed the capital's only bridge across the river, landing on the south side would be . . . pointless." He hesitated. "Even if the bridge was still intact, we would probably be going in on the north bank. A narrow wooden bridge does not inspire confidence." DMC policy was to share as much information as possible about operations with all ranks, to give everyone enough data to permit independent action when necessary, and to give the men a sense of participation. During the planning stage, the men were encouraged to make any suggestions that came to mind. In the field, orders were still orders, though. Discipline had to be tight.

"Alpha Company will be first in," Taiters continued. "Our immediate job will be to secure the LZ"—landing zone—"for the rest of the battalion, to neutralize any rebel forces close enough to pose a hazard to the landing. That *should* be fairly simple, since the plan is to put us down far enough away from any concentration of rebels that they won't be able to reach the LZ before the entire battalion is on the ground. That would mean the only possible problem would come by chance, if a rebel force should happen to happen by where we want to land while we're on the way in."

He went on to display photographs and charts of three possible landing zones, talking about their locations and differences. "If possible, we'll go in at one of these places. Familiarize yourselves with all three."

Taiters turned the platoons over to the platoon sergeants and squad leaders. The noncoms drilled their men on the map data, all three potential LZs, and the territory between them and the enemy circle around Norbank City.

"We're scheduled to land just before sunset. That will give us the entire night for operations," Corporal Girana told his squad. The darkness promised to be a big advantage for the mercenaries. Their night-vision systems would allow them freedom of movement and action. According to the available information, only a small percentage of the rebels had any night-vision gear. And it was a basic tenet that untrained men would fight poorly in the dark, especially against fully equipped veteran, professional soldiers.

There would be no physical training, drills, or work details for the men during the last twenty-four hours. Apart from meals and the recurrent briefings, they had nothing to do but make final checks of their weapons and combat gear . . . and to get as much sleep as possible—with pills if it would come no other way. Once they were on the ground, sleep might he hard to find. Sleep, food, and equipment checks were the important things. Going into combat, every bit of electronic gear was subjected to intensive testing to make absolutely certain it was working. Anything that was in any way questionable was replaced.

"Nolan, from the minute our shuttle kisses dirt, I want you at my elbow, all the time," Girana said when he finally dismissed the squad—sent them for a meal, "unless the lieutenant or captain have other plans. If you're not with them, or doing something one of them tells you to, you're my shadow for as long as we're engaged in combat operations on Norbank. Understood?"

Lon nodded. "I understand, Corporal," he said quietly. He was no longer concerned about showing his . . . nervousness. Since the ship had arrived in Norbank's system, most of the men in the platoon had become quiet, almost withdrawn. The familiar banter appeared only rarely and seldom lasted for long.

"A man has to think," Janno had told Lon. "We've all been through this before, more than once. No matter what the job is, there's always that . . . chance." No one openly talked of the possibility of dying, not so close to action.

"We don't know yet how this contract is going to go," Girana continued. "It could be hairy as hell, or a beer run. The rebels might fight to the end, or give up as soon as they know there's a professional army on the ground ready to take them on. We won't know until it happens. So stick close and we'll get us through this with as little difficulty as possible.''

I'll get through it, Lon promised himself. *Whatever it takes.* All of the concern over his performance was becoming more annoying than reassuring. *It's like they all think I'll be useless without someone to hold my hand and tell me what to do every step of the way,* he thought. *Like I'm five years old and this is my first day at school.* At first he had welcomed the solicitousness. But it had gotten old in a hurry.

Then Lon chuckled softly. *Maybe that was the plan,* he thought. *Get me so mad that I'd forget to be scared.*

6

There were a thousand things to remember. Lon no longer had time for fear or nervousness. On the trek to the hangar, he occupied his mind with the plan for deployment, what was *supposed* to happen in the first few minutes following touchdown. In his mind he looked over the LZ again, recalling the photographs and the topographical overlays. The shuttles would land six miles northeast of the center of Norbank City, two miles from First River, which bent northeast east of the capital. The landing zone was a rocky clearing at the foot of a string of small hills that extended to the river and grew to the east and northeast. Only one significant creek would be between the mercenary battalion and the rebel lines around the capital, and the creek was shallow enough to ford.

Now that an assault landing was imminent, third and fourth platoons of A Company were quiet, each man alone with his thoughts. Many had the faceplates down on their helmets even before they left the armory after picking up their weapons, shutting themselves off from scrutiny. The noncoms were subdued with their instructions, speaking softly, using few words, showing no emotion. Even Phip had lost his usual ebullience.

One member of *Long Snake*'s crew stood just inside the hangar for the shuttle that third and fourth platoons would use. The hangar chief counted heads coming through the doorway, watched as the men filed into the shuttle, then confirmed his head count with the shuttle pilots and with

Lieutenant Taiters. Only when he was satisfied that no one was unaccounted for did the hangar chief step back through the doorway, seal the airlock, and move to his control station in a small room with a heavily shielded window that looked into the hangar.

Inside the shuttle, the men strapped in. The hatches were sealed. The lander's crew chief checked pressurization, then retreated to his post between the troops and the cockpit. Weapons were secured, clipped next to their owners—who also kept a grip on them. Safety harness straps were tightened. Squad leaders and platoon sergeants checked their men before they themselves strapped in. Finally, only Lieutenant Taiters was on his feet.

"Alpha Company will be first in," he said. "Colonel Flowers and battalion headquarters will be in right on our heels. It's up to us to secure the LZ. The rest of the battalion will be coming in almost immediately, so time is of the essence. We want to be on the ground and in position before the opposition even knows we're coming. The other shuttles will be touching down one after another, even as we're setting up our perimeter. Stay alert, and be ready for anything." He paused for a second, then finished with an ancient military cliché. "Good luck, and good hunting."

Lon Nolan took in a long, slow breath, held it for thirty seconds, then let it out just as slowly. There was a strange fluttering in his chest, something between fear and excitement. He looked over to where Corporal Girana sat, and reminded himself to stay right with the squad leader. Girana looked toward Nolan and nodded, as if he could read the cadet's thoughts. Neither man could see the other's eyes. The faceplates of their helmets were down, and the plastic was tinted, concealing the faces underneath.

No one said anything about hurrying up and waiting now. The entire battalion had to get into their shuttles before the launch process began. Hangars had to be depressurized; massive outer doors had to be opened before the landers could be ejected.

Lon became aware of a rhythmic thumping noise that seemed to grow in volume, but he needed half a minute to realize that it was the sound of his own heart. He did another breathing exercise to try to slow the rate. When that did not work, he tried humming "The Ballad of Harko Bain" softly, but could not get away from the distraction of his pounding pulse.

It'll be easier after you've been under fire for the first time and survived, he told himself. *Don't worry about it now. You've done everything possible to prepare.*

He went back to picturing the LZ, rehearsing in his mind the things he was supposed to do when the shuttle touched down and the doors opened. He concentrated on recalling every detail of the pictures of the LZ—hills on two sides, trees on the other sides, the direction that the squad was supposed to go to establish its section of the LZ perimeter.

"The hangar has been depressurized," the shuttle crew chief's voice said over a speaker. "We're opening the outer door now." Lon could feel, rather than hear, the heavy gears that lifted the door open. With no air in the hangar, the vibrations were transferred through the metal of lander and hangar floor. The door was eighty feet by a hundred, seventeen feet thick.

The grapple lifted the shuttle from the hangar floor and moved it out through the door, its boom telescoping to full extension. As a final gesture, nozzles in the grapple head released bursts of compressed air to move the shuttle farther from the ship before the lander's own maneuvering thrusters were used. The motions were gentle, easy. The hangar crew and the shuttle's pilots were all experienced, capable.

We're on our way, Lon thought as he felt himself moving against the straps of his safety harness when the shuttle lost the ship's artificial gravity. More than thirty minutes had passed since he had strapped himself in. He tried not to think of the next wait, while the entire battalion formed up near *Long Snake*. This one would not be as long. There were only nine shuttles in the assault group—two for each line company, the last for Colonel Flowers and battalion headquarters.

Eight minutes later, Lieutenant Taiters announced, ''Hang on, we're going in hot,'' over his all-hands radio channel. Twenty seconds after that, the shuttle's main engines throttled up and the craft started accelerating toward Norbank.

A civilian passenger shuttle would let gravity do most of the work of taking it from orbit to the surface of a world, perhaps taking half an orbit of the planet to get to the ground. A ''hot'' landing by military assault shuttles was different. They would nose over, aiming almost directly for the landing zone, and use their rockets to push their acceleration well beyond that of gravity, trusting in the materials they were constructed of to resist the incredible heat and stresses as they entered the atmosphere. Air would do some of the braking for the shuttle. Then it would spread air brakes and fire retrorockets—as late as possible—to slow it for a short landing. The idea was to give any waiting defenders as little time as possible to react.

The push and pull of gravity stresses were calculated to the limits of human endurance. For troops in the back of a shuttle there could be thirty seconds of near grayout. Lon felt as if he were being compressed into a two-dimensional object as the shuttle's acceleration peaked. Then the pull was reversed. He hurt. Blood pressed against his skin, as if seeking to escape. His face tingled painfully, as if thawing from frostbite.

Then the shuttle was on the ground. The craft continued to use its engines to brake. Lon was thrown against his straps, then back. For the first time in what seemed like an hour, he was able to take a full breath without difficulty.

''Lock and load!'' Lieutenant Taiters shouted over his all-hands channel. Bolts were run on rifles to put a round in the chamber; safeties were switched off. ''Up and out!'' Noncoms echoed the call. Hatches opened. Squads started moving toward their assigned exits. Everyone knew which door to use.

Lon stayed right on Tebba Girana's heels as they left the shuttle. The corporal veered left, and trotted toward the tree line some eighty yards away. Lon moved in perfect formation, bringing his rifle up to port arms. Weighed down with more than sixty pounds of equipment, neither man moved particularly fast.

For one brief moment, Lon had the vertiginous sensation of having stepped into a photograph. The angle was not the same, but there was enough in the view that clicked for the feeling to grab him. He squeezed his eyes shut, just slightly longer than a blink, and looked around, forcing himself past the moment.

The rest of the squad was close by, moving in a shallow wedge on either side of Tebba and Lon. They could all hear the sounds of the other shuttles starting to come in, before they reached the treeline and the perimeter they were to establish. The one thing they did not hear was gunfire.

I guess it worked, Lon thought as he went to ground. *We got down safely, away from any rebels.* The window of vulnerability was already near its end. The last shuttles were landing. Half of the battalion was moving to defensive positions, while the shuttle crews manned their guns and rocket launchers. An enemy attacking now would find its hands full.

The line of afternoon shadows encompassed most of the clearing, but sun still shined brightly on the slopes of the hills on the other side of the landing zone. It was not yet *dark*, even under the trees, but the shadows were thick, the lighting dim and green-tinged. There was a thick, earthy smell—soil and rotting organic debris. Where the duff was disturbed, the odor was more noticeable. Lon's nose twitched, and he fought the urge to sneeze.

He concentrated on scanning the forest in front of him. The squad, the entire company, was down on the ground in a loose line twenty yards inside the forested area. There was little undergrowth. The life here was high, in the canopy, where there was sunlight to fight for. Most of the trees showed no branches lower than fifteen feet, and some extended twice that high before branching. Most of the trees were deciduous. They appeared something like oaks or maples from Earth, though Lon thought that they were almost certainly species native to Norbank. The colony had not been in existence long enough for imported species to take over a wild area so completely and grow to such heights.

There's nothing moving out there, Lon thought, looking over the barrel of his rifle. He had more than just his own eyes to base that conclusion on. Sensors in his helmet, cameras and directional microphones, were far more sensitive—in both frequency and range. They were showing nothing man-high moving in the shadows, where Lon could not see. Nor were there any alarms from anyone else.

"Okay, people, we're moving," Platoon Sergeant Dendrow said over third platoon's channel. "The vector is two-six-five degrees. First and second platoons, skirmish line. Third and fourth, follow thirty yards back. The shuttles are ready to take off. We've got to make sure there are no surprises close enough to be dangerous." The shuttles were too important, and too inviting as targets, to leave them on the ground idle. They would return to the ship, although—with no enemy flyers to worry about—one or two might be kept available to provide close air support, flying a pattern over the area high enough to be safe from ground-fired rockets.

Lon got to his feet as soon as Corporal Girana did. The first two platoons moved away from the initial perimeter. As soon as they were thirty yards out, Lieutenant Taiters had his two platoons moving into position behind them. Lon checked the compass reading on the head-up display on his visor, making certain that they were on the right heading. Then he noticed Girana turning to make sure that the cadet was where he had been told to be. Tebba nodded, just slightly, satisfied.

"Keep your eyes open, Nolan," he said over a private

channel. "This may look like a piece of cake right now, but things can change in a hurry." Lon nodded back, and Girana turned his eyes to the front again.

The first skirmish line had gone only a hundred yards before Lon heard the shuttles throttling up and taking off. There was little separation between one and the next. They took off toward the east, away from Norbank City and the greatest concentration of rebel forces. Once they were out of the atmosphere, and far away from the threat of rebel attack, they could stooge around until all of them could dock with *Long Snake*, or be assigned to stay out to provide surveillance and ground support.

At least we'll have a ride out of here when this is over, Lon thought, trying to combat the irrational feeling that they had been deserted by the shuttles.

The advance of A Company was stopped by Colonel Flowers. The four platoons took up defensive positions, first and second across the front, third and fourth on the flanks and rear. The men were told not to dig in. "We won't be here that long."

The wait seemed long enough to Lon. He was prone, looking around one side of a tree. Corporal Girana was next to him, his rifle on the other side of the tree. If an attack came, there was not much cover for either man.

"They're getting everyone situated so we can move toward the city," Girana explained to Nolan after getting that information on a noncoms' circuit. "Delta Company has the farthest to go. It'll be ten minutes before they're in position." The corporal switched to his squad channel before he continued. "Get a drink, whether you're thirsty or not. And keep your eyes open. Bravo Company will be moving up on our flank. I don't want anyone getting trigger-happy and shooting at them."

The battalion would move in three separate columns, A, B, and C companies. D Company would provide rear guard, spread across all three columns. In the center would be Company A, B to the left, C to the right. The latter two companies would send flankers out. A Company would be responsible for sending scouts out in front. The platoons would take turns, if necessary, providing a squad for scouting. Fourth platoon would be followed by third. Corporal Girana had already been told that his squad would get the call. "We'll catch all the pit scraps this contract," Girana had told Nolan aboard ship. "That goes with having a cadet to baptize."

The shadows were deepening into darkness. Twilight faded rapidly under the forest canopy. Night-vision systems switched on automatically, giving a more garish green tinge to the scene. The system was not perfect. It gave a man about 70 percent of daylight vision. Contrasts were reduced, and resolution faded with distance, more rapidly than it did in daylight, but there was enough to let an infantryman operate freely in the dark.

Lon looked around. In camouflage battledress and helmets, it was impossible to distinguish who was who. Janno and Gen were easy. They were the largest men in the squad, Janno thin and Gen Radnor stocky. Phip was the shortest, but only by a narrow margin; still, Lon was used to the way Phip moved, the way he held himself. He was close to Lon, as was Janno. The man just beyond Janno was probably Dean Ericks, but only because that was the usual arrangement.

There was movement, finally, off to the left, in the distance. Lon tapped Tebba Girana on the shoulder and pointed. Girana nodded. "That's Bravo moving in," he said. "We've already verified that."

Meaning I didn't spot them soon enough, Lon thought.

Less than a minute later, Girana was on the squad channel. "There's been one slight change in plan. We're going out on point first instead of fourth platoon."

My fault, Lon thought. *They want to get me out where something's likely to happen as soon as possible. See what I do.*

"On your feet; let's go," Girana said, matching his own

actions to the words. "Two columns, by fire teams. Keep the columns close until we pass first and second platoons. Then we'll separate, thirty yards between columns, ten yards between men." He switched channels to talk to Lon. "I don't want you quite that far from me, Nolan, five yards, right behind me."

Inside their thin camouflage gloves, Lon's palms were sweating. "I'll be there, Tebba," he said.

Girana was the third man back in the left-hand column. He put Janno and Dean out in front, on point. They were the squad's best men for that job. They would alternate positions if the squad remained on scout duty for long.

"We've got to move fast until we get out where we're supposed to be," Girana said after his squad had started moving. "Then we play it slow and cautious, the way it's supposed to be. But the battalion is going to be ready to move in four minutes. Anything past that is our holdup."

The scouts would determine the speed of the advance. It was up to the advance squad to search for any enemy or their land mines and booby traps, to trigger any ambushes, or spot them before they could be sprung, and make certain that the route was as safe as possible.

"We're not picking up any enemy electronics," Girana said as they neared the line that the first two platoons of A Company were holding, "but we can't count on that as meaning anything against amateurs. They might not have electronics for most of their people."

It would be different up against a well-equipped enemy. Standard battle helmets with their radios, sensors, and computers provided a means of locating and identifying them, unless their shielding was better than the detecting ability of the enemy.

Lon's squad passed through the gap between first and second platoons and spread out. Intervals were easy to measure—the sensors in each battle helmet could give it to within inches—but everyone knew not to make them *too* exact. That would make it too easy for an enemy to target them. The "ten yards" between men varied between eight and fifteen. The columns varied the distance between them as well, only partly in response to changes in the lay of the land, getting closer or farther apart.

As soon as he passed the line of prone infantrymen that marked the front of A Company, Lon felt a difference. He knew that it was all in his mind, but the forest *felt* different once the squad was out in front of the rest of the battalion, alone, exposed, *expected* to make first contact with any waiting enemy. His pulse quickened. His senses seemed to become more acute, more alert. He kept his eyes moving from side to side—not erratically but in a careful pattern—searching for anything that might be the harbinger of trouble. He strained to hear even the softest sound in the green darkness.

Once they were well out in front of their comrades, the squad did not move at any great speed. The pace was more that of a casual stroll, with the man on point stopping occasionally to scan a hundred and eighty degrees. When the point stopped, the rest of the squad stopped as well, waiting for the man in front to signal that all was well and to start moving forward again.

There shouldn't be any mines or booby traps anywhere along here, Lon reasoned. *The rebels didn't have any warning where we would set down. They couldn't know where to plant them, and they can't have so many that they could put them everywhere we* might *land.* The logic was irrefutable—but almost irrelevant. It would only take one. Lon swallowed. His mouth was dry. The rest of him was bathed in sweat.

He glanced over his shoulder. The rest of A Company was moving now, more than a hundred yards behind the last man in the point squad. *The other columns must be moving as well,* Lon thought, but he could not see them. Their points would be a bit behind A Company as well. The overall deployment would look something like an arrow, with the center column's point squad a barb on the tip of the arrowhead.

In the first half hour, the battalion covered little more than a single mile. When Colonel Flowers ordered a five-minute halt, the point squad went on another fifty yards, giving themselves that much more of a lead over the rest before stopping—just long enough for the men to squat and take a drink of water, arranged in a semicircle, everyone looking out, still watching for the enemy.

"Remember, don't count on spotting electronics first," Girana warned the squad. "There could be several hundred of them waiting without anything to give them away."

A half dozen rifles opened up at once—semiautomatic weapons—and without the warning of helmet electronics. Fifteen minutes had passed since the battalion had finished its break and started moving again. The point squad was a hundred and fifty yards in front of the rest of A Company. The gunfire came from their left, and farther ahead, at about a thirty-degree angle to the line of march.

Lon heard someone fairly close to him grunt in pain, but he could not tell who it was. He was already diving for the ground, and bringing his rifle into firing position. He had seen the bright dots of muzzle flashes.

"About a hundred and twenty yards," Lon said on his channel to Corporal Girana. "I saw where they were."

Girana did not answer directly. On the squad frequency, he said, "Return fire, and get yourselves into the best cover you can." There was a pause before he asked, "Who got hit?"

"Me, Raiz," a voice said, obviously through clenched teeth. "Left shoulder. Something's broke."

"I'm with him, Tebba," Harvey Fehr's voice said. "I'll get him patched up."

"Right," Girana said. "Dav, you stay with them. The rest of you, let's go. We've got to keep those guns occupied until Bravo Company can get a platoon around to the side."

As soon as they got to their feet again, moving low, bent over almost double, the men of Lon's squad came under fire again. There were more than six rebel weapons being shot now.

7

The squad shifted into a skirmish line as they got up and started running, and they spread out. Lon stayed close to Tebba, never more than five or six yards to the side, and usually a step or two behind. They all ran from cover to cover, firing on the move, stopping to get better shots whenever they had a tree to shelter behind. Half of the squad would lay down covering fire with rifles and grenade launchers while the rest moved forward to the next cover. They did not charge directly at the enemy positions, but angled to the right, closing only slowly, more interested in taking the least dangerous route.

Air came hard to Lon. *I shouldn't be gasping for breath,* he thought as he squatted behind a tree and dragged in a lungful, and then a second. *We haven't run* that *far.* He held his breath long enough to sight in on a muzzle flash and fire a short burst toward it. He repeated that with the next spot of light he saw in the distance. Then it was time to get up and move again.

Girana gave no indication that he was aware of Nolan. The corporal had enough to do, his own firing and running, and keeping track of the squad while he received updates on the advance of B Company. But Lon worked hard to stay where he was supposed to be.

The enemy gunfire was wildly inaccurate. Despite the closing range, no one else in the squad was hit during the advance. They moved to within eighty yards of the nearest muzzle flashes before Girana told his men to find the best cover they could and stay down. At that range, it was incredible that more men had not been brought down.

"We just need to keep them in contact now," he said. "Bravo has a platoon moving in on the left. Watch for the blips of their helmets. And keep your heads down."

Lon had already spotted the four dozen bright green dots on his head-up display. Green for friendly forces. If any enemy electronics had been spotted, they would have shown as red blips. A few seconds later, the other platoon started firing on the enemy. Then their first volley of rifle grenades started to explode. There were a half dozen or more, the sounds of their blasts too close together for Lon to be certain how many there were. The enemy gunfire dropped to almost nothing, quickly.

"Okay, let's go!" Tebba shouted, pushing himself to his feet. "Suppression fire."

"Suppression fire" meant to spray the enemy positions with automatic rifle fire. The concern was not so much to inflict additional casualties on the enemy as to keep them from shooting back—if there were any of them left to shoot.

Lon continued to trigger short bursts—the ideal was to fire off three shots at a time—moving his rifle's muzzle from side to side, while the rest of the squad did the same. At first the platoon from B Company also continued to pour rifle fire into the enemy's last known positions, but as Lon's squad got close, the other platoon quit firing, to avoid inflicting casualties on friendly forces.

There was dense undergrowth around where the Norbanker rebels had been, ground cover growing along the bank of a small creek. Much of that had been blasted loose by the grenades. And the trees and bushes that remained had shredded leaves near where the grenades had exploded. Trunks were pitted with shrapnel wounds. The smell of explosives remained. Little else did.

Girana came to a halt, gesturing for his men to circle the site and keep watch to make certain that no other rebels were near. Lon saw two bodies that had been mutilated by the explosions, missing extremities, one almost torn in half. He stopped, and swallowed against the rise of bile in his throat. Then he saw more bodies.

"Belzer, Ericks, Steesen, move across the creek and set up to make sure they don't come back," Girana said. "Keep on your toes. We sure didn't kill all of them."

Tebba moved slowly through the area, counting bodies, checking to make certain that there were no living left among the dead. Lon stayed close to the corporal, watching for both of them. He had fitted a new magazine to his rifle, and ran the bolt to put a round in the firing chamber.

"Eight dead," Girana said when he finished counting. "There were at least a dozen rifles firing, maybe half again that many."

"They couldn't have expected that few men to stop us," Lon said. "Did we just happen on a patrol, or were they scouting for a larger force?"

Girana grunted. "You've got the right question, but I don't know the answer any more than you do. Hang on a minute."

Lon waited, guessing that the corporal had to change channels to answer a call. It lasted for thirty seconds.

"We're off the point," Tebba said when he returned to the private channel with Lon. "As soon as Bravo's people get here, we go back to pick up the men we left behind and let fourth platoon send out its point squad."

"Any word on Raiz yet?" Lon asked.

"He'll live. Dav says it looks like the shoulder is busted, maybe the collarbone as well, so Raiz is going to be out of action for a while."

"They gonna take him back up to the ship?"

Tebba shrugged. "If possible. For now, I guess they're going to have to put him in one of the portable trauma tubes, leave a few men with him."

"Us?"

"No. The medics with battalion will take care of him. And one man from Bravo Company who was hit as well."

Lon felt that it was strange to be moving in the opposite direction to the rest of the battalion, withdrawing while others were advancing. The men Lon's squad passed turned their heads to look. Lon noticed, but did not dwell on the curiosity. He had an itch in the middle of his back. He did not like the withdrawal for the simple reason that he did not like facing away from where the danger had been. There were still Norbanker rebels out there, somewhere— *behind* him for certain, maybe all around.

Frank Raiz had already been removed by the medics. Dav Grott and Harvey Fehr rejoined the squad. "He'll be okay," Grott assured the others. "They've already got him in a tube."

The trauma tube was the mainstay of medical help, the crowning success of nanotechnology combined with the latest gross life support equipment. If a wounded man could get into a tube alive, he had more than a 98 percent chance of surviving even the most extensive damage. After just three minutes in a tube, the odds improved to virtually 100 percent. While life support machinery maintained the injured or sick individual, the body was flooded with organic repair units, molecule-sized factories that compared what they found with what they *should* find, correcting anything that did not match the template. Four to six hours would correct most problems, even compound fractures and deep bullet wounds. Only neurological damage—to the brain or spinal cord especially—could take more tube time. And only that and regrowing amputated limbs would keep a victim out of action more than eight hours. The collapsible portable units that troops could carry into the field with them were not as elaborate—or elegant—as hospital units, but they could still do the job properly.

The rest of A Company's third platoon cycled to the rear of the column. Its second squad took a break, waiting for them. Phip sat next to Lon and lifted his faceplate. "Well?" he asked.

Lon shrugged, not knowing how to put his feelings into words. "Now I've been there," he said, his voice flat. He had not started to think back over the experience. There was no hope of making any sense of his feelings yet. The question had opened a jumble of images and impressions, none coherent, none ready to gel. "I don't know what to think," he added after a long pause. *Maybe that's best,* he decided. *Don't analyze it to death. Just let the experience be.*

"You ever figure it out, let me know," Phip said, getting to his feet. "I've been through twenty firefights, some a lot bigger and worse than this one. I still don't know what to think. It's just, well, every once in a while, I get to thinking that it's a hell of a way for a man to make a living."

By choice, no less, Lon thought. One of his hands was trembling. He held it out and stared at it until he could force the shaking to stop. *I wasn't afraid,* he told himself. *Not while it was happening. There was no time for fear then. No use in letting it start now, after it's done.* But the trembling was slow to recede, and even after it was gone, there was a hollow feeling in his stomach—a feeling that had nothing to do with hunger.

"You did good," Corporal Girana said, just behind Nolan. Tebba had his helmet visor up. He was not speaking over the radio. His voice startled Lon.

"I didn't hear you coming," he said, lifting his faceplate as he turned and looked up.

Girana squatted next to Nolan. "It's okay, kid," he said. "I've been at this nearly half my life and I still get the shakes afterward, almost every time."

Lon shook his head. "It didn't seem, well, *real* until I saw the bodies of the men we killed. I heard bullets whizzing past. I knew about Frank getting hit, but . . ."

"I know. Don't beat yourself over the head with it,"

Tebba said. "We're in the business of killing. Kill or be killed."

"And trust that we're on the right side?" Lon asked.

"Trust that we're on the right side," Tebba agreed.

"At The Springs, I had patriotism to give me all the reason I needed. The NAU, right or wrong, was my country. I expected to defend my country. What are *we* defending, the right to make money, to take the best offer we can get for using our guns?"

"We fight for Dirigent, for the Corps, for our mates," Tebba said. "Don't get too hung up on the word *mercenary*, kid. We fight because we're Dirigent's stock in trade, important to the survival of our world. We're serving our world, the same way you would have been serving your country if you had made it to the Army back home. We fight because we're Dirigenters. It doesn't matter if you're born here or immigrated. You're as much a Dirigenter as any of us, even those whose families have been here since the world was first settled."

Lon nodded, slowly.

"And now it's time to get moving again, before the rear guard walks over us."

They got to their feet. The rest of the squad was waiting, some standing, some still sitting. But as soon as Girana gestured to the others, everyone was up and ready to move. They moved back into their two columns with the rest of third platoon, and hurried until they had closed the gap that had opened up between them and the rest of the company.

Lon resumed his post near Girana. Lon worked hard at concentrating on the terrain around them, trying not to let his focus fade because they were—supposedly—in the most secure spot in the line of march, at the rear of the center column, with a sizable rear guard behind them. *Keep your eyes and ears open,* Lon told himself. *You've got to stay alert.*

It was only a few seconds later that Tebba was on the squad channel telling everyone the same thing. *Stay alert.*

Keep your eyes moving. Don't assume that we won't be the first to contact the enemy, even where we are.

The battalion was within two miles of where surveillance had placed the rebel lines facing Norbank City when the next attack came. This attack was in more strength, and came against the column on the right, C Company. The rebels hit behind the first platoon, staging along the flank. Somehow C's flanking patrol had missed the rebels. They had gone right past the ambush without seeing anything.

Lon could not guess how many rebels were in this attack. It sounded as if hundreds of rifles started firing before C Company could respond. But Lon did notice something that he had not in the earlier ambush. The battalion's rifles sounded different from the rebel guns. The report of one of the Corps' 7mm rifles was higher in pitch and shorter in duration.

"Let's go," Sergeant Dendrow said on the platoon channel. "We've got to try to box in these rebels."

The unexpected call sent a flutter—almost of excitement—through Lon. He got back to his feet. Everyone had gone down at the first sound of gunfire. Now it was time to move. Trotting off toward the tail end of C Company, Lon was able to reason out why the rear platoon in the center column would be chosen for the job. Charlie Company was pinned down by the attack. Bravo had the other flank to protect. Delta had to hold the rear, and the rest of Alpha had the front, along the line of march. This might not be the only enemy force in position to attack. So Alpha's third platoon was the logical choice.

I guess, Lon thought. His mind was brought back to more immediate concerns by several explosions. They were not DMC grenades exploding in the rebel positions. These sounds were louder, closer, and deeper, somewhere along Charlie Company's front. The rebels had grenades, or rockets, of their own.

"We go out around the end of Charlie, then turn the corner once we get a hundred yards out," Dendrow said on a circuit that included Lon as well as the platoon's non-coms. "Turn the rebel flank and put the squeeze on."

Nice plan, Lon thought. *I hope it works.* Plans always looked good going in. It was so simple to chart movement and assume results. But all too often it seemed that the success of a plan depended on the enemy being compliant.

Sergeant Dendrow was heading well to the right, through the gap between Charlie and Delta, trying to give the rebels a wide berth. But it did not work. As soon as the first squad approached the line that Charlie Company was defending, the entire platoon came under fire. The rebels had apparently anticipated the movement.

Dendrow's shout of "Cover!" was scarcely needed.

Now what do we do? Lon wondered once he was down and had his rifle pointed in the right direction. The rebel gunfire had stopped as the platoon went to cover—the rebels who were facing this one platoon at least; the rest continued to fire on C Company. *Send the rear guard around even wider?* The decision was not Lon's, but he could hardly help but think what he might do if it were. He *was* in training to be an officer. Someday he might be faced with a similar situation. *No,* he decided. *That wouldn't be my first choice at least. If they expected us, they might expect that as well. I'd try to get air support in to make a run along the enemy lines, rockets and guns, thin them out and pin them down, soften them up first. Then move in to clean up.*

"Stay down and return fire when you've got a target," Girana said over the squad channel. "Don't waste ammo."

The men knew the drill—basic operations tactics. Even Lon could respond automatically to the conditions. He remembered that most night fire tends to be high, so he lowered his point of aim to compensate. Even a bullet hitting the ground in front of the enemy had a chance to do damage—by ricocheting or kicking up bits of rock or wood—while rounds sent way over the enemies' heads could do nothing.

Several minutes passed before there was any news. "One of the shuttles is coming in to make a pass over the enemy," Girana relayed to his men. "Another four minutes."

Lon glanced at the time line on his visor. *This could be a long four minutes,* he thought. He wondered how many casualties the battalion was taking in the meantime.

He felt fear, but it was inconsequential because he was too busy to worry about it. There was a knot in his stomach, a passing awareness that he might die and not even know it—or worse, that there could be minutes of horrible suffering before death came. But he watched his front, firing when he spotted muzzle flashes or anything that seemed to be movement out in the distance, where the enemy was. His hands were steady, his aim true. Although he could not see targets going down, he was certain that he must be scoring at least an occasional hit.

The attack shuttle, coming in at supersonic speed, arrived ahead of its sound, screaming as it came out of a power dive, throttling back and deploying its braking flaps to avoid overrunning its own bullets and rockets and to give itself a little longer time over the target. Lon glanced up, but there was no chance of seeing the shuttle. Even its heat signature was masked by the forest canopy between them.

Lon did hear the first missiles that the shuttle launched, and then the exploding chain sound of its two Gatling guns spewing bullets as it strafed the rebel position. Each six-barreled gun could fire eighteen hundred 12mm rounds a minute. Rockets exploded. Bullets chewed gaping lanes through the canopy, and through everything they encountered below. The din was almost physically painful, pressing against eardrums and brains. When it ended, there was a hollowness to the remaining sounds, the insignificant-by-comparison noise of rifles firing on the ground.

Then there was a screech from the air as the shuttle pilot tortured his craft through a tight turn to return and make a second run, from the opposite direction. *The metal complaining that too much is being asked of it,* Lon thought.

He had to resist the urge to put his hands over his ears. With a helmet on, the gesture would have been futile.

The second run by the shuttle was as painfully loud as the first. When it ended, there was an order for the platoon to move forward again. Three of C Company's four platoons were advancing as well. A frontal attack was not the preferred method of dealing with the situation, but after the assist from the shuttle, it might not be too costly.

Fire and maneuver: It was the most basic of tactics, one that the soldiers drilled in every week in garrison. The platoon moved by squads, two advancing while the other two laid down suppressing fire. There was still shooting coming from the rebel positions, but much less than before, and less organized. The rebels had obviously been seriously damaged by the air attack.

This time, though, the surviving rebels did not retreat, did not abandon the battlefield, as the first ambushers had. They stood and fought. At the end, it came down to hand-to-hand combat, hands and knives as well as guns.

Lon saw a figure rise from the ground, just in front of him. The man wore a helmet, but it had no faceplate, nothing to disguise the look of naked hatred on the face. The man held his rifle in his left hand, like a shield. His right hand held a machete. Lon could not get his rifle around in time to shoot the rebel. He swung at the arm holding the knife and moved in closer, trying to bring his rifle up to use the butt against the man's head. But they collided and went down together. Lon found himself on the bottom, his rifle out of his hands, holding onto the wrists of his assailant—who had also lost or discarded his rifle. The man still had the long knife, though, and was doing everything he could to use it against Lon.

After a moment of struggling in which neither of them seemed to get anywhere, Lon got his feet under him, knees bent, and propelled the rebel up and over his head. Lon rolled to his left, reaching for his pistol at the same time. The rebel was up and scrambling for him again, still holding the machete, swinging for Nolan's neck. Lon pushed himself farther to the side as he brought his handgun up and fired, twice. The first bullet staggered the rebel. The second caused him to fold up and fall, half against Lon, their faces only inches apart.

For just an instant, Lon stared into the open eyes of the dead man, smelled his sweat—and death. Although the look seemed to stretch on endlessly, he knew that it could only have been a couple of seconds. Then he pushed the man off, turned, looked for his rifle, and retrieved it. The first thing he did was glance at the muzzle, looking for any sign that dirt might be plugged in it. He saw nothing, but without a more thorough check, he could not be certain, and a plugged barrel could be deadly.

Lon looked around. There was still fighting going on, but not especially close to him. He got to his feet, slowly. His right knee ached—a dull pain, not enough to sideline him even momentarily. He had run races hurting worse.

"You okay?" Phip asked, coming over and grabbing Lon's upper arm. "I saw you down with that rebel."

Lon nodded. "I'm okay, just a little sore."

"Jeez, you've got blood all over you," Phip said, moving back half a step.

"Not mine. His." Lon gestured vaguely toward the body of the man he had killed. The first enemy he *knew* he had killed. Lon looked around. "Where's Tebba?" he asked.

"Over there." It was Phip's turn to make a vague gesture. "One of these mothers got a swipe across the back of Tebba's legs, right behind the knees. Looks like he mighta cut some tendons or muscles. Medics got him already."

Lon looked around again and saw two men working on someone lying on the ground. He went over. Tebba's visor was up. The face showed no pain, though. He had already been given something for that, and the anesthetic had started to work.

"You okay?" Girana asked when he saw Nolan. That

was not until Lon knelt next to him and got close. With his visor up, Tebba had no night-vision help.

Lon nodded. "I got tied up for a couple of minutes. Looks like my guy wasn't the only one with a machete."

The corporal grunted. "I'll never be able to carve a leg of lamb again," he said, failing to get a smile on his face to go with the attempted jest.

For the moment, the medics had done what they could. They had stopped the bleeding and immobilized Girana's legs. Now they had to wait for a trauma tube to put the corporal in. Those were suddenly in short supply. The wounded had to be triaged to make sure that they went to those who might not survive without them.

"Hell of a way to start a contract," Tebba said. He closed his eyes, squeezed them tight, as if feeling a sudden pain.

No commander liked to start a contract with a pitched battle. It made everything else more difficult. And it wasted men. Open combat was always something to be resorted to only when nothing less . . . costly could be found to do the job, but to start that way. . . .

"Looks like the opposition is a bit more formidable than we were led to believe," Lon said.

Tebba opened his eyes again. "I think you could say that," he said. "Now leave me alone. Find Dav. He's the squad leader until I get back. Stick with him."

8

"I imagine they'll think twice before pulling another stunt like that,'' Lieutenant Taiters said, speaking with his noncoms and Lon by radio. Third and fourth platoons were together again, part of the defensive perimeter that the battalion had established after putting to flight the last few dozen of the rebels who had attacked. After digging two-man foxholes and piling the dirt up in front of them, the men were on half-and-half watch, spelling each other so that everyone could eat and take at least a few minutes to rest. ''The shuttle must have been more than they bargained on.''

Twelve mercenaries had died in the attack. The bodies of eighty rebels had been found. A dozen wounded and four unwounded men had been captured. Two platoons of D Company were escorting the Corps' own wounded and killed to a clearing where two shuttles could put down to evacuate them. The wounded Norbanker rebels would have to take their chances with the care the Corps' medics could provide—without trauma tubes. There were not enough of those for the wounded of the Second Battalion. They would not be ''wasted'' on the enemy.

''What's next for us, sir?'' Sergeant Dendrow asked. ''We keep on the way we planned?''

''The colonel hasn't decided, I think,'' Taiters said. ''We're still picking up the pieces and regrouping. We do need to get into the capital, make contact with the government, one way or another. But we need intelligence as well.

With the assets the rebels have put against us already, there must be a hell of a lot more than a thousand of them under arms. And they've got more than hunting rifles. They've managed to get some fairly good equipment from somewhere.''

''Think they've got anything more than equipment from outside?'' one of the squad leaders in fourth platoon asked.

''We weren't up against professionals tonight,'' Taiters said, knowing what the corporal was hinting at. Dirigent was not the only source of mercenaries—merely the largest and best organized. At least three other worlds specialized in providing hired armies, and several others dabbled in the service.

''Any chance the old man will decide to sit tight and call for reinforcements from home?'' Platoon Sergeant Weil Jorgen of fourth asked.

Taiters hesitated before he answered. ''I don't think we're in that bad of shape yet, Weil. Besides, I'd hate to laager up for a month while we waited for help.'' It would take twelve days for a message rocket to reach Dirigent, and another two weeks or more for the reinforcements to arrive—even if they were dispatched immediately. ''Even if the Norbank government were willing to amend the contract for additional manpower.''

''You think the Norbankers knew the opposition was so much stronger than they told us?'' Lon asked. ''Or is their intelligence that poor?''

''I don't know, Nolan,'' Taiters said. ''Even if they did know, we'd play hell proving that they gave us phony data.''

''Hell, Lieutenant,'' Dendrow said, ''if we told them to pony up for sufficient manpower to do the job, and threatened to pull out if they didn't, they wouldn't have much choice, would they? They gave us bad dope, whether they knew it or not. That gives us an out. I know how the escape clauses in our contracts read.''

''And you know what the Council would think if we

pulled out without being able to prove that we were intentionally suckered,'' Taiters said. ''Anyway, it's bad for business.''

Business? We lost men tonight, Lon thought. *Don't they enter into the equation?*

''Enough of this,'' Taiters said. ''I'll let you know as soon as I hear something. Get yourselves a few minutes off, just in case the rebels don't know enough to stay away yet.''

The shuttles that took the dead and wounded back to *Long Snake* had also brought in ammunition for the men on the ground. Lieutenant Colonel Flowers and his company commanders spent a considerable time in conference—talking face to face in the center of the defensive position that the battalion had formed instead of simply using their helmet radios—trying to decide what to do next. There were, however, no additional rebel attacks on the battalion during that time. The conference broke up a few minutes before midnight.

When Captain Orlis returned to his command post, he called Lieutenant Taiters, then switched them to a radio channel that included the noncoms of third platoon—and Lon Nolan.

''The battalion is going to stay put for now,'' Orlis said. ''We're going to improve our positions and give ourselves clear fire zones around. We've got shuttles flying recon, and that will increase after dawn. We'll also send patrols out to plant bugs and mines, try to buy a little time. The colonel wants one platoon to try to infiltrate, get through the rebel lines into the capital, and make contact with the government.''

Lon guessed what was coming before Orlis told them. *Everybody gets sucked in because of me.*

''Third platoon gets the draw,'' the captain said. ''Taiters, you'll lead. Leave fourth platoon to Sergeant Jorgen, have them spread out to cover your section of the perimeter.

I'll have more instructions for you, Arlan. For the rest of you, be ready to move out in ten minutes. You'll have to find a way into Norbank City before first light.''

No one said anything to Lon about it being his ''fault'' that they were chosen. He waited during the few minutes while they were getting ready to leave. *They all have to know,* Lon thought. But no one even gave him a sidewise glance. The men used the time to eat and make certain that their rifles had full magazines attached. They had drawn new ammunition from the stores brought in by the shuttle that took off the wounded.

With just three minutes left of the ten, Lieutenant Taiters called a conference with the platoon's noncoms. Lon was with Tebba—who had just been released for duty by the medics, his wounds had not been serious enough to require a full session in a trauma tube—looking at Girana's mapboard while the lieutenant discussed the route they would take.

''We'll leave here and head north,'' Taiters said. A yellow dot on all of the mapboards showed what Taiters was pointing at. ''Once we get across this creek, we'll turn due west. That should put us far enough out that anyone watching the battalion won't spot us, providing we're not seen on the way out. When we get here''—he indicated a spot not quite a mile from the city, just outside the reported position of the rebel perimeter—''we'll loop around to the north again and try to enter Norbank City somewhere along here, depending on the deployment of the rebels.'' He moved his cursor back and forth along a small section of the city ''wall''—part stockade-type construction surviving from the early years of the colony, part barricades thrown up between buildings as the rebels approached. ''The rebels are more concerned with us right now. They can't have every point around the city guarded equally well. We'll just have to find a gap.''

He did not sound overly troubled by that. Lon wondered

if the lieutenant was truly so confident or if it was just some of the acting he had been told about.

"Okay, let's get moving," the lieutenant said. "First squad has the point. And, all of you, think sound discipline. If the rebels don't *hear* us, there's no reason why they should *see* us."

The platoon took its time leaving, moving with exaggerated care, going through the lines one squad at a time. The men moved on their stomachs, crawling out to a shallow gully that ran at an angle across the front, following that for fifty yards before getting out and moving into the heavy undergrowth near the first small creek. Once the entire platoon had transited that stretch—where they were most likely to be observed—first squad got up and started moving again.

First squad set the pace, moving single file, five to eight yards between men. At the beginning, there were frequent pauses. If the rebels had the battalion under observation— as was likely—it was in the first few hundred yards that the platoon was in the greatest danger of being seen. And attacked.

Lon had the external microphones in his helmet set to maximum gain, listening for any sounds in the forest. He scanned off to either side as well, alternating that with watching Corporal Girana in front of him and watching where he stepped, each movement slow and deliberate, anxious not to make a leaf crackle or a twig snap underfoot. His focus on the fundamentals kept him too occupied to listen to the voice of fear at the back of his mind.

For the most part, there was no talk on the radio. The communications system the DMC used would transmit even subvocal "whispers," and the helmets were insulated well enough that they would not carry, but other than an occasional word from the point or a terse command from one of the noncoms, there was silence.

Lead Sergeant Dendrow was behind first squad, near the front of second squad. Lieutenant Taiters was farther back, between third and fourth squads. In the event of a rebel ambush, it was unlikely that both of the platoon's top men would be taken out. Within second squad, Janno and Dean were in front of Corporal Girana. Phip was right behind Lon, with the rest of the squad behind him. Lance Corporal Dav Grott was at the rear, making sure that the squad did not get spread out too far or bunch up.

Time lost its normal cohesion. Each step felt as if it were a frozen frame of time, bounded by indefinable gaps. Even a breath seemed to be a distinct entity, existing in separation from all of the other breaths and steps, a series of independent bubbles rising through a viscous liquid. After a time, Lon felt as if he were wading through some glutinous morass that grabbed at his feet and legs. The strain started to become apparent in his knees and calves, a dull ache that he could not shake.

Lieutenant Taiters did not call for a break until they reached the near bank of the creek that was to mark where the platoon would change direction. "Five minutes," Taiters told the platoon before switching to the noncoms' channel and saying, "I want you all watching the other bank for any hint of trouble, upstream and down." The creek was not much, ten feet wide where the platoon would cross, and—according to the aerial survey—no more than two feet deep over a rocky bed. Both banks were lined with dense underbrush, vines and bushes taking advantage of the water and a narrow avenue of sunlight.

Third platoon settled down for its rest in a loose box formation, ready to meet trouble if it should come. But there was no interruption, other than the call of some night-flying bird that passed by overhead.

Lon was startled by the sound. Then he realized that it was the first bird, or animal, he had heard since landing on Norbank. *Well, the sound of the landers would have scared any off then,* he reasoned. *And the gunfights. I guess a thousand men moving together must have done it the rest of the time.* Then he started to think that he really knew little about the native wildlife of Norbank, not even the predators that might be dangerous to humans. But before he could pursue that thought, the break was over. It was time to start moving again.

Fourth squad took the point, with the other squads in the same order they had been before, third squad now bringing up the rear. Taiters and Dendrow shifted to remain in the same relative positions they had held before.

The farther we get from the battalion, the less likely it is that we'll come across rebel patrols looking for us, Lon thought. That deduction did not make him any less nervous. This was enemy territory, and the rebels might have men moving anywhere in it, for any purpose. If third platoon was spotted, it would not matter if the men who found them were looking for them or not. *We get caught out in the middle of nowhere, we might never get back.* That thought was enough to keep the edge sharp.

I could have run from the battalion to the center of Norbank City in fifteen minutes in full battle kit, Lon told himself after the patrol had been out for more than an hour— and had covered less than half of the distance their route would require.

The platoon changed direction again, starting the counterclockwise loop that would bring them near the north side of Norbank City. When they reached the apex of that semicircle, the platoon stopped for another short rest, and third squad took the point for the final stretch.

The one time my being here doesn't stick the squad, Lon thought. *They don't want me out on point to make noise and bring disaster down on all of us.* It was a relief not to have the strain of being on point, but at the same time Lon felt a little miffed at the thought of being considered too much of a risk.

"This is where it gets hairy," Lieutenant Taiters whispered on a conference call with his noncoms before the platoon started moving again. "We don't want to trip over any sleeping rebels. That would be almost as bad as running into troops they've got on watch. There's a chance that they won't have more than a few sentries posted, but we can't stake everything on that hope. So far, they've shown themselves to be better than we might have expected.'' The noncoms and the lieutenant had mapboards out again, holding them close so that the faint green glow from the screens would not give them away.

''We'll stop when we get here,'' Taiters said, noting a position on his mapboard. ''Then first squad will go on alone to find an avenue for us. Once they spot a gap, the rest of us will follow through.''

Again, he's passing us by, Lon thought.

Just after starting out again, the platoon came across one of the few roads leading to Norbank City. It was just a wide dirt track through the forest, but trees had been cleared, leaving an open space twenty feet wide. The platoon hit the road at an angle. Crossing occupied nearly fifteen minutes as the platoon crossed one or two men at a time, watching and listening for any sign that they might be seen.

The platoon reached the spot that Taiters had chosen. Just in front of them, no more than a hundred yards away, was a rebel camp. From what they could see at that distance, it appeared that there might be more than a hundred men bedded down with no more than six or seven sentries—and those were concentrated on the far side, facing Norbank City. The three squads of the platoon who were to wait went prone, facing the rebel position. Lon was almost afraid to breathe, even though that could not give him away at such a distance unless the rebels had advanced sound-detection equipment and knew how to use it properly.

We've got one more problem the lieutenant hasn't mentioned, Lon thought during the interminable wait for fourth squad to find a way through the rebel lines. *The people inside Norbank City don't know we're coming.* There were no absolutely secure communications links between the battalion and the local government, no codes they shared. Anything on the radio, even on a tight beam, might be intercepted by the rebels. *If we tell the people inside that we're coming through the lines, we might be telling the rebels at the same time.*

Getting shot by the people the battalion had come to help would be no less painful than getting shot by the rebels. *Dead is dead. We've got to infiltrate two sets of lines, and the second might be the hardest. The people inside are apt to be a bit paranoid by now. They're on the defensive, and getting the short end of the stick.*

Thirty minutes passed—*slowly.* The first signs of morning twilight would be showing in the east in less than two hours. If the platoon could not get into Norbank City before then, they would have to pull back into the forest, hide through the day, and try again that night. *And the colonel wants us in the city before first light,* Lon reminded himself. *We don't get in, we've failed.* And that would mean, at least to him, that *he* had somehow failed, even though—logically—there was nothing that he could hope to do to make sure that the platoon succeeded.

"Okay, we've got our path," Taiters' voice whispered over the noncoms' circuit that Lon was monitoring. "It's not much, but first squad is between the rebel lines and the city, and they think they see a way in there as well. Once we get that far, we'll try communicating with the folks inside."

"I don't want to even hear water sloshing," Girana told his squad after the lieutenant had finished. "Use part canteens to fill others, then dump any water that's left over."

That only took a minute, and that was all the time there was. Second squad was put in the middle of the three. They moved to the right, going past the encamped rebels, then turned toward Norbank City again. During part of the passage, while they were closest to the enemy camp, the men moved on hands and knees. Then they were back on their feet, at a crouch, staying as low as possible, and even more attentive to sound discipline.

Their pace now made the earlier slow walk seem like a sprint. It was rare for any of the men to take more than three or four steps before squatting for a moment, waiting. Then the squad in front would start forward again. There were no oral messages now, not even subvocal commands. Everything was done with cautious hand signs. When they got close to the rebel line, it was down on hands and knees again, and then flat on their stomachs for thirty yards of slithering across the most exposed stretch of their route.

Lieutenant Taiters had moved to the front of the three squads, and when they finally reached the squad that had been sent ahead to find a route, he went up to join the squad leader just behind the point. There was a long pause, with the rest of the platoon lying motionless, heads down.

In a brief glance ahead, Lon had seen the outlying buildings and part of the old wall that had once completely surrounded Norbank City. Trees had been felled and arranged across one gap, almost directly in front of him, not fifty yards away.

We'll be sitting ducks if we have to go over that, he thought. He closed his eyes briefly. Even at night they might be visible to rebel sentries, and taken under fire. *We could lose half of the platoon in seconds.* He turned his head and lifted up just a couple of inches. Things looked more promising to the left. There appeared to be a gap— or a barricade too low for him to see it from his snail's-eye perspective.

He lowered his face to the ground again, wishing he could burrow into it. They were between the warring factions now, and if the lieutenant could not clear the way in front of them, they might be taken under fire by either side—or both.

Is he going to get on the radio and try to raise someone inside? Lon wondered. It would have to be on an open frequency, one that the rebels might be monitoring as well. In that case, there was no telling who would get the word first to the nearest armed men. *Maybe he's going to send one man in ahead,* Lon thought then. *Hope one man can get to the barricade and get the message to the defenders. And be believed.*

Twenty minutes. Twenty-five. Lon felt as if he were about to drown in his own sweat. He noted when thirty minutes had passed—half an hour of waiting, not knowing what was going on. If they did not get going soon, and get into the city, they would be out in the open between the lines when daylight finally came.

Let's do something, he thought. *Anything.* The waiting was nearly unbearable. Lon felt an urge to get up and run for the city, knowing that he could not—would not. But the desire grew and demanded more and more of his attention.

Thirty-five minutes. Thirty-six.

"Okay," Taiters' voice whispered in Lon's earphone. "We're going in. Take it very slow. We're going under a barricade at the end. The defenders have opened a spot. Close up. I want everyone head to foot. And stay down."

Another three minutes passed before it was time for Lon to move. He followed Girana, keeping his head within a few inches of the corporal's feet, moving exactly with him, shifting one arm and leg forward and then the other, scooting his body along the ground, dragging through the dirt like a snake, even lifting his head as little as he could get by with.

Fifty yards was a long distance to crawl that way, with a rifle over one arm and equipment on a web belt dragging every inch of the way. Before he had covered half the distance, Lon's arms and legs ached. He felt as if he had skinned both knees and elbows, and his upper arms seemed ready to cramp. He had gone another ten yards before he could see where the barricade had been opened. Girana started moving a little faster. Nolan picked up his own pace, though it also increased his aches. Twelve yards to safety. Ten. Lon wanted to close his eyes and scurry as fast as he could over the remaining yards, or get up and run for it.

But he did neither. He continued to follow Girana, holding his position, getting dirt kicked up against his faceplate more than once.

Some of the grass had been worn away under the column of crawling soldiers. It would leave a clear path, once daylight came, to show the rebels where the platoon had passed—an insulting finger pointing straight at the rebels.

As soon as Lon was under the barricade, there were hands on his shoulders, pulling him up and pushing him to the left. A few feet away, Corporal Girana was gathering his squad, counting men as they came through the barricade. Lieutenant Taiters came over and directed them to places along the wall, while the rest of the platoon continued to snake through the opening. It took another five minutes before the last one was through and two locals moved the logs back into place, closing the gap.

We made it, Lon thought. His hands started to tremble again. He worked to hide that until he could force them to be still.

9

They aren't very disciplined, Lon thought, looking at the defenders who had gathered to stare at the mercenaries. *They should be watching the enemy, not us.* The Norbank government troops seemed to be quite nervous. They had been under siege by a determined enemy who might overpower them at any time. And they were amateurs. *The rebels weren't very disciplined either,* Lon conceded. *They fought hard but not well.*

The Dirigenters broke into squads and moved apart—a safety measure. It would not do to have everyone clumped together in case the rebels chose to attack with rockets or artillery—if they had artillery, which was unlikely but not impossible. Lieutenant Taiters talked to two militiamen. Then everyone seemed to be waiting for someone else to arrive.

"Nolan, come to me," Taiters said on a private link. Lon went over to where the lieutenant was standing with Sergeant Dendrow and several Norbankers. "We're waiting for the garrison commander and a representative of the planetary council," Taiters explained, still using the radio, and speaking softly enough that none of the locals standing nearby could hear the conversation.

"Yes, sir," Lon acknowledged. "What do you want me to do?"

"For now, just stick with me. This is a part of the job you need to learn about."

Lon nodded, then took a moment to study the faces of

the nearest Norbankers. None of them wore a helmet or night-vision goggles. There was nothing to hide their drawn faces, with lines of tension and fear. The faces and bodies were uniformly thin, as if they had gone far too long on too little food. *Are they still dependent on grown food?* Lon wondered. *After a hundred years they should be getting most of their food from replicators.* Throughout the worlds that humans had settled, food replicators were the primary use to which nanotechnology had been put. Molecular assemblers could take raw materials—recycled waste products as well as any "fresh" organic material available—and produce any food known to mankind and programmed into the system. That avoided the necessity of taking months to grow specific crops or to raise livestock, which consumed food during the entire inefficient process of reaching slaughterable size.

The group was clustered next to a building, away from direct exposure to anyone outside the perimeter. Lon could see the sky beginning to show a strong hint of dawn. Daylight would come quickly. Norbank City was only four hundred miles north of the equator, even though the climate was more subtropical or temperate than tropical because of the prevailing winds off of the ocean and a polar current that followed the coastline.

Lon had been standing near Lieutenant Taiters for ten minutes when two men approached from the direction of the center of the capital. Norbank City was not excessively large, and it was fairly narrow from north to south.

"I'm Ian Norbank," one of the men said as he reached the group, "Vice Chairman of the planetary council. This is my cousin, Colonel Alfred Norbank, commander of our militia."

Lon quickly smothered his grin. *What's so magical about the title of Colonel?* he asked himself.

Taiters lifted his visor and identified himself—rank, name, and unit. He introduced Lon only by name.

"We're glad to have you here," the vice chairman said.

"We were beginning to fear that you wouldn't arrive in time. But where is the rest of your battalion? These few men you brought won't make much difference."

Taiters hesitated before replying. Lon fancied that he could almost hear the lieutenant counting to ten before he would trust himself to speak. "The rest of the battalion is close, sir," he said finally. "It appears that your rebels are considerably more numerous, and better equipped, than we were led to believe by your representative."

"Their numbers have grown of late," the vice chairman said. "To be honest, we no longer have any real knowledge just how many rebels have taken arms against their lawful government. We're unable to get reliable intelligence."

"There is still the question of where they obtained military weapons," Arlan said. "We were told that they had only hunting and sporting weapons of local manufacture or of early import. But they've used rockets, grenades, and military rifles against us. Those are hardly the hunting weapons."

"I don't know where they might have gotten them, unless they're making them themselves," the vice chairman said. "It has only been in the last week that they started firing an occasional rocket into the city here—maybe a dozen altogether."

Taiters decided to postpone continuing that part of the discussion. Instead, he turned toward the other Norbank, Colonel Alfred. "Colonel, just how many men do you have under arms, under your command?"

He hesitated before replying. "As of sunset yesterday, three hundred and eighty-two."

"All here in the city?" Taiters asked.

The colonel nodded. "I had men south of the river before, but we've had no contact with them in . . . weeks. Everyone who could still move was brought into the city, to defend it. As far as we know, the rebels haven't bothered the outlying communities. But we can't get men or supplies in from those locations."

"What is your logistics status?"

The two Norbanks glanced at each other before Vice Chairman Ian answered. "We're running short on just about everything but water. The rebels haven't been able to cut our supply of that, not with First River handy. But food is getting scarce, and we have very limited supplies of ammunition for our weapons."

"How limited?" Taiters asked, looking at the colonel again.

Once more, Alfred hesitated before answering. "On average, perhaps thirty rounds per man. But since we have no standardized issue, that varies widely. For a few of the rifle types, it may be less than ten rounds per man."

"Hunting and sporting weapons?" Arlan asked.

The colonel nodded. "They run the gamut from .22-caliber to 9mm big-game rifles, with quite a few shotguns in the mix. All but a few are either semiautomatic or bolt-action. We have no more than ten rifles capable of fully automatic fire, and those are among the group with the least ammunition available, old 7.5mm military weapons that were surplus when this colony was founded."

Museum pieces, Lon thought, closing his eyes for an instant. A museum was the only place he had ever seen the old European 7.5mm assault rifle. *They weren't only surplus a century ago, they were obsolete. You couldn't get ammunition for them on Earth today without having it special-made.*

"We are in dire need of the weapons and ammunition you have for us," the colonel added.

"That's beyond my purview, Colonel," Taiters said.

We're not supposed to land those until we're sure that there's no chance of them falling into rebel hands, Lon recalled. *This could get ticklish.* He was not surprised that Taiters had sidestepped the question. The only man who could change that directive was Colonel Flowers, the battalion commander and contract officer.

"The more immediate problem is breaking the siege on

Norbank City so that we can begin to operate on the offensive," Taiters said. "Since we landed here last night, we have faced several attacks by your rebels, one of those in considerable numbers."

"We heard that," Ian Norbank said.

"We were sent in to coordinate our operations with your militia," Arlan said. "We had no secure radio channels before. Now, with us here, we can communicate and be certain that the rebels won't be able to intercept our transmissions."

"You want us to provide covering fire so that you can bring the rest of your troops into the city?" Alfred Norbank asked.

"I don't know what Colonel Flowers has in mind," Taiters said, thinking, *I know damn well he's not going to move the battalion into a besieged town. That wouldn't get us anywhere.* "You'll have to discuss that directly with him. That's why we're here, to permit that sort of communication."

"The sooner the better," Colonel Norbank said.

"Perhaps we should move inside first, closer to the center of town," Vice Chairman Norbank said. "It's almost daylight, and the rebels like to use snipers."

Taiters nodded. "Very well. I need to see to my men first, get them settled down out of the direct line of fire."

"It would help considerably, Lieutenant," Alfred said, "if we could put your men straight into the perimeter."

"I'm sorry, Colonel. I don't have the authority to permit that. We might be ordered to rejoin the battalion as soon as it gets dark this evening, and they've already had twelve hours of hard duty. If there is someplace we could let them get a little rest, out of the line of fire?"

"I'll have the sector commander see to it," the colonel said, with obvious ill grace. But he was unwilling to argue the point. He called someone over and gave the order.

"Now, Lieutenant, if you'll come with me?" the vice chairman suggested, gesturing to the south.

Taiters nodded. Lowering his faceplate again, he said, "Nolan, I want you and Tebba to wander around town for a bit. I need an independent assessment of the situation. You tell him what I want. I'll go with these people."

"Yes, sir." Lon remained standing where he was as the others walked away. Colonel Norbank stopped and looked back at him for an instant, then continued on with his cousin and Lieutenant Taiters.

Lon switched channels to his link with Corporal Girana. "Tebba, the lieutenant has a job for us." He repeated what Taiters had said.

"I'll be right with you, as soon as I see that the others are in place," Girana replied. "Just a minute or two. Time to let the big shots get out of sight."

"Just what are we supposed to look for?" Lon asked as soon as Tebba got to him.

"Everything," Girana replied. "All we've had so far is what they've told us. Time to see for ourselves. Keep your eyes open. We want to know what shape they're in, any weak spots in the defenses, anything that might help us."

"You mean like the fact that they all look hungry?"

Girana grunted softly. "Yeah. I noticed that too."

Nolan told the corporal what Colonel Norbank had said about ammunition, and wanting the weapons that the Dirigenters were bringing them.

"I bet they want to get their hands on good stuff," Girana said. "What's more likely, right off the top, is that we might be able to make ammunition for the rifles they've got, especially if they've kept cartridge casings. Get a listing of the calibers they need, make sure the specs our replicators have match the weapons." He shrugged. "Once we're in a position to get shuttles in and out of here regularlike."

They started walking, heading east, ready to do a clockwise tour of the city. They generally stayed away from the perimeter—keeping at least a single line of buildings between them and the defenses, moving carefully across the gaps where they might come under the sights of a rebel rifle. But they made frequent trips to the barricades, looking at the defensive works that the government had erected, and looking at the people who were manning them. The defenders watched Lon and Tebba. Only rarely did any of the Norbankers speak to the mercenaries first. Girana did talk, being friendly, asking men what it had been like for them, occasionally getting in a question that would be of more direct use, but being casual about it all.

"Got to be careful about this," Tebba explained to Lon. "Act too damned curious and they'll clam up faster than spit."

Before the insurrection and siege, most of the men who were defending the walls of Norbank City had lived beyond them. All of the homes and farms near the capital had been taken over by the rebels—or destroyed. The city had been fairly small. Most Norbankers still lived in more rural settings, overwhelmingly to the west and southwest of the city, near First River. The majority had farms or large gardens. Even within the city there were extensive gardens. But the edges, the areas with most room between homes or other buildings, had been indefensible. The people loyal to the government had been forced to concede the outskirts and pull back into the more densely built-up sections of town. Women and children were crowded into every available shelter, while most of the men either bore arms on the perimeter or did other work to help, building ramparts, carrying supplies and messages. There were more men than weapons—by a large margin.

"Everything's built of wood," Lon observed after they had gone around nearly half of the defended area. They were near First River. It was only there, along the river, that there appeared to be any stone structures at all.

"I noticed," Tebba replied. "For being here a hundred years, they sure haven't gotten very far. Little stone, and I haven't seen any brick or concrete block construction

·yet, and not a hint of anything modern, like plascrete.''

"You figure they've stayed primitive by choice or just circumstances?"

"Beats the hell out of me," Girana said. "It's not like they don't have any money. They came up with enough to hire a battalion of soldiers and buy a lot of munitions. They must have had the money to import small factory systems."

"Or did they just save it all for something like this?"

"Whatever. I've been on worlds that looked a lot more advanced after no more than twenty years. I've only counted a dozen floaters''—ground effect vehicles—''so far. More carts and wagons, vehicles that need animals or people to pull them."

The entire perimeter was dangerously undermanned, a very thin dotted line. There was no sign of reserves posted behind the perimeter, just an occasional building where perhaps a dozen men might be sleeping, although Tebba and Lon did not enter any of them. "Fewer than four hundred armed men to guard the entire city," Tebba muttered, shaking his head. "They couldn't stand up to any kind of direct attack. A platoon could break through before they could gather enough guns to stop them."

"Then why haven't the rebels done it? They sure hit us hard last night. If they'd hit the town like that before we got here, we wouldn't have anyone to work for."

"Maybe they don't *know* just how weak the government forces are," Tebba said. "Or they just lacked the confidence. They hit us because they had to. Their best hope was to weaken us before we could join forces with the government militia and go on the offensive. Every day we're here will make the odds against the rebels that much worse. Even if they don't have any military advisors in, they could probably figure that much out."

They stopped for several minutes to look at the destroyed bridge across First River. It had been made of wood, a narrow lane of planks on wood pilings—tree trunks that had been sunk into the riverbed. Only one section of the bridge, about twenty yards long, had actually been destroyed, closer to the south bank of the river than the north. The rest still stood but did not look very sturdy.

"Just as glad that's out of action," Tebba said. "I'd have hated to have to cross that buzzard under fire."

"I see what you mean," Lon said. The river was a hundred yards wide. The water beneath was no more than fifteen feet deep in the primary channel, and the current was not particularly swift, but the bridge would have been deadly to soldiers burdened by more than fifty pounds of equipment even if it did not expose them to fire from both banks. "Can you imagine getting cut off somewhere in the middle, not able to get to either shore?"

"I can imagine a lot of men drowning before they could shed enough weight," Tebba said, very softly.

Along the river, the government forces were spread especially thin, but no more were needed. There were sentries posted a hundred yards apart. If the rebels attempted a waterborne assault on the city, there would be more than ample time to move troops to repel it.

"You know, the only hint I've seen of night-vision gear is a few 'scopes on rifles," Lon commented after they had traversed about half of the riverfront. "I know it was near dawn when we got inside the perimeter, but you'd think the men would still have them with them if they had them."

"I imagine there are a few," Tebba said. "But, you're right, there can't be many."

"The rebels didn't seem all that troubled by fighting in the dark. You think maybe they had more of them?"

"We didn't find any among the dead. If they do have them, they're more worried about retrieving them than they were about their dead and wounded." Tebba stopped walking then. "Far as that goes, we didn't find a lot of ammunition or weapons with the dead either. I guess the rebels are doing what they can to conserve equipment." He stopped and looked around.

"Let's rest here for a few minutes. Take time for lunch

where no one's likely to see us and where there's the least danger of snipers.'' They had heard occasional shots through the morning, always at a distance, never close enough to pose a hazard.

The two men spent four hours circumnavigating the defensive perimeter. They never saw any sign of a changing of the guard. Men slept at their posts, while neighbors continued to watch. Nor did there appear to be a midday meal. Water was plentiful, and consumed frequently. The day was hot enough to demand that.

All around the city, unarmed men worked at improving the defenses. Buildings away from the perimeter were being dismantled to provide materials for the ramparts. Behind that perimeter, men were also working on a second line of defense, digging ditches and piling the dirt up in front of them, filling bags with dirt and sand for redoubts, erecting new barricades, linking remaining buildings, lining walls.

''Setting up a shorter perimeter is a good idea,'' Tebba told Lon. ''With as few men as they've got, especially. But unless they've got the explosives to destroy the outer line when they do fall back, it won't do them much good.''

''Even if they do, wouldn't that just postpone the inevitable?'' Lon asked. ''Unless they've got more troops coming in to relieve the siege, we're it. If it's too much for us and the men they've got.''

''The colonel will never let the battalion get cooped up in here,'' Girana said, hoping he was right. ''And as long as we're on the outside, free to move, the rebels won't be able to squeeze this town too hard. If worse comes to worst, we can hold on for the month it would take to get a message rocket back to Dirigent and for reinforcements to reach us.'' He paused, then added, ''But that would be one hell of a hairy beast.''

10

Lieutenant Taiters listened to Girana's report, with a few additions by Nolan. He asked questions. After Taiters was satisfied that he had learned everything of value from their tour, he called Colonel Flowers. Tebba and Lon waited; the lieutenant had not dismissed them.

"We have problems here," Arlan told them after he finished his conference with the colonel. "You've seen some of them. The government has fewer men under arms than we were led to expect. The problem is more a shortage of weapons and ammunition than warm, willing bodies. They've got more people who could fight if they had something to fight with. And food is a problem. The people cooped up in this town have been on half rations for three weeks, and it's going to get worse. They don't have enough armed troops to defend their perimeter, so we can't co-opt any of them to move against the rebels. And we can't count on being able to land weapons and ammunition inside the town. First of all, the rebels have surface-to-air missiles capable of bringing down a shuttle. Secondly, there's too much chance of Norbank City falling, and we don't want to hand the rebels enough of our weapons to arm another battalion."

"So it's going to be up to us to face the rebels alone?" Lon said, turning it into a question.

"It could come to that," Taiters admitted. "But the surveillance that's been done overnight and this morning shows that there might be a lot more rebels under arms than we thought, even yesterday. The latest estimate is that there are between a thousand and fourteen hundred rebel troops maintaining the siege here. There is another group, nearly as large, working to get into position to attack the battalion again. Colonel Flowers is doing some maneuvering as well, trying to make sure that we choose the time and place for the next engagement. The rebels appear to be moving more people this way. Our shuttles detected a number of small groups between their town and here, split up and using the cover of the forest and hills to their advantage. We can't even estimate how many more soldiers they're bringing in. At least several hundred, perhaps a lot more.''

Tebba Girana whistled softly. ''We're talking odds of at least three to one now, aren't we, Lieutenant? Maybe worse?''

''Maybe worse,'' Taiters agreed. ''The government is finally willing to concede that the rebels are more numerous, better equipped, and better trained than their own forces. If they could get all of their troops together, they might total ten thousand or more—out of a population base of under sixty thousand. That assumes that the entire second wave supports this rebellion, something that the government has yet to concede.''

''You mean basically all of the adult men,'' Lon said.

''If we have normal colonial population distribution,'' Arlan said. ''And if that sixty-thousand number is accurate. There's no reason to suspect that it's any more accurate than the other numbers the government here gave us.''

''I know I'm outta line, sir,'' Tebba said, ''but hasn't the misinformation reached the point where we could walk away honorably? I mean, the Norbankers gave us a lot of bum data, maybe lied to us. This is a job for a full regiment or more, not just one battalion, even us.''

Taiters shared Girana's opinion, but the decision had already been taken. ''The contract has been amended again,'' he said. ''We're going to stick it out.'' He did not share all of the information with Girana and Nolan. Colonel Flowers was taking precautions. An MR—message rocket—had already been sent to Dirigent with the latest information. Flowers had not requested reinforcements—yet—but he had included a conditional request: "If any six-day period goes by without a progress report, we will almost certainly be in big trouble and require substantial assistance."

"So what do we do now?" Lon asked.

"The Norbankers are going to assemble a company of men who are willing and able to fight but who don't have weapons. We're going to break them out of the perimeter, get them someplace where we can bring in weapons, ammunition, and food. I know that goes against the idea of not putting our weaponry in danger of falling into rebel hands, but they'll be outside the city, and the locals won't be operating independently. Our people will be with them. If it works the first time, we'll do it again, a company at a time. Do what basic training we can in too little time. Altogether, there are probably a thousand, maybe twelve hundred, men available here in the city. If we can get to some of the outlying villages, we might be able to find even more people who are loyal to the government, but we only brought enough weapons to equip one battalion, so there wouldn't be much point in the rest—unless we capture significant stores of rebel weapons, and once we do that, the danger might be over."

"The rebels aren't likely to sit back and let us do any of that, sir," Lon said. "We might get away with it one time, but once they see what we're doing. . . ."

"The rest of the battalion won't be idle, Nolan," Taiters said. "We'll hit the rebels hard, on the ground and from the air." The head of the planetary council wanted the Dirigenters to use their shuttles to attack the rebels' town and the villages around it, to force them to withdraw troops to defend their families. Colonel Flowers had vetoed that immediately, almost angrily: *"We don't make war on unarmed women and children."*

"We're still holding the aces, even if we prove to be up against five-to-one odds," Taiters continued.

"You know, sir, it's really not the rebels who worry me the most right now," Tebba said. "It's the idea of baby-sitting a couple of hundred unarmed men until we can bring in guns and ammo, and then having them with us when we fight the rebels. They could be as dangerous to us as they'll be to the rebels."

Taiters laughed. "Then it'll be up to us to make sure they get enough concentrated training to minimize that danger."

"Us, sir?" Lon asked. "Our platoon?"

"The first time, at least," the lieutenant replied. "We're the ones inside the perimeter."

"We're not going to try to sneak them out the way we came in, are we?"

Taiters laughed again. His helmet was up, and Lon could see that the laughs were helping to drain tension from the lieutenant. "No. The battalion is going to attack to open up a route for us. I don't have the details yet, but it should be this evening, not too long after dark. We'll want to be well clear of the closest rebels by daybreak tomorrow."

There was time to rest then. Lon slept for more than three hours. It was a deep slumber, almost unconsciousness, not the light, troubled sleep that the veterans in the squad had told him about, disturbed by the slightest noise and kept from being satisfying by fear and uncertainty. When Phip woke him, past midafternoon, Lon had difficulty getting his mind fully alert, struggling out of the sluggish stupor.

"What is it?" Lon asked, yawning and stretching, trying to force his mind back to full function.

"Our shot at sentry duty," Phip said. "Time to let some of the other guys get a little shut-eye."

"Anything happen yet?" Lon sat up and looked around. He rubbed at his eyes. That made them burn, so he used a little water from his canteen, leaning back to pour it on them.

"Nothing much—not in here, at least. They're starting to assemble the locals we're to take out with us."

"You heard about that."

Phip grunted. "Yeah, we heard about it, in gory detail." In the DMC, knowledge was shared, as far as practical. Dirigenters were not mere cannon fodder, but professionals. Even the suggestions of a private would be listened to, evaluated, and—if warranted—adopted.

"That gory detail include anything about the operation the battalion's going to run to give us a clear shot through the lines?" Lon asked, getting up to a squatting position. "When, where, and what?"

"No, but I guess the colonel has something in mind. There have been a number of firefights. One was awful damned close."

"Any word on what happened?"

Phip shook his head. "Not that's got down to us. What I'd *like* is for the whole battalion to show up. Let us move the locals into the middle of a diamond and get out to somewhere the shuttles can get into."

Lon shook his head. He figured that he was as alert as he was going to get without more sleep. "I don't think it'll work like that. There are too many hostiles around. It'll do more good if the battalion works to keep them away from us."

"I hope they at least cut loose the rest of the company to help," Phip said. "We're going to be leading the blind, taking them out after dark without night-vision gear. They'll make a racket, and we'll be lucky to cover a mile an hour, even if the rebels aren't on our butts every inch of the way."

"Sounds like you're not too happy with the arrangements," Lon said. It worried him too.

"Not a damn bit happy," Phip conceded. "Not with any of it. I think we should go back to the ship until we can bring in enough men to do the job the local yokels want us to do. Or just leave them to their own devices after the bum information they gave us.''

Lon looked at the ground, then shook his head slowly. ''No, it's better to get it over with. Weren't you the one who told me that we'd be able to take ten-to-one odds against the sort of opposition we're likely to meet on a contract like this?''

''If I did, I wasn't sober,'' Phip said. ''Look, we're in this like it's just a business, remember? Last stands are bad for business, and they don't do the soldiers on the ground a damned bit of good either.''

''Put in for two weeks' furlough,'' Lon suggested. ''I'm sure the lieutenant could use a good laugh.''

''Furlough? This town hasn't even got a bar that's open. They've commandeered all of the alcohol for medical use. That's how primitive this rock is.''

The squad did not walk sentry tours, or stand at specific guard posts. The platoon was away from the perimeter. It was just necessary to keep a few men up and ready to use their weapons to protect the rest of the platoon for the minute or two it would take them to wake and respond if an attack came.

They were not far from where the company of unarmed Norbankers was being assembled, where they had cover from the buildings between them and the front line. They were not *completely* unarmed, but their weapons were knives and clubs. Lon saw one man with a compound bow and a quiver of arrows. *That might come in handy,* Lon thought, nodding to himself. *I can think of times when that might be the weapon of choice. Be better with night-vision goggles, though, or a helmet.*

He stared at the archer for a moment, wondering if the Corps ever used weapons so primitive. *Can't hurt to mention the possibility,* he decided. That would have to wait, though. Lieutenant Taiters had finally decided to try to get an hour's sleep himself. Lead Sergeant Dendrow was awake but occupied, talking with one of the groups of men who would be trusting their lives to the mercenaries that night. That left Girana. Lon went to Tebba, pointed out the archer, then asked his question.

Girana made a sound somewhere between a grunt and a chuckle. "I don't know if we've ever used archers. That some of your Cowboy-and-Indian stuff from Earth?"

"I never thought of it that way," Lon said. "Maybe it is, subconsciously. I just thought that there might be times when a silent weapon like a bow might be just the ticket. Even a beamer isn't totally silent, and if the enemy has the right gear, a beamer targets the shooter every time he pulls the trigger."

Girana shook his head. "I don't know. It sounds like a cockamamie idea to me, but it can't hurt to make the suggestion. Hell, maybe you're right."

Lon went back to where he was supposed to be, with Phip, Janno, and Dean. Thinking about bows let Lon avoid thinking about what might happen that night—for a minute or two at a time. He had been uneasy about the prospects even before hearing Phip's dissatisfaction. *I've had my blood rite. I've been in combat. All I have to do now is get back to Dirigent alive and without disgracing myself to get my commission. Let's not make it any harder than it has to be.*

He watched as the sun dropped toward the horizon. Somewhere, fairly close, a firefight was going on—rifles, grenades, and rockets. It built in volume and then, suddenly, dropped to almost nothing. For several minutes Lon looked around the corner of a building toward the perimeter. He could see the smoke of this latest firefight, smoke from the grenades and rockets, smoke from fires they had started in the woods. With sunset just minutes away, there were even occasional glimpses of orange flames against the shadows of the forest.

"That's nothing, really," Phip said. Lon almost jumped,

he was so startled by the voice speaking close to him. He had not heard Steesen get up and move. "When the whole horizon is smoking, burning, along one side, then you've got something. Lucky it's not the height of the dry season here. A wildfire could really raise havoc."

"I think this will do, for me," Lon said. "We don't have to try to set any records along the way."

Phip laughed. "Now you're getting the right idea. Do the job and get out as easy as possible."

"I don't think there are any easy ways out of this," Lon said. Phip did not reply, but only because there was a call from Lieutenant Taiters on the all-hands circuit.

"The action should be starting in about an hour," Taiters said. "Listen up, this is what we're going to try to do . . ."

11

There were limits to the practical routes out of Norbank City for the Dirigenters and the unarmed militiamen. The only forest cover was north and east of the defensive perimeter, where the terrain was uneven. From north-northwest around to southwest, to First River, most of the ground had been cleared and used for farming. The city's spaceport was on that side as well, thousands of acres of cleared land. There was not enough cover on that side of the city to hide two hundred men—only occasional small groves of trees, mostly fruit and nut trees of terran species brought along by the original settlers. The nearer of those all held rebels now, as did the port.

After sunset, gunfire was almost constantly audible inside the perimeter. A series of small firefights, initiated by the Dirigenters—a squad or a platoon at a time—was intended to disrupt the rebels while the rest of the mercenaries moved into position. The main force made every effort to avoid contact with the rebels, to ''get lost'' long enough to provide an element of tactical surprise when the attack was finally launched.

Inside Norbank City, Sergeant Dendrow and his squad leaders briefed the Norbankers who would be traveling with them, telling them what would be expected, warning them to stay close together and to remain as silent as possible. The militia ''company'' numbered only one hundred and forty men, thrown together just that day. They had no training or experience as a unit.

"It's going to be like trying to keep a flock of hungry geese quiet," Arlan Taiters told Lon.

The loyalists manning the perimeter were all alert now, kept awake and nervous by the gunfire outside—some of it less than a half mile away. But there was no shooting from inside the city. All of the defenders were under orders to conserve ammunition. They were to fire only if there was a direct assault on their lines. With the fighting going on out in the forest now, there was not even any sniper fire coming in.

Colonel Alfred Norbank now had a DMC radio that would allow him to confer with Colonel Flowers. And he had unarmed runners to keep him in contact with the sections of the perimeter.

An hour after sunset, Lon's platoon and the Norbankers who would be going through the perimeter with them moved east, toward the point where they would make their breakout. They were careful to avoid exposing themselves to any rebels who might be watching through nightscopes on their rifles.

Once they were in place, Lon took a moment to lift the faceplate of his helmet and look up at the sky. *Too many stars and not enough clouds,* he thought. The night would not be dark enough to suit him. Then he shrugged. *At least there'll be a little light for the locals. They won't be totally blind.*

He lowered his visor and glanced at the timeline on his head-up display. It would be an hour before the order to move came, maybe ninety minutes. The battalion would attempt to drive a wedge into the rebel lines northeast of the city to open a corridor for Lon's platoon and their charges. Once they were through, the battalion's actions would depend on the prevailing conditions. They would attempt to do as much damage to the besieging forces as possible. If they could roll up a significant section of the rebel line, they would do that before moving to help establish a secure landing zone for the shuttles that would bring in supplies for the Norbankers. Otherwise they would withdraw immediately, continuing to screen the group coming out of the capital.

Ninety minutes after sunset, the second element in the preparatory work started. Two shuttles attacked rebel units. One worked over the force that had been trying to contain the main force of the Dirigenters. The other worked over the rebels besieging the city. Guns and rockets. Each attack shuttle made two passes, with twenty minutes between. Then those shuttles burned for orbit and rendezvous with *Long Snake* while two more shuttles came in to cover the main action.

"Get ready, but keep down," Taiters warned over his platoon circuit once he got word from battalion. "If everything goes right, we'll be moving out in fifteen or twenty minutes."

The start of the battalion's attack was clearly audible. Colonel Flowers hit the rebel line with everything he had. The squads and platoons that had been cut loose from the main body to make harassing attacks earlier resumed, wherever they were around the rebel lines. Thirty seconds later, the latest pair of shuttles added their rockets and gatlings to the fray.

"That'll give them all something to think about," Phip whispered. "I know I'd hate to be on the wrong end of all that."

"Don't feel sorry for the rebels," Lon whispered back. "The more hell they catch now, the less we'll catch when we go out."

The unarmed militiamen looked uncomfortable. Lon wondered if they were thinking of the men on the receiving end of the barrage . . . or if they were simply facing their own fears, knowing that the attack meant that the time for them to go out through the enemy lines was getting that much closer.

"The battalion is pushing forward now," Lieutenant Taiters said on the channel to Lon and the platoon's noncoms.

"As soon as they get the path open for us, we'll be moving. Squad leaders, tell the locals you're responsible for."

The militiamen had been divided into four platoons. Each Dirigenter squad was assigned to escort one of them. Lon tagged along when Corporal Girana went over to "his" Norbankers.

"We'll be going out pretty soon," Tebba told them. "I know you're nervous, but we'll get you through the best we can. All that noise is designed to open a safe path through the rebel lines. Just remember to stay as quiet as possible, and stay together. When one of us gives an order, don't ask questions. We'll explain if there's time, but there probably won't be. Just do what you're told and save the questions for later.

"When we go through the lines, we'll be moving as fast as possible for the first few hundred yards," Tebba continued. "Jogging, not an out-and-out run, so it shouldn't be too difficult even if you're not used to heavy physical exercise." The men who had been chosen for this militia company ranged in age from eighteen to forty, but none of them had appeared to be hopelessly out of shape. "Stay low, but stay with the group. We won't be able to dawdle to collect stragglers."

They should be able to keep up, Lon thought. *We're carrying full combat kit, and they're not carrying anything but themselves and maybe a knife or club. If they can't keep up like that, they won't be much use even with guns.*

He turned his head as the sounds of fighting drew closer. *Can't be more than a couple of hundred yards out,* he thought. *We'll be going very soon now.* Lon looked at Tebba. Girana nodded, as if he had read Lon's thoughts. *Very soon.*

"Get the squad over here, Lon," Tebba said. Lon lowered his faceplate and made the call on the squad channel. The others moved quickly, taking up the positions that Girana had assigned them before. One fire team would stay on each flank of the platoon they were covering. Girana would be at the front. Dav Grott would be at the back, trying to prevent stragglers. The other squads were also moving into position with the locals they were to escort. All that was needed now was the order from Colonel Flowers to move.

Three minutes later the first order came, to move up to the barricades. "Stay down, out of sight," Girana warned the Norbankers. "When I give the word to move out, *move.*"

Once he got to the barricades, Lon could tell that the fighting had started to move to either side. Directly in front of him there was relative silence. The gunfire had broken into two distinct segments as the rest of the battalion worked to provide a wide corridor out of town for them.

Anytime now, Lon thought, looking toward Lieutenant Taiters, who was thirty yards away. The lieutenant's head was slightly bowed, in the attitude that many soldiers almost habitually adopted while they were talking on the radio. Lon's hand moved along the side of his rifle, the fingers feeling to make certain which position the safety was in: *on.* That was where it was supposed to be, until they headed out.

Anytime. Lon turned his attention to his breathing, long, slow breaths, using that to help relax him, just a little. He did not want to be *too* hyper when they started out. That would come soon enough, as soon as bullets were coming close and they were running the gauntlet.

Lieutenant Taiters lifted his head and looked around, scanning his platoon and the Norbankers. Lon caught a breath on the way in and held it. *Here it comes.*

"By squads," Taiters ordered over the platoon channel. "Ten yards between sections. Go!" He brought his right arm up and back in a gesture, pointing over the barricade. A dozen Norbankers from the perimeter force pulled two sections of the barrier out of the way. First squad went through the nearest opening, herding their militiamen along a little roughly.

"Let's go!" Tebba ordered over his squad channel as

soon as the first group was nine paces out. "Nolan, stay with me."

Lon went through the gap right at Girana's heels. The two of them stopped just beyond the barricade as the Norbankers and the rest of the squad came through. Only when Tebba saw Dav in the gap did he start running to get back to the front. Nolan stayed with him, dropping back only a few feet, running crouched over, rifle at port arms, the safety now switched off. For now, there was no question of maintaining normal separation between men. The mercenaries had to stay close to the Norbankers.

The ground in front of the barricades was open and relatively flat, and, with the available starlight, it was no great challenge for men without night-vision equipment. The few buildings that had stood between the current perimeter and the forest had been razed, the rubble burned or dumped into cellars.

Lon and the other members of the squad stayed close to the Norbankers, urging them on with gestures and, when necessary, with a hand on an arm, tugging, pushing. *Sounds like a herd of stampeding buffalo,* Lon thought. He *had* heard buffalo running, if not stampeding. The Springs had maintained fifty of the animals on one section of the military reservation, a tenuous link to an all-but-forgotten past. *I hope the rebels don't have sound detectors planted.*

It was more than a hundred and fifty yards from the barricades to the edge of the forest. The nearest trees were young, saplings, some no more than five or ten years old. There was also undergrowth along the verge, where vines and shrubs could fight for a share of the sunlight.

Out in the open, Lon could feel a strange crawling sensation along his spine—a nervous response to danger. Enemy fire might start coming in at any time. With the Norbankers so bunched up, gunfire could scarcely avoid finding targets, unless the shooters were abysmally bad marksmen. Professional soldiers firing automatic weapons would butcher the group. The chance of survival would be small.

They're not pros. They don't have a lot of automatic weapons, Lon told himself as he stopped to urge on the Norbankers nearest him. He hoped that the second statement was as accurate as the first. The rebels did have *some* automatic weapons. The Dirigenters had learned that in their first large-scale firefight. But most of the rebel rifles had appeared to be semiautomatic or even bolt-action—the same variety of weapons that the loyalists in Norbank City were armed with.

Lon felt as if crossing the open range between city and forest were taking forever, as if the men were running on a treadmill. They ran, but the forest appeared to come no nearer. Lon was not paying attention to the timeline on his helmet display, but by the time he was halfway to the first line of trees, he would have guessed that ten minutes had passed—more than ten times the actual elapsed time. Seconds ticked past in preternatural slow motion. He felt that he was aware of every iota of sensory input, every breath, every heartbeat. It seemed almost as if he could hear each individual gunshot in the battle that was raging to either side, now at least two hundred yards off to left and right.

"Drop back and help Dav keep the stragglers in, Nolan," Girana said on his private channel.

Lon stopped instantly, glad for even a few seconds' respite. The platoon of unarmed Norbankers had strung out over forty yards. Lon dropped in next to the assistant squad leader and they picked up their pace, crowding the last of the locals, urging them forward, almost stepping on their heels. Dancing around to avoid actually tripping over the rearmost of the militiamen occupied Lon's attention. The last stretch of the run seemed to take much less time than the first. He heard the leaders crashing through the underbrush, into the forest, and almost immediately he was going through it as well.

They did not stop even then. Lieutenant Taiters did slow

the pace for a few minutes, but the group kept going, in a hurry to get away from the city and the fighting, anxious to avoid detection by the enemy.

Past the new growth, the forest floor opened up and the group moved past visible reminders of the fighting that had taken place in the past hours. Two Norbankers tripped over bodies of rebel soldiers, starting a chain reaction that nearly brought down half of the platoon running with second squad.

Lieutenant Taiters finally gave the order to halt. The rest was no more than two minutes for the men in the first two groups, less for those in the other half of the assembly.

"Now we go for quiet," Corporal Girana explained to the Norbankers he was responsible for. "We're going to be walking, an easy pace, but we've got to keep moving, and we've got to keep quiet. We're through the bottleneck, but out here, there's always the chance we'll run into rebel patrols." *Or a whole damn force of them,* he thought uneasily.

This time, when the group started moving, the soldiers of Girana's squad were spaced evenly along the flanks of the Norbanker volunteers. The pace was only half that of a marching cadence, sometimes less, with frequent pauses—not rest stops, just a few seconds of everyone standing motionless while the professionals listened for any sounds of enemy activity.

"Tebba, any word yet on how far we're going, or what the rest of the battalion's doing?" Lon asked. They had been moving inside the forest for nearly thirty minutes.

"The rest of the company is moving to shield us," Tebba replied. "The other companies are still engaged. The section of the enemy line to the right of our breakout has collapsed, I guess just about all of the way to the river. The colonel's trying to exploit that. Not for too long, though, I guess. The entire battalion is still supposed to rendezvous so we can get the supplies in for our militiamen before dawn.''

Lon glanced at the timeline on his helmet display. Local dawn—first light—was a little more than five hours off.

12

A Company was almost back together. While its third platoon continued to shepherd the Norbankers, the rest formed a screen around them, one hundred to two hundred yards out on either flank and in front, no more than fifty yards behind. They moved slowly and stopped frequently, making ample allowance for the militiamen who had nothing to augment their vision in the dark.

At least with the rest of the company as outriders, the noise these guys are making isn't quite so dangerous, Lon thought. Even to him, the Norbankers seemed to be making a racket as they stumbled through the woods. The forest floor was relatively open. The only places where bushes or shrubs could establish themselves were near creeks and treefall gaps. Away from those openings, there were only the trunks of canopy trees and the rotting detritus that covered the ground. But the canopy robbed the Norbankers of the starlight they had enjoyed out in the open, leaving almost total darkness. Each column had to be led by a Dirigenter with the night-vision system built into his battle helmet. Behind him, the Norbankers followed, jammed up as close as possible, often walking with a hand on the shoulder of the man in front of them.

They headed almost precisely north from Norbank City, averaging less than a mile an hour. But luck held. There were no run-ins with rebel forces, not even a patrol.

"Bravo and Delta are catching us up," Sergeant Dendrow told the noncoms of his platoon during a brief halt at about three o'clock in the morning. "The colonel's leaving Charlie behind to harass the enemy through until we get the shuttles in and out. We've got two miles to go to reach the LZ, and only an hour and twenty minutes before the shuttles touch down. I know," he said quickly, anticipating the objection. "There's no way to move the Norbankers that fast in the dark. But we have to push harder than we have been. First platoon is going to move ahead and set up security around the LZ, but we still need to get there fast, pick up the goods, and get away before any rebels move in. We've got two birds coming in, and they'll be bringing in ammo and food for us as well. And the wounded coming back to duty after the first night's action."

"We got any wounded for them to take out tonight?" one of the squad leaders asked.

"I guess, a few at least. They're getting moved forward too. The shuttles won't be able to stay on the ground long."

Squad leaders explained to the Norbankers that they were going to have to speed up. "You've had plenty of practice the last few hours," Tebba reminded his group. "We've just got to make it a little faster so we can get you to the rifles and stuff. We *don't* get there in a hurry, your rebels might beat us to them. I'm sure you don't want that."

Increased speed brought increased noise, even an occasional oath. Men stumbled, sometimes fell. The lines broke and needed assistance to reform. The Dirigenters moved closer to the men they were guiding, coaxing, helping, making their own contribution to the sound level. For the moment, speed was more important than silence.

I hope we don't get stuck with baby-sitting again, Lon thought—for about the dozenth time. *There are plenty of other platoons in the battalion. No need to stick us twice.*

"There's a cold front moving in," Tebba relayed to Lon just after three-thirty. "Clouds building up to the north and west. They might be over the LZ by the time we get there."

"Clouds, that's good, isn't it? Give the shuttles cover?"

"As long as they don't come in hot," Tebba said. "I

imagine they'll come in soft, and from the north, slide in to the LZ slow, use the clouds as long as they can. We're likely to have rain before the morning gets too far advanced, according to CIC." CIC was the combat information center aboard *Long Snake*.

"Myself, I wouldn't complain if we got monsoon rains," Lon said. "We can handle it better than the opposition."

"But our militia can't. That makes it a wash." Girana did not bother laughing at his pun, and Lon did not notice it.

When the rendezvous time arrived, the platoon of mercenaries and the militia were still a quarter mile from the LZ. But part of A Company and most of B and D were there. The supplies were unloaded. The men returning to duty got off. A half dozen men wounded during the evening's fight were loaded. So were the corpses of the four Dirigenters who had been killed.

By the time the Norbankers reached the LZ, the shuttles were already gone. There was a rush to distribute weapons, ammunition, and food. The loads had to be spread around. There were no trucks. The Norbankers were given hasty lessons on the rifles they were handed—just the essentials, loading, safety switch, and so forth. Magazines were fitted to rifles, bolts were run to put a round in the chamber. The Norbankers were also given five minutes to eat a meal pack, Dirigent combat rations. None of the Norbankers complained about the taste.

"Not even a chance to sight in the weapons," Phip said in an aside to Lon. "They'd be lucky to hit the ground if they had to." He shook his head. "The only safe place will be behind them once they start shooting."

"They'll make noise, though, and that will help if we get into a firefight," Lon said. "They'll make the rebels keep their heads down, give us more chance to fire for effect."

By the time everyone was ready to move away from the LZ, there was vague illumination back under the forest canopy. With clouds moving in, it was a diffuse gray light, dim, straining eyes—but it was sufficient to let the Norbankers move without tripping over each other.

"We get time to train 'em right," Girana told Nolan after they had started moving again, "we might actually make decent soldiers out of them."

"If enough of them survive that long," Lon said.

"It's our job to make sure that they do," Tebba reminded him. "So let's make sure we do our job."

For the moment, they were still moving north, farther from Norbank City. During the short rest stops that Colonel Flowers permitted—the entire battalion, less C Company, which had remained closer to Norbank City, was moving more or less together now—the militiamen were given some help with organization and the rudiments of maneuver doctrine. The Norbanker platoons were broken into squads. The Dirigenters made no attempt to choose leaders. The Norbankers had to do that for themselves. But each militia platoon was, temporarily, assigned to one of the mercenary platoons, mostly with B and D companies. They marched together, and the Dirigenters did what they could to give the militiamen training on the march and during the stops.

For once, Lon's platoon was spared. "We've done our bit," Taiters said when Lon mentioned it. "For now, at least."

"How long are we going to stay away from the action?" Lon asked next. "We're not completing the contract out here."

Arlan shook his head. "This is just a guess, but I imagine we'll go back in tonight. We don't want to give the rebels too much time to regroup. It would be nice if we could take even two or three days with these locals, give them a chance to sight in their weapons and get used to firing them. But we don't have time or ammunition to spare."

"They're still not going to be able to see at night." Lon shrugged, even though he was not close to the lieutenant.

Taiters sighed. "They didn't ask for night-vision gear,

and our contracting officer apparently didn't mention it, or didn't push it. Goggles or helmets might have made all the difference.''

''And we don't have enough spares to give them some?''

''Not nearly enough.''

Freed of their responsibilities for herding the Norbankers, third platoon rejoined the rest of A Company and moved out to the left flank of the battalion. When Colonel Flowers finally called a halt shortly after nine o'clock, they were a dozen miles from the nearest point in Norbank City, in old-growth forest.

''We won't be here long, but dig in,'' Captain Orlis told the company's noncoms. ''Recon doesn't show any hostiles within four miles but we can't be certain. The rebels don't have enough electronics for us to be sure of spotting them. They could have a company or more within spitting range if they tailed us out.''

Lon shared a foxhole with Corporal Girana and Janno Belzer, which meant that Lon and Janno did the digging, piling the dirt along the front and sides of the hole.

''At least this isn't rough ground for digging,'' Janno said. ''Not like heavy clay. I've seen some dirt you almost needed to blast to scratch a hole out of it.''

''This day and age, there's got to be an easier way,'' Lon replied. Getting the sod up was the most difficult part of this excavation. Under the decaying leaves and twigs was a bed of a mosslike substance that resisted their shovels.

''There is,'' Janno said. ''Or, at least, there could be.''

''What do you mean?''

''I've got a cousin who works in the research and development department of one of the sutler companies. Some years back they tested prototypes for what they called a sonic shovel. You stick four poles into the ground to mark your corners, as deep as you want the hole. The thing used ultrasonic vibrations to turn any kind of soil into powder.

Then you just had to scoop the stuff out, like shoveling fine, dry sand."

"So why are we still doing it the old-fashioned way? What was wrong with it?" Lon asked.

Janno made a barking laugh. "It worked perfectly, according to my cousin, and weighed less than six pounds. It could loosen the dirt for a hole like this in under a minute, so you wouldn't need more than one per squad. There *was* one slight drawback. The damned thing was so powerful that our standard sound-detection gear could hear it from thirty miles off. Dual-purpose tool. It dug the hole, then attracted the enemy for you to fight. Quartermaster section rejected the idea."

Lon laughed softly. The two men had not paused in their digging while they talked. Below the layer of detritus and moss the ground was dry, with a soft, crumbly texture. Janno stopped digging at one point and picked up a clod of the soil, then broke it with only gentle pressure of his fingers.

"Poor soil for farming," he said.

"What do you mean?" Lon asked. "It's doing all right growing eighty-foot trees."

Janno shook his head. "My guess is this is a very delicate ecological balancing act, poverty soil, all of the available nutrients tied up, everything in use all the time. Rain forests are like that, and this is almost rain forest. Even a slight disturbance to the balance could destroy the system. And farming would be more than a slight disturbance."

"That part of your military training here?"

"No. That was freshman biology in high school. Dirigenters get to see more examples of nature than most folks do, more different ecosystems. Even modest military operations can impact an ecological system, and large-scale fighting can even have a significant impact on weather."

"Come on. You're jerking my string now."

"I'm serious. Look, you had to do a lot of reading of military history at that academy you went to, didn't you?"

"The Springs. Sure."

"Memoirs, that sort of thing, soldiers talking about their battles and campaigns?"

"Some of that. More on the tactical and strategic stuff though," Lon said. "I still don't see what you're getting at."

"A lot of talk about the weather in those memoirs, wasn't there? Too much rain, too cold, too much snow?"

"Well, of course, but soldiers always gripe about the weather. We've done that on field exercises."

Again, Janno shook his head. "There's more to it than that. I don't recall the details, but we had a study done, on Earth. From the time when gunpowder became important in warfare, and especially where the use of artillery or aerial bombardment was extensive, large military operations have induced much higher precipitation levels, rain or snow, and temperature extremes, in many climatic zones. And, no, it wasn't just chance. They studied every conflict from the fifteenth century on through the last major military operation on Earth in the twenty-first century. Once you get more than ten or fifteen thousand soldiers involved, and large numbers of artillery, tanks, or bombers, over anything longer than a few days, the weather tends to extremes."

He used the back of the blade on his entrenching tool to pat down the dirt piled in front of the trench. For a moment, Lon just looked at his friend.

"Hearsay and guesswork," he said finally.

"Statistical certainty, bolstered by a lot of computer simulation."

"You studied that in high school too?"

"Why not? Military subjects are important on Dirigent. The more we know about everything that can influence a contract, the better we're going to be."

The Dirigenters were put on half-and-half watches. In the center of the battalion's defended area, the Norbankers were given two hours of concentrated training—as much as they could absorb. They were taught to field-strip and reassemble their rifles, lectured on the capabilities and limitations of them. Beyond that, they were given simplified plans for responding to the most likely military engagements—again, what they could be expected to learn in such a limited time.

"It's not enough. It can't be enough," Girana commented to Lon when the Norbankers were finally given a chance to rest. "We get any kind of action and they'll get chewed up. They'll be lucky if they only take five times the casualties they should. It could be a lot worse. I just hope it's not bad enough to discourage the lot of them. The survivors," he added after a pause. "Them and the rest of the folks in the capital."

"They give up, there's not much we can do, is there?" Lon asked.

Tebba just shook his head.

Captain Orlis briefed his lieutenants and noncoms. "We'll be moving out at 1500 hours, heading back in. Charlie Company is drawing a rebel force after it, into the hills east of Norbank City. The best estimate we can get on the rebel force is six hundred to eight hundred, that's from Charlie and from aerial surveillance. We're going after them. If we can neutralize this force we'll have gone a long way to leveling the playing field on Norbank."

He went over the expected line of march on mapboards, and showed where Company C would try to stall the rebels, the battleground that Colonel Flowers wanted. "We can't count on the rebels cooperating," Orlis said in a flat aside. "And we can't be certain that they'll respond to any . . . stimulus the way that trained soldiers would, so be ready for anything."

The militia company would be moved to the rear of the battalion once they got close to contact, held back as a reserve, then be brought in when—and if—it could be done without excessive danger to the mercenaries.

"The colonel wants to wait until we have the situation in hand, but he also wants to get the locals involved soon enough so they can feel that they've had a part in the victory. He thinks the morale boost that will give them could be important, not just to the ones we've got with us but to the rest of the loyalists as well. They *need* a victory. We're to make sure they get it." He paused, then added, "Within limits. We're not planning to make foolish sacrifices for anyone's pride."

When the briefing ended, Taiters called Lon over. "Stick with me, Nolan. I've already told Girana. It's time you saw what platoon operations are like. I'm going to patch your comm links directly to mine. We'll have an open line between us, and you'll be in on any calls I make or receive. If you need to make a call out on any other channel, you'll have to use the override—but don't, unless it's an emergency, and warn me first."

The line of march had A Company on the left, B on the right, with the militia behind them. The battalion's D Company brought up the rear. The colonel and his headquarters detachment were in the center, ahead of the Norbankers.

From the start, the colonel insisted on a rapid pace, nearly as fast as the mercenaries would have traveled without the amateurs in their midst. "We've got to cover as much of the distance as we can before dark," Lieutenant Taiters told Lon.

On the march, Taiters generally stayed between third and fourth platoons, but occasionally moved out of the double columns and ranged along the side, keeping an eye on all of his people. Lon heard him talking with platoon sergeants, squad leaders—even individual privates. The conversations were rarely more than a terse question and a minimal answer. More rarely, he would take a call from Captain Orlis, or be part of a commanders' call from Colonel Flowers or someone on the battalion staff—the latest intelligence from C Company and continuing observations of the rebels from the shuttles and *Long Snake*.

All three of the battalion's companies kept patrols out to ensure that they were not surprised by an enemy ambush. Breaks were scheduled well in advance, taking advantage of locations that the point squad found.

"You know every man in both platoons pretty well, don't you?" Lon asked the lieutenant during one silent stretch.

"Part of the job," Arlan replied. "Any commander needs to know the capabilities and limitations of his men, know who has special talents, or who has problems that might interfere with the performance of his duties. The better you know your men, the better you'll do your job. It's a cumulative process, though. Even if they move you to a different company when you get your commission, you'll learn. No one will expect you to know everything about every man under your command the first day."

"How far up the line does that go?"

Taiters chuckled. "I know for a fact that Captain Orlis knows every man in the company. I don't just mean that he can match faces and names. He's got a pretty good idea of the abilities of everyone, some knowledge of their backgrounds and families. I can't be so certain about Colonel Flowers, but I'd bet money that he knows every officer and noncom in the battalion as well as I know my men, and probably recognizes every private's name and face, and can place which company he's in. And for the people he commanded on his way up, and those who've come to his notice for one reason or another since, he'd know a lot more."

"Colonel Gaffney?" Arnold Gaffney was Seventh Regiment's commanding officer. "I mean, there has to be a limit. He has more than five thousand men under his command. He can't know *all* of them. That wouldn't leave him time for anything else."

"Probably not," Taiters conceded, "but I bet he's got a pretty good handle on personnel anyway. Don't forget, before he was regimental commander, he commanded First Battalion, before that, Bravo Company of the First, and so forth. He did a stint as adjutant for the regiment as well. So he's probably got a good idea about at least half of his men, especially those he's been on contract with, and I'll bet he knows every officer and sergeant—probably damn near every corporal. Remember, our turnover rate is a lot lower than in most armies. The average length of service in my platoons is over eight and a half years, and that's with your few months dragging down the average.''

The general direction of the battalion's movement was south-southeast, but it did not move on a direct line. The colonel tried to take advantage of the terrain, which started to change early on from flat land to gently rolling to moderately hilly. As the ground got more uneven, the forest first became less homogenous and then gave way to alternating stands of trees and grassy areas. Occasional outcroppings of rock left some areas almost bare of vegetation. By sunset, the rest of the battalion was within three quarters of a mile of C Company—*and* the rebel force that was chasing it.

''We'll take thirty minutes here,'' Captain Orlis told his officers and noncoms. ''Make sure everyone eats and is ready to go then. The fight could come almost anytime after that.''

13

Lon squatted next to the lieutenant, watching his mapboard during the briefing that Colonel Flowers conducted near the end of the rest stop.

"Charlie has been fighting a series of small skirmishes all day," Flowers said, indicating that company's movements. "Staying just out of reach of this rebel force, doing what they could to draw them farther from the siege and reinforcements. The other large rebel force, the one coming in from the east, coalesced this morning, rendezvousing here." The point he indicated was six miles northeast of the battalion. "They were apparently moving to intercept us. The last fix we had on them was here." This point was four miles from the first, almost directly north of the battalion. "At some point today, they must have gotten word of where we were because they now appear to be coming after us. CIC has intercepted a number of transmissions from that area. We have partial translations, but they're using a lot of code words that we can't identify. As of twenty minutes ago, they were four miles behind us, following the same route we did. The latest estimate is that this force is about the same size as the one that Charlie's been toying with—six hundred to eight hundred. That means that we might have to deal with sixteen hundred rebels, or more, at once if we can't take care of the first force before the second catches up. The estimate is not all that . . . certain. The true numbers could be twenty percent higher and it wouldn't surprise me.''

Flowers paused, then said, "So, maybe two thousand in these two forces, another thousand or more still holding the siege of Norbank City. My own suspicion is that the rebels must have at least another thousand men under arms, either guarding their primary settlement area or elsewhere, undetected. That number could be extremely conservative as well. It behooves us to keep those various forces from consolidating, or getting us in a position where they can all hit us at once.

"For now, that means dealing with the force that Charlie has been in contact with as quickly as possible. When we started this march, I hoped to have complete tactical surprise, but now we have to assume that the enemy knows that we're in the vicinity. Since none of our scouts has reported any contacts with rebel patrols, they shouldn't know *exactly* where we are, but the commander of that force has become more reticent to follow Charlie's lead over the last hour or so. I think they're looking for a chance to move back toward Norbank City. So we're going to let them, and we're going to get in position here and here." He indicated the crests of two low ridges that paralleled each other. "Then we'll let Charlie funnel them in for us. It should be full dark before we make contact, which gives us the edge.

"I want our militia company here, at the right end of the northern ridge. Alpha will be to their left. Bravo and Delta will take the southern ridge and put two platoons down at this end of the valley, to cork the bottle. I want those platoons favoring the sides of the valley, not a line straight across. That could involve us in friendly-fire difficulties, with Charlie moving in behind. As soon as we've got this force accounted for, we'll move to intercept the force behind us, try to give them the same sort of surprise. We'll go into the details of that later, after we deal with our first task.

"If the rebels in the first force don't walk into the trap, we'll make adjustments. Holding both ridges, we'll be able to adapt no matter which way they go. But that could complicate moving to meet the second force on favorable ground. Questions?'' He waited, and when none of the officers on the hookup spoke, Colonel Flowers said, ''I want everyone ready to move in five minutes. Bravo and Delta will lead the way since they've got the farthest distance to travel.''

Even in the dark, the Norbanker militiamen moved with some assurance now. They were armed and had been given a couple of hours of training, enough to make them think that maybe they were not quite hopeless. They were not quite as limited in vision this night because there was more open sky, some illumination from the stars. They were also aware that a fight was near, that they would have part of it, and that they would have the advantage of numbers—for the first time in their civil war.

A Company brought up the rear. Fourth platoon lagged behind, planting electronic snoops and land mines to slow up the rebel force behind them. As long as those rebels continued to follow the battalion's trail directly, they would run straight into trouble. And that would alert the battalion, give them the exact position of the second rebel force.

Lieutenant Taiters, with Lon at his side, stayed with fourth platoon while they were planting the mines and bugs, taking an active part in deciding where they would go. ''Any left over after the fighting,'' he explained to Lon, ''we'll retrieve before we leave. If we can. If not, and if we don't have a chance to teach the locals how to deactivate them, the explosives will degrade in thirty days, making them harmless.''

As soon as the work was finished, fourth platoon hurried to catch up with the rest of the company. The battalion and the Norbanker militia were moving into position, ready for the rebels. Taiters looked over the deployment of his platoons, then conferred with the platoon sergeants before he and Lon took their own positions—just behind the line and between third and fourth platoons. There was no digging of foxholes this time. There was too little soil covering the rocky ridge. Where it was possible, men moved the smaller stones around to give them some cover, but they would have the high ground; the ridges were sixty to seventy feet above the floor of the valley between them.

The gunfire drew closer, but there was never anything like a constant exchange. From reports that were being passed to all of the officers, Lon knew that C Company was maintaining contact with the rebel force, striking and withdrawing, sniping, working the rebels toward the rest of the battalion.

Then there was a more urgent call. "Everyone down and quiet. A rebel patrol is entering the valley."

I hope the militia doesn't screw up now, Lon thought. There were a few mercenaries with them to make sure they received any orders—or warnings. *Just keep down and keep quiet,* Lon thought, as if his mental projections might make a difference. *Patience.*

Lieutenant Taiters edged closer to the line, and raised up enough to give him a glimpse of the valley floor. Lon stayed where he was. *I'm not going to be the one to screw up,* he thought. *The lieutenant knows what he's doing.*

"Their point isn't very far in front of the main body," Arlan whispered on his link to Lon. "It looks like no more than twenty yards between the last man in the point squad and the rest of them." The lieutenant moved back from his observation point. "They're moving fast too, despite the dark."

"No flankers on these ridges?" Lon asked, also whispering.

"Apparently not. They're moving right into the trap."

It'll be slaughter, Lon thought. *Fish in a barrel.* Taking part in what seemed certain to be butchery did not appeal to him—but neither was he deluded enough to think that the battalion should somehow offer a "fair" fight. *It's them or us, and there are still a lot more of them than there are of us.*

"The colonel wants to wait until that point squad gets to the other end, right in the face of the men we've got plugging it," Taiters told Lon. "That might not put the whole rebel force between the ridges, but most of them will be, and Charlie Company will make sure that the rest can't bolt."

Any minute now. Any second, Lon thought. The hair on his arms felt as if it were standing at attention. His right hand moved along the receiver of his rifle, checking to make sure that the safety was off. There was a full magazine in, and a round in the chamber. He glanced at the timeline on his visor: 2053 hours. Lon glanced left, toward where his friends were—forty yards away. That was too far for him to take any comfort. It would help to be surrounded by friends now, on the verge of battle. *This isn't like before, when the rebels hit us without warning. This time we're doing the waiting.*

"Ready!" The single word over the command channel startled Lon. He had become too preoccupied with his thoughts. "Fire!"

Along both ridgelines, the mercenaries opened fire, the muzzle flashes looking like strings of fiery Christmas lights blinking on and off. The sound might almost be mistaken for firecrackers going off on a Federation Day holiday back on Earth. The mercenaries fired short bursts, three or four rounds at a time, looking for targets, not just firing wildly into the valley. For the first ten seconds, the gunfire was all one-way. It took that long before the rebels even started to respond—other than to dive for whatever cover they could find among the rocks and stunted trees on the valley floor.

Taiters and Nolan moved forward, into the line, ready to make their own contribution. Lon got his first look at the killing ground as he brought his rifle up and scanned for targets. They were not difficult to find. He watched for movement, for muzzle flashes, and each time he sprayed a few rounds that way. Those were the most certain indicators of live targets. With men down all over the valley floor, it was impossible to be certain which were dead and which were alive, even with the infrared assistance of helmet night-vision systems; bodies needed time to cool.

Those rebels who could return fire did so, but it was uncoordinated, hardly effective. There was *some* cover in the valley, but little that could shelter anyone from fire coming in from both ridgelines, or from the scores of grenades that were tossed and fired. The rebels tried grenades as well, but they proved ineffective. They had only hand grenades, not grenade launcher rounds like those the mercenaries had. Several rockets were fired by the rebels, though, blasting gaps along the ridges.

Even though they were at an impossible disadvantage, the rebels in the valley fought on. There was no hint of surrender or flight. After several minutes they even showed some signs of trying to regroup, crawling to the best cover available, consolidating, directing their fire first toward one section of the ridges, then to another.

It was not quite a surprise when some of the Norbanker militiamen on the ridge started shooting at the rebels below. Even without orders, they wanted to make certain that they got in on the fight. At first that fire was sporadic, but before long it seemed to be almost general.

Lon's mind had gone almost numb by then. He was focused entirely on doing his job, firing and then reloading, looking through his sights, trying to avoid any broader picture of the scene below. There were only targets on the other end, not human beings. *Aim carefully, then pull the trigger.* The smell of gunpowder made his nose itch, and the acrid fumes dried out his mouth. His eyes burned, but there was no way to rub them, and Lon knew that rubbing would only make it worse.

His radio remained silent. There was no need for orders now. The only call would be if someone in the two platoons was hit and needed help, and—so far—there had been no casualties in A Company's third and fourth platoons.

The sound of two explosions, close together, behind him, startled Lon badly. He needed several seconds to realize that they had come from the mines that fourth platoon had planted.

"You heard that?" he asked Taiters.

"I heard. Hang on." Lon listened while the lieutenant reported the explosions, and their location, to Captain Orlis, and then to Colonel Flowers.

That means the second force is only four hundred yards behind us, Lon thought. *They could have us in range in less than two minutes.* Alpha had very little cover against attack from the north, from behind. Lon glanced at his helmet timeline: 2101 hours. That startled him almost as much as the explosions had. Less than eight minutes had passed since the start of the firefight. He shook his head. He would have sworn that it had been going on for an hour.

"We're turning around and moving down the slope about ten yards," Captain Orlis said on the channel that connected him to his lieutenants and platoon sergeants. "Except first platoon. They'll stay in place to anchor the left end of the line on the ridge. The militia will move across to take our positions. Give them a hand, but hurry them up." After those orders were acknowledged, Orlis said, "Get your men in whatever cover they can find. We'll let the second rebel force close to within two hundred yards, then open up, try to pin them down too far out for any return fire to be fully effective."

Third and fourth platoons each left one squad to help the Norbankers move into position while the rest moved back down the hill toward the north. The slope was gentle, but that still left many of the men in awkward firing positions— prone with their feet above their heads. They wiggled around, getting as comfortable as they could in the time they had. A little cover in front, if no more than a couple of small rocks, was more important than comfort.

Lon and the lieutenant stayed near the ridge until nearly three quarters of the militiamen had filed past and started to settle into the line that A Company had vacated. Then Taiters pulled his last two squads back, sent them down the slope to get ready. Only then did he and Nolan follow. Lon had scarcely got down on his stomach before the second rebel force opened fire—before A Company could start the exchange.

These rebels did not come straight in along the track that Second Battalion had taken. They came in separate groups, from the northeast and the northwest, angling in toward the ridge. The rebels were 180 yards away when they opened fire, well inside the distance that Captain Orlis had hoped to hold them at. They had taken advantage of what cover there was, infiltrating, moving intelligently.

The first volley from the rebels was wildly inaccurate. Some went low, but most went high—not just over the heads of the men of A Company, but also over the Norbanker militia, above and behind them. But as soon as the mercenaries started to return fire, the rebels' aim improved. They had muzzle flashes to target. There were hits. Lon heard one call for help from someone in fourth platoon, and then a squad leader saying he had the man and that his wound was minor.

Lon had no qualms about *this* fight. It was as near to even terms as the rebels were ever likely to manage against trained professionals. They had odds of three to one or more—counting only A Company as their opposition—and they were not boxed into a closed killing zone, like the valley on the other side of the ridge. These rebels came on with the same determination as their doomed comrades, using fire and maneuver tactics to minimize their casualties as they moved closer.

''Charlie's sending two platoons around on our right flank,'' Captain Orlis informed his leaders. ''They're going to hit these rebels from the side. Delta will be moving around on the other flank as soon as they can. It's going to take them longer, though. They've got farther to travel and they need to disengage first.'' Almost as an afterthought, Orlis added, "The first rebel force has about had it. There can't be more than a hundred of them still fighting.''

One hundred left out of six hundred to eight hundred? Lon blinked, surprised despite what he had seen. *How can they keep going? Why not surrender? Are they going to make us slaughter them to the last man?* Lon turned his face to the side for a second, fighting down a surge of bile. He blinked several times, squeezed his eyes shut briefly, then turned his attention back to the enemy coming at him. It was only chance that he noticed the time: 2110 hours.

The new fight would not be ended as quickly, or as decisively, as the other. The rebel force coming in from the north had not been caught unawares and, for the moment, held on the initiative, pushing in on their diagonals, hitting the ends of the Dirigent line.

"They've had some training,'' Lieutenant Taiters observed on his link with Nolan. "And I think we underestimated the number.''

Lon tried to scan the breadth of the battlefield, noting the two concentrations of rebel soldiers moving in. There was more gunfire coming from farther back, in the center— from well past the two-hundred-yard mark. And that more distant gunfire seemed to be more accurate as well.

"They've concentrated marksmen with nightscopes in the middle,'' Lon said. "Maybe two hundred and fifty yards out.''

"Where?'' Arlan asked, but before Lon could point them out, the lieutenant said, "I see. Hang on while I pass this on to the captain.'' Lon listened to the exchange—a twenty-word report and a two-word acknowledgment.

"Good work, Nolan,'' Taiters said then. "You were the first to spot that.'' He called third platoon's first squad and told them to concentrate on the snipers before talking to Lon again. "You might as well take a hand at this too, Nolan. Your baby.''

Lon adjusted his sights, then switched his rifle's selector to single shots. Each time he spotted a muzzle flash, he put one round just below it—at least, that was how he aimed. The squad that was targeting the snipers would be firing the same way. It did not take long before there were no more muzzle flashes to aim at.

Dead or moved, Lon thought. *At least we stopped them.* He watched the area for another minute, head above his gunsights, waiting for the sniping to resume. When it did not, he switched his rifle back to automatic and targeted the rebels moving in toward the hill, almost missing the ''Well done'' that the lieutenant gave him and the squad from third platoon.

The firefight expanded as first C Company and then D Company came in on the flanks. Their sequential appearance stopped the rebel advance—which had reached the bottom of the slope. Many of the rebels had to turn to face the new threats, which decreased the amount of gunfire coming toward Alpha. It was only then that Lon noticed that many of the militiamen were firing over the heads of the mercenaries at their estranged compatriots.

''What the hell?'' escaped from his mouth.

''What?'' Lieutenant Taiters asked quickly.

''Behind us. The militia's shooting over us.''

''No help for that,'' Taiters said. ''Just keep your head down.'' He passed that information to the rest of the company.

Then Captain Orlis came on-line. ''Resistance has ended in the valley behind us. The colonel is moving the rest of the battalion around to get in on this fight. We've got two shuttles on the way down to give us close air support. Four minutes until they arrive.''

Lon looked at the time again. It was 2124 hours. The fight so far had lasted only a half hour.

14

Before the shuttles arrived to add their firepower, the fight was over. The rebels from the second force withdrew into the woods under good discipline, fighting as they retreated, taking as many of their wounded as they could with them.

"It's the kind of thing we would do if we had to," Tebba Girana told Lon—an offer of grudging respect for the enemy.

The shuttles circled at ten thousand feet—high enough to ensure that they could escape any rockets fired from the ground, in case there was more fighting close, but their guns and rockets were not needed, and they climbed back toward *Long Snake* when their short tour was finished.

Few rebels managed to escape from the earlier ambush.

After clearing his action with Lieutenant Taiters, Lon climbed back to the ridge and looked down into the valley. Switching his faceplate to magnify the view, he scanned the length of that battleground. The rebel dead were everywhere. The loyalist militia was on its way down the southern slope, going in to retrieve rifles and ammunition. Several squads of Dirigenters also went into the valley, partly to verify a body count, but mostly to prevent any butchering of surviving rebels.

"I've never seen such a slaughter," Lieutenant Taiters said, joining Lon on the ridge. "There must be eight hundred down there, dead or wounded."

"Plus the ones we got on the other side," Lon said. They

had heard the preliminary casualty reports for their own people, six dead and thirty-seven wounded in the battalion. The militia company had lost four dead and twenty wounded. ''I know we want every advantage we can get to minimize our own casualties, but ... this?'' Lon made a broad gesture that tried to encompass the entire valley. ''Why didn't they surrender?''

''It's a civil war, Nolan. Maybe they didn't see any alternative. Prisoners usually don't fare very well in this kind of fight. I know the colonel would have preferred it end with less killing, but ...'' He shrugged and turned away, then started walking back down the slope. There was simply nothing else intelligent to say, and he wanted to get away from the scene.

The rest of A Company was already near the bottom of the hill, checking the rebel casualties on the north side. Lon stood by the ridge a moment longer, then switched off his magnification, turned, and followed the lieutenant down, then Lon sought out ''his'' squad. None had been killed or wounded, but Dean Ericks had the visible reminder of a close call. His helmet had been damaged by a bullet, just over his right ear. When Lon reached the squad, Dean was sitting on the ground, holding the helmet in his hands, one finger tracing the crack in the side.

''Three centimeters to the side and no trauma tube in the galaxy could have helped me,'' he whispered—speaking to himself. He seemed unaware of anyone else around him.

''Just think if it had been Phip,'' Lon suggested. ''That melon he carries on his shoulders is a better target.''

The reunion was cut short when Lieutenant Taiters called for Lon to return. ''Nobody called time out,'' he told Lon. ''There's still work left to do.''

''Yes, sir,'' Lon replied. ''What next?''

''We've got to arrange pickup for the wounded, and this time it's going to be tricky. I don't think the rebels are going to give us a clear field. The colonel doesn't think they will. We're going to stay put, man those ridges again, and send out platoon-size patrols to try to keep the rebels back."

"They're going to land a shuttle in that valley?"

"That's the plan. I know. It's going to be a mess. There's no time to clear the bodies away first, let alone bury them. But it's our best bet for avoiding additional casualties among *our* people. We can't get squeamish about enemy dead."

"I know that," Lon said, trying to erase the picture of a shuttle's skids coming in hot, racing across bodies. "Where will we be, on the ridge or out on patrol?"

"You and I will be out with fourth platoon. Third is staying with the Norbanker militia. And we're in a hurry."

Lon followed the lieutenant to where fourth platoon was taking a few minutes' rest. He was relieved to be moving away from the carnage in the valley, relieved that he would not have to witness the indignities that would be visited upon the rebel dead, but he would have preferred to remain with third platoon. What friends he had in the company were concentrated there. But the men of fourth platoon were not strangers. His position as Taiters' apprentice had assured that.

Platoon Sergeant Weil Jorgen was waiting for them. The lieutenant spelled out where they were heading on his mapboard, with fourth platoon's squad leaders on circuit, their mapboards slaved to the lieutenant's. Lon squatted next to Taiters, watching over his shoulder. The briefing took less than a minute. "Any questions?" the lieutenant asked. Jorgen shook his head. There were no questions from the squad leaders either.

"Nolan?" Taiters asked over their private link.

"I've got it, sir," Lon replied.

"Good. Stick with me."

Weil Jorgen got the platoon formed up and moving northeast. The platoon sergeant took up his position with the second squad in line. The lieutenant and Lon moved with the third squad. Before they got clear of the battalion's new perimeter, Lon could see one other platoon moving away, to the northwest.

That rebel force should be somewhere between us, Lon thought. *If they haven't turned one way or the other.* He tried not to think of the numbers. This one rebel force might still have eight hundred men—or more—and there were other groups, somewhere. He gave little thought to the possibility that the rebels might suddenly decide that they had had enough bloodshed and surrender or flee back toward their homes. *They're going to be looking for revenge,* he realized. *And they might outnumber us by ten or fifteen to one.* If the platoon ran into the enemy force and could not get away or get quick help. . . .

Lon forced himself to stop thinking about that, to concentrate on his immediate work. *I sure can't afford to daydream, not now.* He took a moment to go through his ritual, checking his rifle and the readouts on his helmet's head-up display, then looked around to make certain where all of the others were.

The platoon's course carried it into increasingly hilly territory to the east and northeast. There were many open areas, rocks and wild grasses, and fewer stands of trees—most of those were a compact species that resembled scrub cedar. The platoon avoided the ridgelines, staying in the valleys or low on the slopes, wherever the cover and going were best. Lon was glad to see patches of clouds moving across from the northwest, hiding the stars as they passed, cutting down on the available light.

Once they were well away from the battalion, Lieutenant Taiters changed the deployment of the platoon. One squad stayed out in front on point. Two squads followed in parallel columns, starting fifty yards back. The final squad was rear guard, with a fifty-yard gap between them and the central body. Lon and the lieutenant were on the right, with the platoon's fourth squad, which had rotated into that position. Sergeant Jorgen was on the left, with second squad. Third had the point; first rear guard. In fourth squad's line of march, the squad leader was in the number three position. Lieutenant Taiters was two spots back, and Lon was right behind him. Except for those two, the interval between men was kept at about five yards.

The platoon's assignment was simple. Barring enemy contact, they were to go out a mile along their initial vector, then turn and head east for a half mile before turning back toward the battalion's position. They were to look for the enemy, plant bugs and mines, try to keep the enemy at least a mile from the valley where the shuttles would be landing. If they ran into the enemy, their first duty would be to report on the location and size of the enemy force. After that, they would try to disengage, or attempt to draw the enemy to one side or the other—away from the LZ. Survival was third on the list of priorities. Protecting the casualties and shuttles came first.

Lon kept his eyes moving, watching where he would place each foot, and scanning his side of the formation, watching the ridges and slopes, looking for any sign of the enemy, any hint of improper movement to branches or grass. *Don't look for the routine, look for the exceptions* was the principle. There was a light breeze, its direction appearing to change as the terrain did, but mostly coming from the northwest, the same breeze that was blowing the clouds in.

The platoon moved silently. It was only rarely that Lon heard anything from the Dirigenters—a twig snapping, leaves crunching. And there were few other noises. The usual night routines of the native wildlife had been disrupted by the firefight and had not returned to normal. Occasionally a bird flew overhead—high, a predator searching for food, or tracking the possible threat represented by men prowling the night. Lon had yet to see any of the larger animals, predators or prey. Even close to the main human settlements the indigenous fauna had not yet been driven to extinction, or away. One of the militiamen had told Lon that the dominant predator in this area was a catlike creature that could weigh up to three hundred pounds. It was strong enough to take a human, or even a cow. Lon had heard one of those, wailing in the distance, the first night on Norbank, but had not known what it was until later, when he had had a chance to ask the militiaman about the sound—something like the cry of a coyote.

The platoon reached its mile limit. There had been no sign of the enemy. Lieutenant Taiters let the men rest for five minutes while they planted electronic snoops and land mines. He rotated the squads again for the next leg of the patrol. But Taiters, Jorgen, and Nolan retained their same relative positions in the formation, moving with different squads.

"If we're going to run into anything, it's most likely along this outside stretch," Taiters warned his noncoms. "That means extra vigilance on the point and along the right flank."

How much extra can anyone give when we're already straining our senses to the limit? Lon wondered. The strain to hear or see anything out to the limits of hearing and vision had already given him a dull headache and burning eyes. Staring into the green-tinted distance shown by his night-vision gear always brought some discomfort, but rarely as much as this time. The volume on his helmet's external sound pickups was cranked around to maximum, magnifying the few noises there were.

"Lieutenant?"

"What?"

"We might have a little extra warning if we put one or two men way out on the right flank, even with the point or beyond it."

Taiters hesitated. "They'd be hung out in the wind with little chance that we could help them if they ran into anything."

"But it might save the rest of the platoon," Lon said.

"You volunteering?"

Lon did not think that his own hesitation was long

enough for the lieutenant to notice. "Yes, sir, I'll go."

Arlan nodded. "I'll ask Roy Bantor to go along with you. He could walk on eggs and not crack a one." Bantor was a lance corporal, assistant leader of fourth platoon's second squad. "Just remember, it's going to be his show. You're still just a cadet. You're not in the line of command yet."

"I remember."

Lon listened while the lieutenant called Bantor and asked if he was willing to volunteer for the mission—and Taiters emphasized that it was not an order. Bantor did not hesitate. He came forward to where Taiters and Nolan were waiting.

The lieutenant spelled out the job precisely. Roy nodded, then turned to Lon. "Your idea?"

"My idea," Lon confirmed. "Your patrol."

"Right, a two-man patrol." Lon could not see Roy's face behind the tinted faceplate and was not certain what to make of the lance corporal's tone. "Just remember, there's no room for mistakes when we get out on our own." Lon nodded. Roy gestured, and they moved away from the rest of the platoon.

Bantor moved quickly, but with assurance. His first goal was to put distance between the two of them and the rest of the platoon, moving a hundred yards to the north before turning. Even then he did not slacken the pace. The idea was for the two men to get even with the point, and that still was a hundred yards to the west when they made the turn.

"We're going to have to loop around wide again when the platoon turns back to the south," Roy whispered over a private channel once they started west. "If this is going to work, we can't just parallel the rest. We're going to have to range about, look for the enemy. It won't do any good if we just walk into a trap and get bagged without a chance to warn the others."

"Right," Lon said. He did not want to waste his air or attention. Staying on Roy's heels and avoiding any noise while they hurried through a wooded area took all of the concentration he could muster. Bantor seemed to move effortlessly through the forest, but Nolan had to work at doing it properly.

As they neared the point squad, a hundred yards to their left, Bantor finally slowed his pace. They were still not moving as deliberately as the platoon, but Lon no longer felt as if he were in a walking race.

We got this far without drawing fire, he thought, then: *Think ambush. Look for the sort of spot you'd pick if you were laying the trap instead of walking into it. Think what you'd do if you were the enemy, and assume he's at least as smart as you think* you *are.*

Roy started to angle a little to the right, farther out. Once he was beyond the level of the point squad, he slowed his pace more, visibly taking care where he set his feet. Lon hardly dared to breathe. They were effectively alone between the enemy and any friendly forces. They were also getting near the track the company had followed on its way south, not quite as far out as where they had left the mines and snoops.

"Watch for booby traps," Roy said. Lon did not bother to reply. There was no need.

Two minutes later, Bantor stopped—went motionless. Nolan did the same, a fraction of a second behind the lance corporal, and looked past him, trying to spot whatever it was that had caused Bantor to freeze in place. Lon scanned ahead and to the side, slowly, looking for the slightest hint—but he did not see or hear anything that did not belong.

After nearly a minute of standing absolutely motionless, Roy shook his head minimally and started moving again. *A false alarm,* Lon thought. But for several more minutes the two men were far more deliberate in their movements, slower, pausing after every step to look and listen. It was not until they finally turned the corner and started heading south again that Roy started to move a little faster. On its "inside" track, the platoon's point squad had drawn even with them again.

If anything's going to happen, it should be soon, Lon thought. In another five minutes they would probably be too close to the rest of the battalion for the rebels to dare anything. If they were going to strike, it would come out here, well beyond the range of the weapons of the rest of the Dirigenters. Lon stopped for an instant, letting Roy get a couple of steps farther ahead of him while he turned and looked back and to the right. *If I was running the rebel force here and had spotted us, I'd move in behind us and aim for the others,* he thought. *Count on that for surprise. Let the two scouts go to get at the full platoon.*

Thinking about that scenario increased his nervousness. Lon started walking again, leaving the extra gap between him and Roy. Bantor had seen that Nolan was farther back and said nothing about it. As long as each man knew exactly where the other was, the extra distance between them was a safety valve, making it slightly less likely that both would be taken out by a single burst of gunfire.

"Nolan." Bantor's whisper was almost inaudible even over the radio. "Stay here. Get down and take a good position. I'm going out a little farther to the side, then I'll come straight back in."

"You see something?"

"No, not really. I've just got an itch I need to scratch."

Lon moved a couple of steps, then crouched behind a tree trunk. Roy waited until Lon was in position and had his weapon set before he started moving off to the west, one very cautious step at a time, his rifle at the ready and tracing arcs from side to side. Lon scanned the forest in front of his companion, his eyes also tracing arcs, farther and farther out.

Bantor had gone less than thirty yards before a single gunshot rang out and he fell.

15

"Roy?" Lon waited five seconds. When Bantor did not reply, Lon started to move toward him. He was snaking across the ground as he reported the downed man to Lieutenant Taiters. There was no need to give their position. The blips of their helmet electronics would show on the lieutenant's head-up display.

"Just a single gunshot so far," Lon said, not thinking that Taiters and the rest of the platoon would have heard that much. They were not *that* far away. He stayed flat on his stomach, his head just up enough to let him watch where he was going.

"Stay where you are, Nolan," Taiters said after Lon had moved about ten feet. "Bantor's dead. I just lost his vital signs. Don't let them get you too."

"Maybe it's just his electronics that went bad, Lieutenant," Lon said. He had stopped at the order, but . . .

"I've still got everything else from the helmet, just no vitals," Taiters said. "Don't expose yourself any further. Do you have cover where you're at?"

"No, sir. I'm about ten feet from the nearest cover, behind me. I got out this far before you told me to stop."

"Try to edge back. Were you able to see anything?"

"Not a thing. I didn't even see the muzzle flash. I can't say if there's just one rebel or that whole rebel force."

"Start trying to get to the best cover you can. I'm going to move first squad halfway to your position. As soon as they get set, I want you to work your way back to them.

Stay down and be careful, but come on back in.''

"Yes, sir." There was no other possible reply.

Staying flat and crawling backward was far more difficult than crawling forward, but safer than trying to turn around. Everything seemed to catch as Lon pushed himself with his hands and forearms, and stretched out to pull himself along with his toes. He was unable to see where he was going, and he did not know when he neared the tree that had sheltered him before until he jammed a foot into it. Then he had to risk lifting up a few inches to be able to look, to see which way he had to shift to get around behind the trunk.

"I'm back to cover, Lieutenant," Lon said. "A fairly good-sized tree."

"Wait two minutes, then start working your way due east," Taiters said. "First squad will be waiting for you, ready to give covering fire if necessary."

I hope it's not necessary, Lon thought, checking the timeline on his visor so he would make no mistake about when to start back. He was still on his stomach, but shifted around so he could look toward the east. He did not have to guess the direction. His head-up display gave him a compass reading. He tried to pick out a route, looking to go from cover to cover—as near as possible. *The shortest possible distance without exposing myself too much.*

"You can start now, Nolan." Lon recognized the voice of Corporal Nace, the squad leader.

"On my way, Wil," Lon whispered.

Turning his back to the unseen and uncounted enemy was difficult. It made Lon feel too exposed, too juicy a target. But he did not want to take any longer than absolutely necessary getting back among comrades. He scuttled along as quickly as he could manage without getting his butt too high for safety, ignoring the growing ache in his knees and elbows as he scrabbled along the ground. *I'd need less than ten seconds to get up and sprint the distance,* he thought. *Maybe three minutes to crawl it like this.* But

Lon was not frightened enough to let himself be panicked into such a foolish attempt.

After he had covered half of the distance, Lon stopped to catch his breath and look both ways. He had not even realized that he had started to hold his breath until he had to gasp to fill his lungs. He did not see anyone from first squad, but he did not raise up more than a few inches to look. They would be there, right where they were supposed to be. Lon never doubted that. He took another deep breath, then resumed his crawl.

"I see you, Nolan," Nace said ten seconds later. "Just keep coming, nice and easy. There's no one in sight behind you."

Despite the admonition and reassurance, Lon tried to crawl faster. He started panting for air but did not stop moving. He finally spotted a little of a DMC battle helmet's camouflage pattern, no more than five feet away. *I made it!* Lon thought, resisting the urge to get up and lunge forward to join first squad. It was just then that the gunfire started behind him.

There was no question of it being a lone sniper this time. Dozens of rifles opened fire almost simultaneously in a ragged volley. Lon got up to his hands and knees and plunged forward, scurrying on until hands caught him from one side and pulled him down. For perhaps ten seconds then, Lon lay motionless, dragging air into aching lungs, before he could turn to face the new threat. First squad had already started to return fire.

Lon got his rifle up, but took a few seconds to scan the front before he bent to the sights and started shooting. The enemy gunfire was coming from along a fairly broad front, at least fifty yards across, and no more than 150 yards away. That might mean thirty men or sixty, and there could be many more nearby.

"We're moving up to you," Lieutenant Taiters said over the squad leaders' channel. "The shuttles are on their landing run now. We've got to keep these bastards busy for ten minutes."

At first, Lon had trouble holding his rifle steady, even in what should have been a rock-solid prone firing position. His hands and arms were still trembling from all of the crawling. But gradually his muscles steadied, and he moved quickly from target to target—from from one muzzle flash to the next, firing his short bursts. The routine helped to steady him, helped Lon forget the aches.

The number of enemy rifles taking part in the firefight rose. The increase was more audible than visible, but unmistakable. He heard one bullet smack into a tree trunk no more than six inches above his head and just off to the side. The bullet ripped loose bark and dropped it on his helmet. Lon shook his head and continued shooting. After seeing Dean's creased and cracked helmet earlier, this did not even count as a near miss.

At a distance, even over the sounds of gunfire, Lon heard the two shuttles coming in for their landing—very close together. *Load the wounded up fast,* Lon projected. *Get them up and out of the way.*

Ten minutes seemed like a very long time, even though the rebels showed no hint of trying to close in on the squad, or run over them. *We're facing at least company strength opposition,* Lon thought, guessed. *Maybe quite a bit more.* Most of the rebels were firing single shots, but not all of them. The military rifles that had been found earlier were capable of fully automatic fire. But none of the rebels seemed to have mastered the short burst. They always seemed to rattle off ten or twelve shots each time they pulled the trigger—a waste of ammunition to any professional.

"I had a man spending ammo that way without good reason, I'd make him pay for his own bullets," Corporal Nace mumbled over a channel to Lieutenant Taiters.

"Maybe there's a reason they're not afraid of running out," Taiters replied. "The loyalists have learned not to waste. They haven't had anything *to* waste.''

''Sir, those weapons we captured, the military ones, do we know where they came from?'' Lon asked.

''They were made on Hanau, but that's not necessarily where the rebels got them. Don't worry about that, Nolan. It can't make any difference to us.''

The volume of enemy fire increased again. There appeared to be at least a doubling of the number of weapons engaged. ''They know about the shuttles,'' Nace said. ''Looks like they want to get close enough to get a piece of them.''

He had scarcely stopped talking when the rebels started moving in against the lone Dirigenter platoon. The Norbankers did show some basic knowledge of fire-and-maneuver tactics—using half of their men to cover the other half as they got up and moved a few steps closer before dropping to cover, one group leapfrogging the other—but their local manpower advantage was so large that it was scarcely important.

The mercenary platoon kept the enemy advance slow—and costly. Four dozen men with automatic rifles, beamers, and grenade launchers took a fierce toll on the frontal attack. Each time a group of Norbanker rebels got up to advance, there were fewer than the time before. But the rebels had started out with a lot more men than one platoon could pit against them, and despite heavy losses, they kept coming. Lon Nolan had no way to be certain, but after the shuttles landed and the rebels appeared to put all of their resources into the attack, he guessed that the platoon was facing at least six hundred men—the equivalent of three DMC companies. That meant twelve-to-one odds.

We can't stop them all. Some of them are going to reach us unless they quit trying, Lon thought—and he could think of nothing that was liable to make them quit soon enough. He emptied one forty-round magazine, then a second. The leading elements of the rebel attack were within sixty yards of the platoon, and the Dirigenters had started taking casualties. Lon was only vaguely aware of the talk going on among the noncoms. He did not keep track of the numbers—seven dead and twelve wounded so far, more than a third of the platoon. There was no time for bookkeeping. He had little time for anything but shooting, and one tortured thought: *How much longer are those shuttles going to be on the ground?*

"Fix bayonets!" Taiters ordered. The shouted command startled Lon enough to throw off his aim. He reached for the bayonet on his belt with his left hand, attempting to line up his next target and shoot one-handed at the same time. The rebels were close enough that they were hard to miss, even like that. The Dirigenters who were still able to got their bayonets—eight-inch-long, double-edged blades— mounted on their rifles, and got ready for the face-to-face fight.

Lon heard the roar of attack shuttles taking off, accelerating quickly into a steep climb. But the Norbanker rebels did not suddenly give up their advance. They might not get a chance to shoot down the landers, but they still had one small group of outlanders they could overrun and destroy.

I guess we've had it, Lon thought. There was no emotion to the realization. Death might be imminent, but until it came, he still had work to do. Right next to him, Wil Nace's head was thrown back, and then the corporal collapsed over onto his right side, hit. Lon spared him only the briefest glance, uncertain whether the squad leader was dead or wounded. Very soon, it would probably make no difference.

Another forty-round magazine was empty. Lon scarcely had time to get another magazine loaded, the first round slammed into the chamber. But he did not resume firing the rifle. Instead, he pulled his pistol and used that. The rebels were within forty yards, close enough for the pistol. Lon squeezed off the fourteen rounds the semiautomatic pistol held, coolly aiming each shot, then dropped that weapon to take up the rifle again.

There was no longer any great advantage to firing the rifle on full automatic. Lon moved the selector to single shots. The enemy was close enough that he could have *thrown* the bullets and been sure of hitting an enemy with each one. The faces of the rebels were clearly visible, most distorted by intense emotion—anger, fear, or some fey humor. Lon was up off of his stomach, kneeling behind a skinny tree trunk. He heard bullets smack into the wood more than once, felt heated air as one round whizzed past him with less than an inch to spare.

But those barely impinged on Lon's awareness. He was caught up in what he had already subconsciously accepted as his own Götterdämmerung. The universe had closed in like a Q-Space bubble to encompass only the area enclosing Lon and the men who would likely kill him. And time had ceased to maintain its orderly progression from present to future.

Like a machine programmed to kill and unaware of its own mortality, Lon went about his work with cold precision. He noted a searing flash through his left shoulder but not the ensuing pain. He did not realize that he had been struck by a bullet, or that he was bleeding. His concentration was too intense, his focus too narrow. He continued to fire his rifle, hardly noticing that his left hand could no longer grip the weapon, that the arm had dropped to his side, useless.

No more than twenty men of the fourth platoon were still able to fire. The enemy—less numerous than earlier—was moving in slowly. At close range, it would not take them long to finish the job.

Then a new sound entered Lon Nolan's universe—the metallic, grating noise of shuttle Gatlings being fired. He was not certain whether he dove for cover or was knocked to the ground by a bullet. There was no pain, but by the time he hit the dirt, there was no awareness either.

16

Death smelled like a hospital, with cloying, antiseptic odors permeating everything. Distant noises were swamped by their own echoes, indistinguishable, unimportant, beyond full awareness. There were no sights, nothing but a dark limbo populated only by ghostly retinal images, or imaginings, flickering amorphous shapes in dark purples or greens, morphing from one fantastic appearance to the next, teasing the mind to find familiar silhouettes in the shapeless blobs.

This must be hell, trying to drive me crazy. That was the first coherent thought in Lon's return from the abyss. Death was assumed, unquestioned. There was *Self* without *non-Self.* There was only the thought, without accompanying images, abstractions beyond representation—a universe without matter, and with little energy.

Through subjective eons there was nothing more, not even cognition of passing time or wonder at the lack of substance to existence. Lon's mind took no special notice of its own—apparent—survival. He gave no thought to future or past, for those concepts did not currently exist for him. Nor was he aware of the lacunae in his tightly circumscribed experience, the recurrent voids, each shorter than those that came before.

Slowly, there was one almost subconscious image. Lon was nearly aware of floating in liquid, secured in some sort of womb. After another passage of nontime, light entered his universe—harsh, bright light—and he felt the circulation of cool air against his cheeks. One layer of muffling was removed from the faraway sounds that he was finally, almost, aware of. Then he felt his chest move as he sucked in air. Awareness was not a flood but a growing trickle of sensory input.

There was an era of discovery as Lon's body gradually made its presence known, encapsulating his awareness, his consciousness. Only slowly did outside referents intrude. Memory was the last constituent to arrive and find its place.

Memory. . . .

Lon found his mind catapulted back to the climax of the battle, to the last rush of Norbanker rebels. They were so close that he could almost have spit on them. And the rattle of Gatling gunfire, the roar of an attack shuttle passing overhead, low, fast, emptying thousands of rounds of ammunition in the few seconds that it could have been in range before roaring skyward on a burn-to-orbit and rendezvous with *Long Snake*.

Recalling the name of the ship triggered associations in Lon's still-expanding mind-universe. He opened his eyes, intuitively certain that he had to be aboard the ship, in its dispensary, its hospital ward.

I'm alive. He experienced a feeling of wonder, surprise, at that revelation. It was impossible but undeniable. His view was restricted to what he could see directly in front of his eyes, above him. He could not move his head—or anything else—and his field of vision was bordered by a rectangular opening not far from his face. Ceiling lights surrounded by a light gray field—the color of walls and ceilings aboard *Long Snake*.

He blinked.

"Take it easy, son," a voice said from behind, above Lon's head. "You're going to be fine. It'll just take a few more seconds to flush the last of the repair units from your system. Just relax, and wait."

Waiting was easy for Lon . . . since he had no choice. He could move only his eyelids and eyes, and the eyes did not seem inclined to obey directions. His mind was beginning to function at something near normal, though, and he had enough to think about. He was obviously in a trauma tube in the ship's dispensary. He was also at the end of his treatment, which meant that he had likely been in the tube for at least two hours, more likely four. The molecular repair units had finished repairing whatever damage had been done to him in the firefight.

I was shot, he realized, and then, *more than once.* He recalled the first wound, in his arm, or shoulder. He had no memory at all of the second wound, the one that had robbed him of consciousness. It took a moment to reassemble his final memories of the battle, the nearness of the enemy, men falling on both sides of him—and the roar of an attack shuttle giving them belated support. At first Lon did not notice when the lid of the trauma tube was lifted and one side lowered. There were two men standing next to him, watching him. One wore the insignia of a surgeon. The other was an enlisted rating, a medical orderly.

"You can get up now," the doctor said. "Good as new. There was no serious neurological damage."

The orderly helped Lon to sit and then stand, and remained close, ready to catch the patient if he started to fall. There was often a brief period of disorientation and dizziness for a patient coming out of a tube. Lon felt the vertigo, but he had planted his feet well apart, and leaned back against the edge of the tube until it passed. He looked down at himself and saw that he was wearing nothing but a disposable hospital gown.

"Just how bad was it, doctor?" he asked, turning his head toward the surgeon—slowly. "How close did I come?"

The doctor blinked once—quite deliberately, it appeared to Lon. "You want the full details?"

"As much as I can understand."

"Very well. There were three separate bullets. The first

creased your right arm here.'' He traced a line across Lon's arm.

I didn't even know about that, Lon thought.

''That wound was . . . relatively insignificant. The other two were serious. One entered here.'' The doctor tapped the left side of Lon's chest, just below the collarbone. ''It fractured the clavicle, then was deflected downward, causing the left lung to collapse, and exited below the fourth rib, about three centimeters to the left of your spine. The other bullet caught you in the side, slightly below the ribs.'' He poked Lon again, in the left side. ''That one damaged the liver, stomach, and small intestine. There was no exit wound. The bullet was lodged against the ilium on the right side—the upper part of the hipbone. We needed a surgical probe to extract that. And between the three wounds, you lost considerable blood. If help had been a little longer getting to you . . .'' He shook his head.

''The others with me. How many made it?'' Lon asked.

''I don't know,'' the doctor said softly. ''We treated nine men. How many were uninjured, treated dirtside, or killed, I don't know. Sorry.''

''I'll show you where your clothes are,'' the orderly said, finally stepping away from Lon. ''Then you get yourself to the mess hall for a meal. After that you can worry about getting back to your unit on the ground.''

Lon nodded, and let the orderly lead him away. Once they were leaving the ward, Lon asked, ''Have you heard anything about how things are going on the ground?''

''Just rumors. All I know for certain is that we haven't received any additional casualties since the group you came in with. I guess that counts as good news.''

They had entered a small locker room. The orderly pointed to one of the lockers. ''You'll find your stuff in there. Most of it's new, except for the shoes and helmet. Your weapons are in the armory.''

Lon nodded, mumbled his thanks, and opened the locker.

"You know how to find your way to your mess hall from here?" the orderly asked.

Lon hesitated before he nodded. "I think I remember." He shrugged. "If not, I know how to use the locators."

"Good enough. Good luck."

Thanks, Lon thought as the orderly left. Lon stared into the locker. The battledress, underwear, and socks were new, but that would not have surprised him even without the damage his clothes had to have taken. It was simpler to recycle uniform clothing than to clean it. The boots had been cleaned, somewhat.

Lon stripped off the hospital gown and dropped it on the floor. Methodically, he pulled on clothing, first donning everything he could while standing, then sitting to pull on socks and boots. When he was finished, he picked up the hospital gown and put it in a chute designated for that purpose. The last item that Lon took out of the locker was his helmet. He carried that under his left arm as he left the locker room.

In the passageway, he looked both ways, trying to make sure that he did know exactly where he was and how to get to the A Company mess hall. He had labored over plans of *Long Snake,* trying to memorize everything that he might need to know about it. The ship's dispensary was a new point of departure for him, but novelty was not an insurmountable complication. At worst, he would only have to look at the wall, down by the hatch through the nearest gastight bulkhead, to see where he was—section, level, and corridor. But after a few seconds he turned left and started walking, striding along at a solid clip, knowing that he had more than a quarter mile to go to reach the mess hall.

The mess hall was staffed by men from *Long Snake*'s crew, not by soldiers. The ship and its crew were part of the DMC, but an ancillary branch, like the fighter wing and the noninfantry elements of the planetary defense forces. They came under the direct jurisdiction of the Council of Regiments.

Only one cook was present in the mess hall, but he welcomed Lon warmly. "Just grab a seat somewhere close," the cook said. "Tell me what you'd like and I'll bring it to you. You're not the first guy to come through this watch. There've been a half dozen others, more or less, just enough to keep me awake till my relief shows up."

The cook seemed desperate for companionship. He scarcely stopped talking the whole time Lon was in the mess hall—while he was fixing the meal, while Lon ate it, and afterward, in the few minutes Lon took to relax before going to find out what to do next from whoever was handling things for the battalion aboard ship. Lon was content to let the cook carry the conversation, contributing only a word or two when it was inescapable. The cook did not seem to mind.

The battalion's Charge of Quarters was an elderly captain who was serving out his final year before retirement as assistant adjutant. He was not frail, or unfit for combat duty. There were no sinecures in the DMC. But after more than thirty years in uniform, Captain Bowman was due the easy posting.

"Only one man left in hospital from your lot," Bowman said when Lon reported, "and he's probably out of the tube by now. For now, my advice is to go to your quarters and catch up on sack time. The general policy is that we don't return casualties to full-duty status for eight hours after they come out of the tube, and it might be longer than that before we send the lot of you down. Depends on what's going on, and whether or not we've got any other reasons to make the shuttle run."

"Can you tell me anything about the others in the platoon I was with?" Lon asked. "How badly were we hurt?"

"You were with Alpha's fourth platoon?"

Lon nodded. Captain Bowman leaned back. "I won't lie to you. The platoon got hurt bad. The last figures I had were nineteen dead and one man missing, besides the wounded.''

''Who was missing?''

Bowman had to check his complink. ''Lance Corporal Bantor.''

Lon shook his head. ''He was dead before the fight, killed by a sniper. That's what put the rest of the platoon in danger. Bantor and I were patrolling out away from the rest. Roy went out farther than I did and was killed. The platoon was moving to rescue me when we came under full attack. How about Lieutenant Taiters, Platoon Sergeant Jorgen, and Corporal Nace?''

The captain consulted his complink again. ''Nace is the last one in hospital. Taiters was out an hour ago. Jorgen wasn't injured. Anyone else you want to know about?''

Lon closed his eyes for an instant, then opened them again. ''Can you read me the names of the dead?''

If I hadn't suggested sending a couple of men out wide, Lon thought. He had returned to his squad bay and dropped onto his bunk to wait for orders. His first move had been to look for Lieutenant Taiters, but the platoon leader was off *somewhere* in the ship. *If we hadn't gotten so fired up about what we were doing. If Roy hadn't gone out those extra yards.* The Ifs. There were a lot of them, and twenty men had died.

I might as well have killed them myself. All I had to do was keep my mouth shut and obey orders. I didn't have to make suggestions. No one would have thought the worse of me.

For a time, then, he managed to blank out conscious thought. He stared at the bottom of the bunk above his. He blinked rarely. The wounded from fourth platoon would be in the next bay over, but Lon could not bring himself to visit them. They had been hurt because of him. Their friends had died—40 percent of the platoon. Maybe they would not want to see him. Or, perhaps even worse, they might act as if it were not all Lon's fault. Eventually, he slept. His slumber was almost as blank as the hours in the trauma tube had been—up until the last minutes before he had fully regained consciousness. Lon was wakened when his bed shifted as someone sat on the edge of it.

"How you doing, Nolan?" Lieutenant Taiters asked.

"I've been better," Lon replied once his eyes were open. "I got a lot of men killed, didn't I?"

"*You* didn't get them killed. Get that nonsense out of your head right now. It was our *job* to find those rebels and keep them occupied so the shuttles could get in and out with our casualties. That's what we were supposed to be doing."

"Not like that. If I hadn't come up with such a brilliant idea, maybe no one would have walked into that kind of hell, and nobody would have been killed."

"Cut that shit. Don't go feeling sorry for yourself, or for anyone else. You had a good idea. And we *did* fulfill our orders. Our casualties got out. We didn't lose any shuttles. Anyway, if there was blame, it would be mine, not yours. All you did was make a suggestion. I vetted it. You're not in the line of command. I am. It was my decision, not yours."

Lon's "Yes, sir" showed no conversion, no abandonment of the guilt he felt.

"If you're going to be an officer in the Corps, you've got to get past this. There is only one constant about war. People die. It doesn't matter if they're good, evil, or indifferent. A bullet doesn't ask if its victim is kind to his mother or kicks dogs. We try to minimize casualties, but there are always going to be some. As long as men have to go in harm's way to fight, some of them won't come back. If you let that tie you up in knots, you'll be useless to the Corps—and to yourself.

"You've got all the tools, Nolan, skills, aptitudes, the things that can be taught and the things you have to find on your own, what you bring to the table. You're a damned good soldier, and you should be a damned good officer. But your attitudes still have a way to travel. That's the one weak spot I've noted. And the only person who can do anything about those is you."

Lon sounded chastened when he said "Yes, sir" this time.

"The Corps doesn't want officers who are going to be spendthrifts, men who'll throw lives or equipment away carelessly. But the Corps also doesn't want—can't afford— officers who will let considerations of cost, in lives or money, tie them up so thoroughly that they can't give any orders."

"I'll work on it," Lon promised.

Taiters stared at him, then nodded. "It's the hardest part of the job," he said more softly. "You get to know your men. You give orders and some men don't come back. It hurts. But if you can't live with the pain, you can't handle the job. I suspect that's one of the reasons some men prefer to remain privates throughout their careers. All they have to do is take orders and risk their own lives. They don't have to order other men to risk death."

"I've wondered about that," Lon said. He straightened up and lifted his head a little. "How are things going dirtside? Have you heard anything?"

"Nothing recent. Why don't we both take a hike up to CIC and see what we can learn."

Long Snake's Combat Information Center was forward of the soldiers' section of the ship, at the rear of the command module. CIC was staffed by both ship's personnel and specialists from the staff of the Council of Regiments. The center of the huge room was a nine-foot-diameter chart table. This was more than just a larger version of the mapboards that DMC officers and noncoms carried, although it was the master unit that linked those devices and updated them. The surface of the table could be used to show flat maps or charts, but the flat surface could also utilize holographic projections to give true topographical information. And, finally, 3-D globes or star fields could be projected in the space above the chart table to cover any planet in the DMC's database or any known section of the galaxy.

A dozen complink monitors and work stations were set around the edge of the chart table, with fixed seats to allow CIC's staff to work even during the short intervals when *Long Snake* was without its artificial gravity. Only four of the positions were occupied when Arlan and Lon arrived. Around the perimeter of the room, several other crew members sat at complink terminals, handling voice communications between the ship and the soldiers on the ground. The computers that managed all of the available data were not in this room. They were located elsewhere, under the care of technicians and their own sophisticated repair units.

Taiters and Nolan waited at the door for some response from inside, permission to enter or instructions to go away. After less than a minute, a lieutenant from ship's crew came to them.

"What can I do for you, Lieutenant?" the sailor asked.

Taiters identified himself and his companion. "We're just out of the infirmary. Any chance on finding out what's been going on down there while we were out of action?"

"I'm Karl Osway, the duty officer here this watch," the naval lieutenant said. "Come on in. You had the platoon that was chopped up last night?"

Lon winced at the verb, but Arlan showed no sign that it bothered him. "Yes," Taiters said. "That was mine."

"Sorry about the men you lost. That was a tough break. Come on over to the chart table and have a look." Osway gestured and let the two visitors precede him. The current projection was topographical, with Norbank City slightly below the middle of the chart. The area shown was about twenty-five miles in diameter.

"Things have been fairly quiet since your set-to last night," Osway said. "Your battalion hurt the rebels badly.

They've pulled out to regroup, apparently, and they have even broken off the siege of the capital. We've been able to land the rest of the arms and ammunition for the government forces, as well as replenish supplies for the battalion, and the locals have started bringing in food and people from some of the outlying areas that were cut off before.''

"Are the rebels retreating toward their own territory?" Lon asked.

"We're not certain, Cadet, but it doesn't look like it. It appears more that they're regrouping, and maybe waiting for reinforcements. They've moved off, here, toward the northeast, to some pretty rough country, but we haven't seen any signs of them moving any farther.'' He indicated an area at the edge of the chart table, ten miles from Norbank City and six miles from where a patch of green blips showed that the majority of second battalion was.

"Any current estimates on rebel numbers?" Taiters asked.

Osway shook his head. "None that you'd want to bank on. This main force here—a consolidation of the troops that were besieging the capital, the remnants of those who fought the battalion, and some of the reinforcements we knew were coming—may number anywhere between nine hundred and sixteen hundred. They chose good ground. It's rough, heavily wooded, and there seem to be scores of caves in those hills. Frankly, they could conceal a couple of regiments in there. And we *think* that there are still more rebel troops moving in from their region, but we can't be certain or get any kind of reliable estimate on numbers. They're moving in small bands and taking damn good care to avoid detection. My own personal guess is that they've had professional training in guerrilla tactics.''

"Well, we know they've gotten military weapons in from somewhere,'' Taiters said. "It wouldn't surprise me if they've bought teachers as well, even if they couldn't afford to bring in mercenaries to strengthen their case.''

"That's the guess,'' Osway acknowledged. He looked

around, then said, more softly, "Look, I may be out of line, but there's something the two of you might be interested in seeing." He moved to one of the complink consoles at the chart table and keyed in a command. "Have a look," he invited when he had what he wanted on the monitor. Arlan and Lon moved closer to read the screen, a selection from one of Colonel Flowers' log entries.

"The men of fourth platoon, A Company, this battalion, under the command of Lieutenant Arlan Taiters, showed exceptional courage and ability while faced with overwhelming numbers of enemy soldiers, holding their position against at least two companies of rebel troops, buying time for the battalion to land shuttles to evacuate wounded men successfully. I want to especially take notice of the heroism, courage, dedication, and ability of the men of the first squad of that platoon, and of Officer Cadet Lon Nolan, who was with them during this action. This squad, which initially faced the entire enemy force, held on at terrible cost to themselves until the rest of their platoon could reach them. Without the efforts and sacrifice of these men, the cost to Second Battalion would have been far greater."

"Mentioned in dispatches," Taiters whispered. Then he turned to Osway and said, "Thanks, Lieutenant. I appreciate it."

"Yeah, thanks, Lieutenant," Nolan echoed. He was shaking his head, surprised by the praise.

Osway smiled. "Just don't let anyone know I spilled the beans before you get your copies through channels. Like I said, it's a bit out of line for me, but—what the hell—I figure heroes deserve special treatment now and then."

"Any idea when we're going to get a ride back down to the surface?" Taiters asked. "Me and my men?"

"You're not on the schedule yet," Osway said. "Sometime tonight, most likely, maybe even tomorrow. I imagine it depends on how things are going."

●　　●　　●

"And you thought you had screwed up?" Taiters said as he and Nolan were walking back toward the troop area of *Long Snake*. "I told you that you did good. Even the colonel thinks so, enough to mention you in dispatches. Back on Earth, you'd get a big medal to hang off your dress uniform for it." The DMC did not, as a general rule, award medals for heroism, only small ribbons for each contract that a soldier was part of.

"It's still going to take some getting used to," Lon said.

"Don't ever get to the point where it *doesn't* bother you to lose men. You may have to fight the emotions every time, but you've got to control it. *I* lost those men too. I knew most of them since I first joined the Corps. But you've got to partition the pain, not let it take over everything. Save it for when we're back on Dirigent. Then there'll be time to deal with it."

If we get back, Lon thought, but he was learning. He would not let even Lieutenant Taiters see that fear.

17

To a man, the wounded from fourth platoon were anxious to get back to the surface and rejoin their unit. They did not speak of their pain, or fear. The trauma tubes and their nanotech medical robots had not left any scars on their bodies. Any wounds to the spirit remained hidden. If necessary, treatment was also available for those, counseling and therapy that could include both drugs and virtual reality sessions to help them integrate the experience.

They did speak of their friends, the ones who had not been lucky, but that pain too was muted, not to be shared. Not yet.

For a time, Lieutenant Taiters stayed with the group. He conducted an informal inspection—functional, dealing with the serviceability of helmets and weapons, and giving him a chance to see if anyone might need immediate counseling. Rifles were cleaned. Helmet electronics were checked and double-checked. Giving them work to do was standard therapy.

"Get a couple of hours' sleep," Taiters told his men when the last check had been completed, the last suspect electronic module replaced. "Then get in a good meal. I don't know how much longer we'll be up here. If we haven't heard anything by the time you get done eating, sack out again."

When the lieutenant left, the men from fourth platoon moved toward their bunks. Whether they felt the need for sleep or not, they would make the effort. On contract, sleep and meals had to be taken when they could be found. Lon stood and looked around. His own bunk was in the next bay, with third platoon. He hesitated to leave, though, not certain that he was ready for solitude. He felt better having others around, men who had gone through the same fight, and the same treatment, as he had.

Corporal Nace got up from his bunk and walked over to Lon. "You did good, Nolan," he said. "All the way. I heard how you stood off the rebels after I got hit, maybe kept them from butchering the rest of us."

"I just did what I had to do, Wil," Lon replied.

"Don't sell yourself short. I wouldn't hesitate to go into combat with you at my side anywhere, anytime. And I'll guarantee that the rest of the squads feel the same way." He turned to look at the men in the room. "Those of us who are left," he added, so softly that Lon barely heard.

"They're not all this bad, are they?" Lon asked.

Nace shook his head. "Very few of them, thank God. You'd better go get some rest while you can."

Lon took off his boots and stretched out on his bunk. Sleep did not come. But even with his eyes open, staring at the springs under the bunk above his, he could not avoid dreams. He had seen violent death before. The first time he had seen it, he had been no more than ten years old.

The Nolans had lived in North Carolina, within twenty miles of what had once been the Cherokee Indian Reservation in the Smoky Mountains. Lon's father, George, had taught college. His students were in Durham, those who did not attend strictly by complink, and Professor Nolan had made the commute to the university campus three times each semester. His stipend provided the extras that BM— basic maintenance—did not. But the family was not wealthy. They lived within a mile of a circus—a slum occupied almost exclusively by families who had only BM. The Asheville circus was not the largest or roughest in the state, but to a curious ten-year-old it had been an irresistible magnet. His first foray into the circus had come two years before. It seemed a completely different universe from the one he knew. The children he met in the circus might almost have been a different species from those he knew from school and the carefully chosen social outings his parents arranged.

Different, and exciting. But it was not until Lon was ten that he found many chances to explore this alternate universe. He was large for his age, and well tutored in self-defense—an essential part of his school's curriculum, the primary excuse for having students actually come in person to a classroom instead of taking all of their lessons on a complink web.

Over a period of several weeks, and through a series of fights, he had found his place in one gang of circus boys. Social standing was determined strictly through physical domination and strength, as purely as if they were not human but some extinct species of predators.

He had been running with the gang one afternoon in April, a school holiday. The sound of a gunshot had drawn them around a corner and down the alley. The boys, eight of them, had seen the culmination of a murder. The victim was on his knees, bleeding. His attacker stood three feet away, a revolver in his hand. The gun had seemed gigantic to Lon, and the blast it made when it was fired a second time sounded as loud as thunder from a lightning bolt that had struck very close. Blood had spurted from the forehead of the victim. He fell backward. Once he came to rest, he moved no more. His attacker went through his purse and pockets, grabbing what little money the victim had. Then he ran off, giving the gang of boys no more than a passing glance, obviously giving no thought to the possibility that they might identify him.

A siren sounded. "We gotta scram," the leader of the pack said. But like the others, he had to get closer first, to see what death looked like. The boys had formed a circle around the dead man. Then a new blast from a police siren brought them out of their shared trance. "Run for it," the leader said, and they ran, getting clear of the area before the police arrived.

With his eyes open, Lon could still almost see that body, smell the gunsmoke and the other odors of that neighborhood and a man who had died violently. He remembered not fear, but the thrill that he had felt, the excitement. Lon closed his eyes. The memories had caused his heart to beat faster. His breathing had become shallower, labored, as if he were running from that death again.

"That was a long time ago, and a lot of light-years away," Lon whispered. He sat up, trying to banish the childhood ghosts. Of the seven boys he had run with that year, two had died violently before their sixteenth birthday, and two had simply disappeared—run off or abducted. Kidnappings in the circuses were never for ransom. No one in them had the money to make that attractive to even the most desperate of criminals. Kidnappings were to find prostitutes, or victims for snuff movies.

"It's a wonder anyone ever lived long enough to reproduce," Lon mumbled. He got up and headed for the latrine. The circuses never faded away to ghost towns. The population always seemed to increase. Kids started having sex as soon as they were physically able, and puberty often occurred when they were ten or eleven years old. Girls often had their first baby—or their first abortion—before their twelfth birthday. Lon had been twelve when he had sex for the first time. It had cost him four bits, half his weekly allowance. That had bought him ten minutes with a girl who was two years older than him, and who already had two children. She had been nursing the younger of the two when Lon was brought to her. The baby had cried the whole time his mother was with Lon. The girl was thin, almost emaciated, and—even through the fog of distant memory—extraordinarily plain-looking, but Lon had visited her almost every week for six months, saving as much as he could from his allowance to give him those few minutes of . . . not-quite-pleasure.

"Hey, Nolan! We're going to eat." Corporal Nace had just come into the third platoon's bay. Lon was sitting on the edge of his bunk again—had been for most of the past two hours. He had not tried to sleep again after his waking dream.

Lon nodded slowly and got to his feet. Now he was tired, his mind almost numb enough for sleep. But that would have to wait—if there was still time for sleep after a protracted meal. *The way my luck's going, the lieutenant will tell us it's time to go back to the surface,* Lon thought as he followed Wil Nace to where the men from fourth platoon were waiting.

They sat together but ate in comparative silence. There was none of the free exchange of jokes and gossip that had marked meals in garrison, or on the voyage out. The little conversation there was was conducted in low tones, with minimal words. Lieutenant Taiters came in twenty minutes after they started. He asked how everyone was feeling and said that there was still no word on when they might be shipped back to the surface, so they could get at least a couple of more hours of sleep. There were no cheers, nothing more than nods from a few men.

"I'm going to head back and sack out now," Lon announced shortly after the lieutenant left. "I haven't got the energy to lift another forkful of food to my mouth." He was slow to get to his feet, though. His exhaustion was real, and more pronounced once he had mentioned it.

Halfway back to the barracks bay, Lon stopped and leaned against the wall. Continuing felt . . . futile. He toyed with the idea of sliding to the deck and resting, maybe even sleeping. Only the thought of Nace and the others coming along and finding him asleep on the floor in the hall made it possible for Lon to resume his walk. When he got to his bunk, he collapsed across it, face first, asleep before he stopped bouncing. This time there were no dreams, or nightmares.

"Nolan!"

Lon felt himself being shaken, but even that could not wake him quickly. He had to fight his way through a stupor. Only when his mind placed him back on the surface of Norbank, perhaps in imminent danger, did he snap all of the way back from sleep. The transition then was abrupt.

"I'm awake!" he announced, too loudly.

"Relax, Lon. It's just me." Lon recognized Lieutenant Taiters' voice then and sat up.

"Sorry." Lon rubbed at his eyes. "I guess I was pretty deep."

"I was beginning to think I'd have to throw cold water on you to wake you."

"What time is it?" Lon looked around as if trying to reassure himself that he was still in the safety of *Long Snake*.

"Oh-two-hundred," Taiters said.

"Wow, I guess I've been out for close to nine hours." He shook his head. "I must have been more unconscious than asleep."

Arlan smiled. "It happens. You go for a few days with little or no sleep and then when you get the chance, your body demands all it can get . . . especially after time in the tube."

"What's up? Are we going back to the surface?"

The lieutenant nodded. "We'll be leaving in a little more than an hour. Time to get cleaned up and get in one last shipboard meal before it's back to battle rations."

Lon got to his feet and spent a moment yawning and stretching. "Any change in conditions dirtside?"

"There's been no major fighting, but CIC thinks that the rebels are gearing up to risk everything on one throw of the dice. It looks as if they're marshaling all of their forces for one pitched battle. Don't worry about that yet. Go get your shower and do whatever else you need to do. I'll wait.''

When Nolan returned from the latrine, Taiters was sitting on the next bunk, leaning forward, forearms on his thighs, head down. But he looked up when he heard Lon coming. Lon went to his locker and started dressing.

''It doesn't seem very smart for the rebels to risk everything on one battle,'' Lon said when he was half dressed. ''I mean, wouldn't the smart thing be for them to, you know, melt into the woods and just stall? They have to figure that we're not here forever. All they'd have to do is wait until we pull out and come back out. Even if we trained government forces, they wouldn't have us to worry about.''

''You don't have to convince me. But maybe they're not using just their brains. It's a civil war. They're making emotional decisions. Maybe they want revenge for what we did to them last night. Maybe they figure their support will erode if they don't force the issue now. Hell, I don't know. Maybe they've got some pickled soothsayer giving orders. Come on, finish dressing and leave the strategy to others. Let's go get that meal.''

The men from fourth platoon had already started toward the mess hall. Lon and Arlan caught up with them. The group was still quiet, but not as completely as before. Sleep and time away from danger had loosened the straps of silence. The table talk was still scanty, but not absent. Mostly they talked about rejoining the company and getting back to business.

''The sooner we get this fight over, the sooner we can get on to the training phase of the contract, and the sooner we'll get home,'' Wil Nace said.

''We've got scores to settle first,'' Tarn Hedley, one of the privates in Nace's squad, said.

''Can that, now!'' Nace said. ''You're no rookie. Don't let emotion screw you up. We've got a contract to fulfill. Period.''

Hedley did not respond, but Owl Whitley, from the platoon's second squad, did. "Don't build a monument out of that 'business first, last, and always,' Corp. This ain't recruit training back home, with by-the-book questions and answers. You feel this as much as we do. We lost good mates down there. Ain't no way in hell we can forget them, and there's no reason we should."

"Every man who joins the Corps knows the price he may have to pay," Nace said, setting down his knife and fork. "It goes with the job. And there's nothing in the *Articles of Charter* about vengeance. You get to thinking about hating the other side, and that leads to nothing but trouble. You been in the Corps long enough to see anyone punished for war crimes, Whitley?"

"Yes, but that was some loser who thought rape and murder of a noncombatant were okay. This is different."

"Before we head out to the hangar, you'd best take a few minutes to reread Section Three of the *Articles*, Whitley. There are damn good reasons why we have strict codes of conduct and severe punishments for violations. It's not just a matter of morality, of philosophical notions of right and wrong, though that's an important part of it. The Corps trades on its reputation—not just our reputation for military ability but also for the honorable behavior of our people. A lot of people wouldn't want to invite a horde of Visigoths to their world. If they think we're worse than what they've got, it's no sale, no matter the danger they think they're in."

"No one's saying you should just forget fallen friends," Lieutenant Taiters said. "But you'll honor their memory more by not losing sight of why we're here, what we're all about. The Corps puts a lot into earning respect. One black mark can take ages to erase. There are still places where what the Corps did on Wellman, nearly a hundred years ago, is remembered and held against us. That was the one time when the Council of Regiments lost sight of what we're about, what we're supposed to be about.

"Now, enough of this. We've got about time for dessert and another drink before we head to the armory for weapons and then go on to the hangar. Let's save the philosophy for garrison."

"What was that about Wellman?" Lon asked the lieutenant after they left the mess hall. The enlisted men were farther ahead, walking to the armory.

"It's why there's no Ninth Regiment anymore," Taiters said. "Didn't they cover that in your recruit training lectures?"

"I don't remember hearing about it," Lon said.

Arlan shook his head. "I thought they made sure everyone heard about that. They did when I joined the Corps."

"Well, what was it?"

"Wellman was a small colony world, I guess not much more populous than Norbank. We were hired by off-worlders to go in and make it possible for our employers to exploit a natural product that existed nowhere else, some sort of organic compound that was a natural superconductor. That was bad enough, against the code of ethics of the *Articles*. But beyond that, the contract was bungled from start to finish. The Ninth Regiment was virtually destroyed by the farmers of Wellman. Then the Council of Regiments compounded the problem by sending in more forces—ostensibly to fulfill the contract, but more to get revenge." Taiters shook his head. "A few men from the Ninth had been taken prisoner. Most went over to Wellman's side. They helped train the world's population and they stood the Corps off again. The Corps' General was removed by unanimous vote of the Council of Regiments, which then resigned en masse after ordering courts-martial for themselves and the deposed General."

"I'm sure nothing was said about that in training. I wouldn't have forgotten *that*."

"I hope we're not forgetting that lesson," Taiters said, more to himself than to his companion.

18

Altogether, a dozen soldiers rode the shuttle down. The rest of the troop compartment was filled with supplies, primarily food and ammunition. Cases were secured using the safety straps that would normally keep soldiers in place as well as added ties to make certain that loads did not shift or come loose. Dirigenter shuttles were designed to be versatile.

There was no talk among the men once they entered the shuttle and took their seats. Each of them had the visors of their helmets down, hiding their faces. Rifles were secured. Safety harnesses were fastened, tightened as far as possible.

Lon listened to the routine warnings from the pilot. The hangar was depressurized, the door opened, the shuttle pushed out into space. Lon expected the shift, anticipated being thrown against his straps. The moments of maneuvering to get away from *Long Snake* seemed routine now, and even the blast of the shuttle's engines did not catch him by surprise this time.

Going in, he told himself as the lander made its first burn. The pilot was not quite so . . . enthusiastic as during the initial assault. The craft accelerated toward the ground, but the gee-forces were not what they had been during the first landing on Norbank—at least it did not seem nearly so extreme to Lon. *Maybe I'm just getting used to it,* he thought. There was never the sense of breathlessness, the feeling that he was near to graying out at the tug of acceleration or deceleration. Lon did not even bother to stare at the nearest monitor to watch their progress.

The shuttle was in the upper reaches of Norbank's atmosphere before a troubling thought came to Lon. *How can we keep all emotion out of what we do? If we kill without emotion, what does that make us—machines, or something worse?* He was distracted by memories of the talk in the mess hall. *Maybe revenge isn't the emotion we should have, but there should be* some *feeling, some realization of what we're doing.* He shook his head. *The lieutenant was right. The time for philosophy is when we're in garrison, back on Dirigent.*

"We're going in at Norbank City's spaceport, just west of the town," Lieutenant Taiters said, breaking Nolan's chain of thought. "It will mean a bit of a walk to get back to the rest of the company, but you and I have orders to report to Colonel Flowers first, and he's in the city now."

"What does the colonel want from us?" Lon asked.

Arlan chuckled. "Major Black didn't provide any details. He just said to report to the old man. You're not still thinking that you're in any kind of trouble, are you?"

"No, I guess not. But I can't help but wonder."

"We'll find out soon enough."

The shuttle braked early, then circled around to land on the improved strip of clay that Norbank City called a spaceport. Coming in for the landing, Lon was certain that the stresses were less than they had been the first time, though the shuttle still came in faster than a civilian shuttle would have.

"Make sure your safeties are on," Taiters told the men. "We're almost in town, at least two miles from any enemy."

They did not race from the lander to take up defensive positions. Lon could see guards—mostly locals but with a few DMC soldiers at key locations—posted along the perimeter of the port, looking outward. A staff sergeant came out to meet them—specifically Lon and Arlan.

"I'm to conduct you straight to the colonel, sir," the sergeant said after saluting. "Sorry, but we don't have any transport but what you're standing on."

"Don't worry about it, Sergeant," Taiters said. "We've had our rest. The exercise will do us good." The lieutenant told the other men to find a spot nearby and get some rest, that he would be back as soon as possible. No one complained about the delay in returning to the company . . . and possibly to fighting.

The walk was not excessive, perhaps a mile and a quarter. Lon saw differences from his first visit to the city almost at once. There were people out and about, even women and children. A few shops were open. A farmers' market had been set up within a block of where the front lines had been. Since the rebels had lifted the siege, produce had been able to make it in from farms west of the city—those farms that had not been burned or robbed by the rebels.

"They'll all be buttoned down tight by sunset," the sergeant said, "but they're making the most of a day with no snipers. Can't tell what'll happen after dark. There might still be rebels close, what with 'em not using electronics the way we do."

"Works both ways, Sergeant," Taiters said. "They can't tell where we are by our electronics either."

Lieutenant Colonel Medwin Flowers was sitting in the shade next to a two-story building that bore the legend "Government House" over its entrances, drinking a pale yellow liquid from a tall glass. Two locals in fresh suits sat facing the colonel. They also had drinks. Major Black stood to the side. When the major saw the approaching trio of soldiers he pointed them out to the colonel, who then set his drink aside. Lon could see that the colonel said something to the two locals; then he stood and moved away from them. Black came with him.

When Lieutenant Taiters took off his helmet, Lon

quickly did the same. Neither of the senior officers was wearing a helmet, though Major Black was sporting the earplug of a radio.

"Forget the formalities, gentlemen," Colonel Flowers said before Lon could snap to attention and salute. "This is informal." He grimaced and shook his head slightly. "You've had a rough go of it. But I want you both to know that I think you did a commendable job under the most trying circumstances. There's no way to be certain, but it may be the actions of your platoon, Lieutenant, as much as what happened earlier, that broke the siege of this city."

"Thank you, sir," Taiters said. "Just doing our jobs."

"Yes, and doing them better than anyone has a right to demand," Flowers said. "It's regrettable that the price was so heavy, but . . . it does happen." Flowers turned to face Lon then. "I'll be glad to welcome you as an officer in the battalion when we get home to Dirigent, Nolan. You've shown your worth. I think you have an excellent future ahead of you in the Corps." He smiled more broadly. "If it were in my power, I'd pin the red and gold pips on your shoulders now, but Corps regs say that can't happen until we get home."

"When we get back to Dirigent is soon enough for me, sir," Lon said. "I'm learning not to rush things."

Flowers nodded as he turned again, including both of them in his gaze. "The other reason I wanted to see you is that I want to pick your brains. I want you to tell me about that engagement you had, just how it went, and what sort of impression you got of the rebels you were facing. The more I can get inside the heads of these rebels, the better things will be for us."

The colonel kept them for an hour, questioning every detail of their memories of the engagement. Drinks were brought for Lon and Arlan, the same fruit ade that the colonel was drinking. Long before the inquisition was over, Lon found himself sweating profusely. It was not just the temperature and humidity. Although both were above eighty, the men were seated in the shade, with a moderate breeze. Remembering what had happened, going back through every minute of the fight and the events leading up to it, brought back some of Lon's fear and tension, and that brought on the perspiration. He started looking around, as if he were concerned that those same rebels might be sneaking up on him again. The only relief that Lon found was that Arlan Taiters seemed to be affected almost as much by the questioning.

"Sir, may I ask a question?" Taiters asked once Flowers indicated that he was finished. The colonel nodded. "It's obvious that the rebels have managed to get military weapons in from someplace, either directly from Hanau or through some third party, and I got the impression that the rebels must also have had at least minimal training by professionals," Arlan said by way of preface. "Do you think that they might have a cadre of mercenaries on-planet, professionals we might come up against ourselves?"

Medwin Flowers' brows curled into a look of concentration, almost a frown. He was slow to answer. "I agree with your assessment about the weapons and training. I've asked myself the same question you asked. We have no evidence of mercenaries operating on behalf of the rebels. There was no indication of that before we came. There is no sign of any other shipping in the system or military aircraft operating, or we would have had opposition to our shuttles. And we have not detected any sophisticated electronics." He paused, shaking his head slowly. "We can't rule out the possibility that there might be a few professionals providing training and advice for the rebels, but there can't be any significant number, perhaps no more than a squad or two. It's more likely that the rebels have a few of their own people who have served as mercenaries somewhere and then come home. That might also explain the weaponry. Those hypothetical veterans might have had the contacts to expedite procurement of military weapons. Either way, it shouldn't impact our operations any more than it already has."

Arlan nodded once, slowly, an unconscious gesture. "Thank you, sir," he said. "I was just wondering."

"We're monitoring this as closely as we can," Flowers said. "We're not taking anything for granted."

"Yes, sir. I guess we should be heading out now. The men we came down with are waiting, and we need to get back to the company." Taiters stood, as did Lon.

"I've never gone through a grilling like *that* before," Lon said once he and the lieutenant were well away from the battalion commander. "Not even back at The Springs."

"I'm sure the colonel is concerned," Arlan replied. "We're obviously up against fanatics, people who aren't deterred by taking heavy casualties. I imagine he's got people trying to find out everything possible about the animosity between the two groups of settlers here. This feels like something more than mere political squabbling. When a conflict gets this bloody, this intense, it's more likely to be over religion, or basic philosophies. If there was rational leadership, the rebels would be looking for peace talks by now, some sort of compromise."

"Are you saying that the fight might go on until there's no one left to fight on one side or the other?"

"It's possible. If neither side is willing to accept anything less than total victory. But I hope we're not stuck in it that long. Our job is to break the armed rebellion and train the government militia. Then we can go home."

"But what happens after we leave?"

"I don't know. The colonel might try to sell the rebels on the idea of a contract to guarantee the safety of noncombatants against reprisals, but if this is really a deep ideological fight, they probably wouldn't accept any offer from us."

"Even if it means they risk being butchered?"

Arlan cracked a grin. "They have one thing going for

them. It may be a good thing that we had to get the weapons and ammunition to the government forces early, before the revolt was put down. They might use most of that ammunition up, not have enough left to do serious damage to the rebel civilians. Especially after we finish training the militia. And I'm sure that the colonel will be in no hurry to put through a contract for more ammunition. We can't guarantee peace here forever, but that would buy the rebels time to think about getting outside protection—from someone else if they won't trust us—or time to recover from the fighting and replenish their own supplies.''

On the rest of the walk through Norbank City, Lon stared at the civilians intensely, as if his gaze might penetrate their masks to discover what they were thinking. They gave no indication of being religious or political zealots. They appeared no different from people he had seen elsewhere, on Earth or Dirigent, or Over-Galapagos—if anything, they were more rustic than people he had seen anywhere else.

What drives you? he wondered whenever the eyes of one of the civilians met his. *And what drives your rebels?*

19

Long Snake's attack shuttles operated in relays. The landers remained above ten thousand feet—high enough to give them time to evade surface-to-air missiles—but kept up an assault on the main rebel positions. Beginning as soon as they had the cover of full darkness and continuing on into the night, the aircraft sent rockets into the hilly region where the rebels were congregating, softening up the enemy for the men of the Second Battalion and the Norbanker militia.

On the ground, at a distance, the explosions sounded like thunder. Flashes of light preceded each thunderclap, completing the analogy. Each group of four to six blasts was separated by ten to fifteen minutes from the next series as one shuttle after another made the descent, two attack runs, and then climbed back into space to rendezvous with *Long Snake*. The timing was never precise, to avoid allowing the rebels to predict with any certainty when the next strike would come. Occasionally, longer hiatuses were left to increase the uncertainty.

Lon Nolan took a cold pleasure from the explosions. *Hit 'em hard,* he urged. *The more you take care of, the fewer there'll be for us to face.* He did not deceive himself that the air attack could obliterate the enemy, or even reduce his numbers enough to make the coming land fight inconsequential. There *would* be rebel casualties, but equally important were the less tangible effects that the bombardment was certain to have. Men would not be able to sleep through it, and that would have to augment the attack's effect on morale.

The mercenaries and militiamen had started to move two hours before dark, using the last hours of light and the short twilight to get the Norbankers as close as possible to where they needed to be before darkness slowed the advance. Three of the militia companies hiked with the Dirigenters. The fourth new company had been held back by the government to help protect the capital, and to help ensure that more produce and livestock made it into town from the western farming area before the rebels could try to reestablish their siege. The government also had civilians strengthening the city's defenses, which showed no great confidence in their militia or in the mercenaries.

Each militia company was paired with a mercenary company. They moved parallel to each other. A few mercenaries marched with the militia, to make sure that the local leaders were not totally without communications. Only the point company, A Company this time, was not saddled with militiamen.

That's one headache I'm as glad not to have, Lon thought during one short rest period. Lieutenant Taiters still kept him close, and Lon listened in on everything that the lieutenant said or heard on the radio or in person. Third and fourth platoons were back together, fourth showing the gaps of men lost in their last fight. Lon found his opinions solicited now, his suggestions listened to—if not necessarily adopted.

I guess I have been accepted, Lon thought. He found no elation in that, no sense of accomplishment. It was more a weight on his back. He felt the need to weigh his words, his thoughts, more carefully before issuing them. He knew the names of the men who had died the first time one of his suggestions had been accepted. If he closed his eyes, he could see some of their faces. Despite the assurances of the lieutenant and the colonel—and the others who had spoken to him—Lon was not ready to grant himself complete absolution for that.

Lon concentrated on what he was doing. The slightest sound or movement, real or imagined, could make him turn his head, his rifle ready if needed. He recognized his heightened nervousness and tried to combat it, but with little success. Telling himself *I'm too damn jumpy* was not enough. There was always *I don't want to get anyone else killed,* to counter it.

It was just after sunset that third platoon rotated to the front, to take the point. "You stay with first and second squads," Taiters told Lon. "I'll stay with the others. Anything happens, get on to me immediately." Maintaining an open link would be impractical while they were operating separately.

It's not leadership, but it's close, Lon decided. And it was one more mark of the new trust that Taiters and the colonel were showing in him. *Just don't screw it up,* he told himself.

The battalion, with its accompanying militia, moved in three columns. One platoon could not hope to scout all three routes, but split in halves, they could cover much of the ground. One squad moved out in front, split into its two fire teams, staying thirty yards or more apart, each team single file, ranging left and right in a zigzag pattern. Behind them, the other squad moved in a skirmish line across the middle, as the terrain permitted. The two squads spelled each other every fifteen or twenty minutes. Lon stayed with the rear squad. The two squad leaders reported to Platoon Sergeant Dendrow, but Lon was included in all of those conversations.

Level ground became a rarity. At times the battalion had to move through three different valleys, cut off from each other by hills that ranged between fifty and two hundred feet in height. Much of the terrain was rough, not merely because of the topology but also because of scrub growth that clogged the land. This was not the tall forest that the mercenaries had originally operated in, but a more mixed growth—trees, grasses, bushes, and vines. The terrain provided excellent locations for ambush at almost every turn. Small groups of enemy soldiers might be anywhere along the slopes of the hills or in the valleys, ready to pick off the scouts.

Like the night before last, Lon reminded himself. Although he trusted the men in front of him to do their jobs, he kept scanning himself, looking for any hint of trouble.

The explosions in and around the rebel positions gradually sounded louder. *I hope they save something for later, in case they have to bail us out,* Lon thought when he realized how long the bombardment had been under way. Scores of missiles had been sent against the rebels.

It was only minutes later that a call from Captain Orlis came. "Hold the point. We're all stopping. The last shuttles in reported that the rebels might have moved."

No wonder they moved, Lon decided. *Too much hell coming at them.* The men of first and second squads moved into a defensive alignment, across the narrow valley they had been following to the northeast and along the slopes above it. No order to dig in was given, but most of the men scraped away a little soil and vegetation to give themselves some cover. Just in case.

Lon went to Corporal Girana. "Let me see your mapboard, Tebba," he said as he got down next to him. Girana rolled onto his side to get the unit out of its pocket on his trouser leg.

"Be careful of the glow," Girana said softly.

Lon nodded as he unfolded the mapboard. He fiddled with the controls until the area he was looking at was centered on the last known position of the rebel force. With infrared images overlaid on the basic chart, Lon could see the hot spots of fires and blast damage from the missile strikes. There was no clear heat signature from the soldiers who had been present before.

They might still be there, Lon decided, *masked by the*

heat of the battle damage. He was not certain how fine the resolution of the shuttle imaging systems was from ten thousand feet.

The screen was updated by CIC aboard *Long Snake* while Lon was looking at it. He thought that one shuttle must have risked coming in much lower than ten thousand feet, looking for the rebels. Running a reconnaissance mission, a shuttle could come in slow and quiet, and—at night—it would be invisible to unaided human eyes on the ground. The resolution of the overlay improved considerably, but it was still impossible to be certain whether the rebels were still where they had been.

The colonel's either going to have to risk a shuttle almost at treetop level or send men in on the ground, Lon thought. *That's the only way to be sure. As long as we're not the ones who have to go in and find them.* He spent a couple of minutes longer studying the mapboard, the battalion's location, their original destination, and possible places for the rebels to have moved—memorizing as much as he could. *They can't move as fast at night as we could. That limits how far from the original position they can be.*

That still left plenty of areas the rebels *might* have moved to. Every ridge, slope, and valley provided its own opportunities. *And there are supposed to be caves in these hills,* Lon remembered. He called Lieutenant Taiters and mentioned that. "We haven't been looking for caves," he added. "I sure don't recall seeing any. And caves would make ambushes harder to spot."

"I forgot about the caves too," Arlan admitted. "Hang on." The lieutenant kept Lon on the line while he called Captain Orlis to mention caves and to ask if anyone had been looking for them.

"Not specifically," Orlis said. "I guess it's something we'd better start doing. I'll pass the word back to battalion, so that the rest know there may be gaps we haven't checked. You'd better make sure all your men know about them now, and put men along the slopes to look for openings."

"Sir, I think we ought to actively check this area where we're at," Lon said. "It won't do much good to watch a perimeter if we've got enemy inside it."

"You're right, Nolan," the captain said. "Arlan, get your people busy. Make sure there aren't any snakepits inside your perimeter, then check out about fifty yards around you. Tell the men to be damned careful. The opening might be just big enough for a man to get through, and if the enemy has got men stashed, they'll probably have those openings camouflaged."

Taiters assigned half of his men to look for caves while the rest stayed on the perimeter. Lon went with Girana's squad while they quartered the area.

"I messed around in caves a little back on Earth," Lon told the corporal. "There were a lot of them around the part of North Carolina where I grew up. The one thing that might give away an opening is that the temperature in it should be quite a bit cooler than outside."

Tebba passed the tip on to the rest of the squad. He put his men in line, little more than an arm's length apart. They went back and forth over the area inside the perimeter the two platoons had set up, then started along the slopes of the hills on either side, beyond the perimeter.

The only holes they found were too small to harbor enemy soldiers. The largest that Lon saw was wide enough for a human for only the first two feet. "A good place to duck if shooting starts," he told Tebba.

"As long as there aren't any nasty creepy-crawlies in there first," Tebba replied.

"Norbank have anything like that?" Lon asked as the squad moved back inside the circle of guns.

"Don't know. None have tried to crawl into my pants yet anyhow," Tebba said. "That's the way I want to keep it."

Before Lon could say anything more, several shots sounded from the next valley east. Lon and the rest dove to the ground immediately, not waiting to discover what the shooting was about.

"I think maybe somebody found an occupied cave," Tebba said when no additional gunfire sounded.

"Or somebody just got too nervous," Lon suggested.

Over the next fifteen minutes, there were two additional series of shots, in different locations. Word came down that a few snipers had been found in caves. And disposed of. Then there were orders to get up and start moving again.

The rebels *had* moved—exactly where was not yet certain.

20

"We've got more than six thousand years of military experience and innovation behind us as a species, and here we are operating much as the earliest soldiers did—sending a few men out ahead to try to find the enemy.'' Arlan Taiters had the faceplate of his helmet halfway up, giving him room to rub his face with the fingers of both hands. His two platoons were together. He was sitting with his back against a tree, his position hidden from three sides by the trunk and by a thicket. Lon Nolan sat next to the lieutenant.

''Some things may never change completely,'' Lon replied. ''At The Springs, they taught us about battles that happened thousands of years ago, and tactics that have been obsolete for millennia. We studied phalanxes and Roman battle squares. We read Caesar and Thucydides, and dozens of other ancient authors. We re-created famous battles on 3-D chart tables, with infantry and horse cavalry charging and wheeling. Swords and spears. Most of us thought it was a horrible waste of time.''

Taiters stopped rubbing at his face and lowered his head so he could look at Lon with the night-vision enhancements of his visor. ''I used to think that, too, but it isn't. Look at it this way. We're on the peak of a pyramid built of all of those battles, weapons, and tactics.'' He shook his head. ''No, not the peak of a pyramid—we're part of a continuum, built on the past, with the future to be built as much on what we do as on what those other soldiers have done before. The more links of the chain you know, the easier it is to extrapolate, to improvise, when you come up against something new, or something not covered by orders.''

''Like now?'' Lon asked, and Arlan nodded.

''Exactly. We've got the best surveillance gear in the galaxy. We can pick up a helmet's electronics from two hundred miles out in space and take photographs from that distance with enough resolution to identify an object no larger than your hand—day or night. We have computers that can track the positions of twenty thousand individual moving traces in real time, as well as monitor and record their conversations and helmet telemetry. We can fire an MR halfway across the galaxy and know it will arrive within two hundred yards of its target. But here, up against an enemy without electronics to trace, and with a forest to hide in, we're right back to where the Greeks and Persians were four thousand years ago, stumbling around trying to find the other guy before he finds us first and clobbers us.''

''I'd have thought that we'd be able to at least get thermal images of that many warm bodies,'' Lon said. ''We've got the advantage of infrared cameras and our own night-vision gear.''

''You know the limits of that, especially here. The basic material the Norbankers use for clothing has just enough thermal insulation to make spotting them difficult at any distance. It's not as efficient as the stuff they make our battledress out of, but enough with the temperature conditions here.''

The men of A Company were still in their defensive positions, half of them on watch while the other half slept— or tried to. Lieutenant Taiters was ''up'' while his two platoon sergeants rested. Other companies were doing the scouting now, a squad here and a squad there, while one or two shuttles kept up the search from the air. It had been nearly three hours since the discovery that the rebels had moved.

Occasionally there were short bursts of gunfire, never particularly close. Each time it triggered a quick alertness in the waiting men, but turned out to be the discovery of rebels in yet another small cave. It was not clear whether those men had been sent in to snipe at the mercenaries and government forces or if they had simply been cut off from escape.

Midnight passed, then one o'clock. There was still no word from battalion headquarters. Lieutenant Taiters checked to make sure that his platoon sergeants were awake, and told them that he was going to try to get a little rest.

"You too," he told Lon after his radio conversation with the sergeants. "Get it while you can."

Lon lay down. He had scooped out a shallow depression under a thick tangle of brambles. (*A fine nest for a paranoid,* he had thought at the time.) As long as he did not try to sit up, he would be fine. He made himself as comfortable as he could under the circumstances. He left his helmet on. The webbing inside did not make a perfect pillow, but it was better than bare ground. Lon turned down the volume on his earphones and dimmed the head-up display on his visor. If an alarm came, he would be ready to respond instantly. In the meantime, sleep would ease the waiting.

But sleep would not come.

He was exhausted. His mind had slowed, his thinking dulled, the way it always was when sleep had been too long delayed. But he could not slide below something close to a trancelike state. He was aware . . . but not fully, neither truly awake nor asleep—almost like the way he had been aboard ship after coming out of the trauma tube. His ears continued to strain for any hint of danger. Questions continued to plague him.

Will we ever finish here? Images floated by, at the periphery of his mind, at the edge of perception. At one point he started, shivering, feeling as if he were falling, but lying on the ground in full gravity left nowhere to fall. All the episode did was drag him farther from the void of sleep.

Sleep! For a time he thought he was back at The Springs,

studying for final examinations his first semester. He had stayed up all night, two nights in a row—afraid not just of not making high marks, but actually worried that he might totally bomb one or more of the tests, fail a course . . . and perhaps find himself washed out of the academy. The memory was so vivid that he could see the bright light of his desk lamp, feel the eyestrain caused by his complink monitor, smell the coffee he had consumed in a vain effort to maintain alertness.

"Huh?" he said, half aloud. He had thought he had heard his roommate asking a question about one of the courses. *This isn't The Springs.* He looked around quickly, disoriented by the dark and the greenish cast to everything through his helmet faceplate. He needed a moment to recall where he was, and to realize that it had been Lieutenant Taiters' voice he had heard.

"I'm awake," Lon mumbled, trying to force himself to live up to the claim. He felt groggy, almost drugged. "What is it?"

Arlan gave him a few seconds before he said, "We've got orders. We're going to move out in twenty minutes."

"Yes, sir." Lon started trying to sit up, only to run his helmet into the thorny vines he had camped under. He dropped back to the ground and took a deep breath. Then he slid to the side, out through the only exit his position offered. Lon took off his helmet and rubbed vigorously at his face with both hands, still trying to shake off the effects of the almost-sleep he had . . . suffered through. "They found the rebels?" he asked.

"Some of them, anyway," Arlan said. "About four miles northeast of where they were before."

Lon blinked several times as he put his helmet back on. "The terrain gets even rougher off that way, doesn't it?"

"A little," the lieutenant said. "It doesn't get really bad until farther out, though. This is all just foothills stuff."

"Were they still moving, or had they set up camp?" was Lon's next question.

"We'll know if they're still there when we get there," Arlan said. "We can't get in position before dawn, though."

"You mean we're going to run a daylight attack?" The idea before had been to get into position early enough to take advantage of the dark, to hit the rebels while they would still have difficulty seeing them.

Arlan shrugged. "If the colonel's made up his mind, he neglected to tell me. Once you get yourself pulled together, trot over to Corporal Nace. This isn't what I had planned, but I need you to help fill the gaps in fourth platoon."

Lon nodded.

"I'll try to keep you filled in about what's going on. I probably don't *need* to say this, but I will anyhow. You're still just a cadet, out of the line of command—no matter how well you've proved yourself."

"Yes, sir. That's not something I'm likely to lose sight of," Lon said.

"I know. It's just that we're all tired, and tired men make mistakes. Go on, get over to Nace and see where he wants you."

Even with the addition of Lon, Nace's squad was still four men short. Every squad in fourth platoon was shorthanded, but first squad had suffered the worst casualties. Wil Nace put Nolan between Tarn Hedley and Owl Whitley, and—most of the time—kept the three of them in the middle of the squad.

"It's not that I don't trust your abilities," Nace told Lon on a private channel. "I've seen you in action. I know that you know your stuff. It's just . . . well, I don't want to lose an officer cadet who's ready to get his pips, not if there's any way to avoid it without putting the rest of the squad in extra jeopardy. That's laying it on the line."

"I appreciate the honesty, Wil, and you'll have my fullest cooperation. I don't want to lose me either." Between them, they managed about half a chuckle.

Captain Orlis held a short conference with his officers and noncoms. Lon shared Corporal Nace's mapboard while the captain outlined the plan. Second Battalion would move in two elements, a mile apart, following parallel tracks toward the northeast in an effort to outflank the rebels. Somewhat behind the mercenaries, the local militia would come up in the center, with just enough of the Dirigenters to maintain communications.

"Are we going to put people in behind the rebels to keep them boxed in?" Lieutenant Hoper asked.

There was a pause before Orlis said, "No. If they want to keep retreating, we let them. Colonel Flowers insisted on that, even though the government wants us to do to this batch what we did to the others. If we drive them off, too far away to be an immediate threat to the capital, that gives us time to give the militia some real training, get them to the point where they're not as dangerous to us as they are to the rebels."

I don't think that's the only thing the colonel has on his mind, Lon thought. *With the militia in the center the way they are, they'll be coming straight up the valley at the rebels. If we attack after daylight, they'll take heavy casualties.* He was hesitant to ascribe motives to the colonel, but it looked like one more way to prevent wholesale slaughter of the surviving rebels after the battalion left Norbank.

Alpha and Bravo companies were on the left flank, Alpha in front. Its first platoon provided advance scouts. Second and third platoons took turns on point. Fourth was not purposely excluded. Its turn would have come next. There just was not time for them to rotate to the front. After third had been on point for fifty minutes, the advance was halted. One of the patrols had come upon a rebel outpost. The three men in the outpost were killed—silently, two by a beamer and the third by a knife across the throat.

We've got to be close, Lon told himself when he received

the news from Lieutenant Taiters. *Amateurs wouldn't put sentries out farther than easy shouting distance.* He cranked the volume up on his helmet's external microphones. *Someone will hear something.* Lon knew how good the Corps' sound detection gear was. On Dirigent, during a field exercise, he had picked up the local equivalent of a squirrel biting open a nut at ninety yards, gnawing his way in and then chewing the nut meat. It had taken him some time to figure out what the noise had been, using his helmet's pickups like direction finders, then scanning the vector until he spotted the only possible target.

Alpha Company was ordered to hold its position, to switch into a skirmish line facing up the slope to its right. "Look for caves," Captain Orlis ordered, "but be quiet about it, and try to handle any enemy you find the same way."

Two openings were found along the company's new front, but both were vacant of anything larger than a scaly creature the size of a house cat. The men who found that unknown animal decided to leave it alone. Its teeth appeared fearsome.

Dawn was near. Even with his visor up, Lon could pick out shapes on the forested slope above him. *We'll never get close enough to the main body of the rebels in secret,* he thought. Although there might be rebel patrols on the ridge atop this slope, the main body was—or was believed to be—another ridge over. Even when Alpha got to the top of this hill the enemy would be more than two hundred yards away, within range of rifles and beamers, but beyond the range of the grenade launchers that one man in each squad carried.

As long as they keep their heads down and don't do anything stupid, we'll still have to go in after them, Lon thought. In daylight, that could be suicidal, depending on how much—or how little—cover there was between this ridge and the next. *And the Corps doesn't believe in suicide missions. So the colonel must have something else in mind,* he reasoned. He shook his head then, recalling the Norbanker militia advancing along the valley, moving directly toward the rebels. *It can't be that; Flowers can't intend to use three companies of militia as sacrificial lambs to let us get in.* Colonel Flowers might not be too heartbroken over some militia casualties, but he could not be callous enough to offer up more than four hundred loyalist troops for certain slaughter.

What's the alternative? What am I missing? Lon asked himself. It was part of the education of any aspiring military leader to look at situations and seek the optimal solution. Wargaming had been an integral part of the curriculum at The Springs, as well as a major extracurricular activity ranked equally with physical sports.

Thinking about the tactical problem did not keep Lon from paying attention to his more immediate responsibilities, guarding his section of the squad's front. He tried to recall the details he had seen on the mapboard earlier, the terrain, the supposed positions of the enemy force. At the same time, his eyes continued to scan the hillside in front of him, and his ears strained for any untoward sound.

The valley that the rebels were thought to be defending was a little more than a mile long between lower passes between hills. The nearer crest was eighty feet above the interior valley, not quite that high above the valley between Alpha Company and the rebels. The far ridge was higher on both sides. The distance across the valley that the rebels held, crest to crest, averaged twelve hundred yards.

Room for an army and a half, Lon thought. CIC's estimate of the number of rebels was extremely vague. There might be as few as six hundred—or more than two thousand. *Hell of a way to run a war. It could be two-to-one odds in either direction, and we might not know which until we're in the middle of the battle.*

Company Lead Sergeant Jim Ziegler ran a radio check of platoon sergeants and squad leaders. Lon was hooked into the noncoms' channel. Nothing seemed to be stirring

along A Company's front. No one was picking up any iden-
tifiable sounds from the supposed rebel positions.

"I want one squad from each platoon to move up to just
behind the ridgeline," Ziegler said. "We need observation
posts. If you run into opposition, try to handle it quietly,
and try not to show yourselves to the rebels across the
way."

Before fourth platoon's sergeant could assign one of the
other squads, Wil Nace volunteered his men. "We need
this, Jim," he said.

Jorgen scarcely hesitated. "Okay, Wil, you've got it. But
be damned careful. Watch your heads, and your butts."

Lon was waiting for Nace's call on the squad channel
when it came. He had already started to choose his route
up the hill.

21

Lon Nolan was just a few paces to the right of Corporal Nace as the squad started up the slope. The pitch was not steep enough to cause any difficulties, but it was enough to put a strain on the muscles of calf and thigh, even though the line stopped after almost every step forward to search for the enemy, and for any mines or booby traps he might have planted. In some ways, the slope was a help. Eyes were closer to ground level, nearer to where any booby traps were likely to be set, nearer to any sign of men who had traveled the route recently. And if the Dirigenters had to dive for cover, the ground was that little much closer.

The crest was silhouetted by the brightening glow of dawn, a sharp line above the mantle of shadow that the mercenaries climbed through. The upper reaches of the trees on the hillside were already in sunlight.

Climbing toward morning, Lon thought. As the skirmish line got closer to the light, he crouched forward a little farther, subconsciously delaying the time when he would lose the cover of the shade and failing night. Many of the other soldiers reacted similarly, and well before the line reached the summit, the men were virtually crawling toward it.

"Down!" Nace ordered his squad when they were still six feet below the crest. "That next hill is higher than this one. Slide up into position carefully."

The soil near the top of the hill was thin, fighting to hold scrub growth in among the rocky mass of the extrusion.

The ridge itself was nearly devoid of vegetation, a naked spine of rotting limestone. As Lon slid up against it and took his first careful peek over, he found himself looking through the upper branches of trees growing along the opposite slope of the ridge. Farther off, across the next valley, another ridge—forested rather than bare—ran parallel to this one. From a distance, it looked to be more than the twenty to thirty feet higher that the charts said it was. Lon pulled back from the edge, feeling too exposed for comfort.

Within seconds, things began to go wrong. Lon heard gunfire far off to his right. With the hills creating echoes, he could not be positive, but he suspected that the gunfire came from where the Norbanker militia was—or was supposed to be. At first there were only a few scattered shots, but the volume built up. It took no more than a minute or two before it had crescendoed into a major firefight.

"What is that?" he asked Lieutenant Taiters.

"I don't know. Keep your mind on your own area."

Lon edged up to the crest again to look at the next hill. There was no trace of activity there, even when he switched his faceplate to maximum magnification and scanned the opposite ridge slowly. He saw no sign of any rebel positions, not even a sentry. *We wouldn't be visible,* he thought, *or not very. But that's with good equipment and better training. If these rebels* are *amateurs . . .*

"Lieutenant, I don't think the rebels are over there, at least not many of them. I think they've moved again."

This time Taiters did not answer immediately. He left Nolan hanging while he made a number of calls that he did not include the cadet in. When he finally returned to his channel with Lon he said, "You may be right. No one's spotted any activity there since we got in position. Keep your eyes open. The colonel is checking with CIC before he decides what we do next." The lieutenant paused, then said, "That shooting you hear is at the rear of the militia. A company or more of rebels hit them from behind. Delta Company is moving to relieve them."

Lon raised himself a little higher, but not enough to offer a good target in case he was wrong—if there *were* rebels across the way. He wanted a look at the eastern slope of the hill he was on, and at the floor of the valley. If the rebels were not behind that next ridge, they might be anywhere, including right under the noses of Lon and the other Dirigenters.

The firefight to the south abruptly decreased in intensity. Lon glanced that way. *One side or the other managed to disengage,* he thought, the best guess. *The rebels must have pulled back before Delta got to them* was more of a stretch, but reasonable. The remaining fire finally stopped altogether.

Almost simultaneously there was a new locus of gunfire, behind and below Lon, and slightly to the north. His own company was under attack. He slid away from the summit and turned, bringing his rifle to bear, and scanning for targets. He saw no muzzle flashes, and there did not seem to be very many guns in the attack, off near the end of the company's defensive perimeter.

"It's just a patrol," one of the squad leaders said over the noncoms' channel. "First platoon is dealing with them. Mind your own fronts."

Lon was already moving back to the ridge before Corporal Nace passed that order along to the squad. "Stay on this side of the ridge," Nace added, "just in case this is a trick to try to get us to expose ourselves to a larger force on the other side."

I guess amateurs might try something like that, Lon thought. He scanned the slopes and valley floor east of him, with an occasional glance behind him. The action was some distance away, but gunfire in back of him was difficult to ignore. *Why don't they get that put down?* he wondered. *A small patrol shouldn't be hard to handle, even if they're playing hide-and-seek.*

The gunfire seemed to get more distant before it stopped. In the silence, Lon could hear the echoes of far more distant shooting, bounced around so much that he was not even certain where the original sound was coming from.

"Mount up. We're moving out," Captain Orlis said on the company noncoms' channel. "Pull your squads back from the ridge and get ready to head southwest."

Lon stayed back with Wil Nace, following the rest of first squad back down the slope at an angle. Without the need to discuss it between them, they divided zones of responsibility, each watching half of a circle around them.

Once all of the company had reached the bottom of the slope, Captain Orlis wasted no time getting his men moving back the way they had come. Third platoon was in front, with fourth behind it. Lieutenant Taiters was with fourth's first squad, in the middle of his two platoons. He called Lon up to him.

"It looks like the rebels want to play cat and mouse," he told Lon on their private channel.

"Either they've learned fast or there's somebody different calling the shots than there was when we first landed," Lon said.

"It does seem awfully obvious," Taiters admitted. "It's got battalion and CIC thinking in circles, wondering what's next."

"You think maybe there's an outsider running things for the rebels now?" Lon asked.

"Someone who's had professional training, at least."

They moved in silence for a couple of minutes after that, watching the flanks. Taiters ran checks with his platoon sergeants and squad leaders.

"You know, if it were me calling the shots on the other side, I think I'd do what I could to draw us away from the capital, then hit it with everything I could cobble together, try for a *coup de main* to overthrow the government," Lon said. "Hope that would be enough to get us out of the action."

"Present us with a *fait accompli,* no one to pay the bills," Arlan said, nodding. "If they were feeling generous, they'd offer to let us leave peacefully, save themselves some grief.'' He shrugged. ''If not . . . we could have one hell of a problem getting out safely.''

''You don't think it will come to that, do you?'' Lon asked.

''Probably not,'' the lieutenant said, almost too quickly. ''If nothing else, we could pull back into defensive positions and wait for relief from Dirigent. Between our weapons and the assistance we can get from the shuttles, it should be possible to hold on for the four weeks or so it would take.''

''You ever been on a contract that hairy?''

''No, and I don't expect this one to go that far, either. We've got the numbers to force the issue, if we have to.'' The unspoken qualification, *I hope,* was understood. ''There's another possibility,'' Taiters said. ''The rebels might be trying to convince us to retreat into the city with the militia so they can renew the siege, keep us all bottled up for however long it takes them to finish us off or convince the government to seek terms. I imagine that the local authorities are already pressing the colonel to defend their capital.''

Fat chance, Lon thought. The DMC was light infantry, meant to be mobile, not a static defense force. Whatever the circumstances, the preferred response would almost certainly be to keep the battalion out where it could maneuver freely.

''The government might pull all of its militia back into the city,'' Lon said. ''That might even be to our advantage.''

Over the next hour and a half, while the battalion rendezvoused with the three companies of militia, the rebels continued a series of harassing attacks—striking, then retreating before they could be trapped, or destroyed by the mercenaries. There never seemed to be more than a short-handed squad—eight to ten men—involved in the attacks, and they disappeared into the forest as soon as they had fired a few rounds. The rebels did not inflict many casualties; only one Dirigenter was killed, but there were a few wounded, with no immediate chance to bring in a shuttle to evacuate them. The risk was too great. All that could be done was to get the wounded into portable trauma tubes and take them back to Norbank City under strong guard.

Doesn't make us look very good, Lon thought after one attack came close to Alpha Company. *It's like we're the amateurs and they're running rings around us.*

On several occasions, the sounds of shuttles passing overhead came through. The landers were staying high, out of harm's way, as they searched for the main enemy force—hidden somewhere in the forested hills, according to the best estimates that CIC could arrive at. The morning had dawned clear, but clouds had started moving in from the west almost immediately after sunrise. Two hours later there was about 80 percent cloud cover, a heavy layer that bottomed out at about four thousand feet. The shuttles did not come below the clouds, which eliminated any chance that their crews might see anything useful, and the more technical gear—infrared cameras, radar, and radios—remained only marginally effective.

As soon as Colonel Flowers had gathered his forces, he sent out a number of patrols, hunting the snipers who were continuing their nuisance attacks. In thirty minutes there were three more small engagements as Dirigenters caught rebels and forced fights.

Alpha Company was pulled from the perimeter, into the center of the region that the battalion and the three militia companies had formed. "We've got work," Captain Orlis told his platoon leaders and platoon sergeants. "Get ready to move. I'll let you know what's up as soon as the colonel gives me our orders."

It was only four minutes before the captain came back on the channel. "We're moving east. The idea is to send one platoon with a company of militia on a course aimed directly at the rebel capital at Fremont. The colonel expects that that sort of threat will force the rebels to respond.

When that happens, the rest of the company will move in to keep the rebels engaged until we can bring more people in to help—if we can't handle it ourselves. Third platoon will go with the militia. Taiters, you stick with third, and keep Nolan with you.''

The militia company showed more organization than it had when the platoon had escorted it out to get weapons several days earlier. The company commander was introduced as Captain Eustace Molroney. His four platoon leaders were all designated as lieutenants, and they had platoon sergeants at their sides. What they did not have was uniforms or insignia of rank. The militiamen were dressed in whatever outdoor clothing each had available.

When the combined unit moved away from the perimeter, the militia showed that they had learned the basics. They moved in good order, keeping proper intervals and paying attention to their flanks. The mercenary platoon provided point, rear guard, and flankers—one squad for each. Taiters, Nolan, and Platoon Sergeant Dendrow remained with the Norbanker militiamen, sticking close to Captain Molroney.

The militia captain appeared to be in his late twenties or early thirties, although—in a colony at the basic level that Norbank was—he might have been no older than Lon. Unlike some of the men under his command, Molroney appeared to be fit, and used to outdoor life. He was tall and well muscled; his face and arms were deeply tanned, as if he routinely spent much of his day outside. The important quality, though, was that he appeared to inspire respect and obedience in the men under his command.

''They'll do what I tell them,'' he told Lieutenant Taiters before the group marched through the perimeter. ''Even if they don't agree, they'll do it, and save the arguments for later, when it's safe.''

I hope so, Lon thought, not totally convinced, but all that Taiters and Dendrow did was nod their heads, accepting—

or appearing to accept—what Molroney said at face value.

Taiters went to some pains to make certain that the militia captain understood the mission precisely. "We head in the direction of the rebel homeland. We're supposed to be a magnet, a threat they can't ignore. Once we draw the rebels against us, we hold on until help gets to us, first the rest of our company, and then whatever other forces we need."

"Suits me," Molroney said. "Far as that goes, I'd just as soon march all the way to Fremont and finish the job right. With all the men they've shipped this way, they can't have left all that many to home."

"Even Governor Norbank isn't ready to try anything *that* ambitious," Taiters reminded the captain. "We don't have the manpower or equipment, and the governor doesn't want to leave Norbank City undefended."

"I know, I know," Molroney said, making an impatient gesture with the hand that held his rifle. "I was just saying what I'd like, not what I think we should do. There is a difference."

There is indeed, Lon thought, hiding a grin.

"Anyway," Molroney continued, "the sooner we get going, the sooner we'll get finished, don't you think?"

And so they had started moving east—not directly, but as the lay of the land allowed. In the hilly country, no choice of route was completely satisfactory. It was not just that none of the easy physical routes went precisely in the right direction. Taking the ridgelines would expose troops to enemy observation, often from a long distance. Following the valley floors would put the men at a tactical disadvantage in any fight, conceding the high ground to the enemy. And the compromise, following a contour along the slope, had its own problems, including additional strain on legs and backs. But, for the most part, it was the least objectionable choice.

To some extent, the route was chosen by Molroney. He knew the area, the most direct (or least indirect) paths to take them where they wanted to go. The choice of a hillside path was Taiters's, the uncomfortable compromise. He kept his flanking squads out as far as possible, on one side as near the ridge of the hill the rest of the troops were on as possible without having them silhouetted against the sky-line, on the other side sometimes also near the top of the opposite ridge. And the point squad was typically two hundred yards in front of the main body.

"We're looking for enemy contact, but I want to know about them as early as possible," Taiters explained. "And I need to know how many there are. If it's a patrol, we don't laager up and wait for the cavalry, we deal with them and keep going. If it's a larger unit, I want some choice in the ground we defend."

In the first two hours, there was no contact at all, not even with one of the roving patrols that had been hitting the mercenaries and the local allies earlier in the day.

"They must have seen us leave," Lon said to the lieutenant during a brief rest. "We didn't try to sneak out." They had traversed one valley, heading toward the north-east, then turned and were going almost southwest on the next declivity over, aiming for a pass that would allow them a more direct route east.

"They're watching us," Taiters said, an affirmation he could offer no evidence for. "They may be staying clear, but they have to be watching."

"Just keeping track of us?" As long as the two spoke softly and used their radio gear, they could exclude Mol-roney from the conversation without being noticed.

"Whatever. We haven't gone far enough for them to get the idea that we're headed for Fremont. So far, it might just look as if we're out hunting, or trying to get behind them. A couple more hours and they should get the mes-sage. By nightfall, at least. Then we wait for the fun to start." There was grim seriousness in the lieutenant's voice.

"A night attack? Without night-vision gear?"

"They've done that before," Taiters reminded Nolan.

"In any case, people fought at night for thousands of years before anyone came up with anything to help them see better in the dark. But maybe a dawn attack is more likely. A lot depends on how long it takes them to move troops to intercept us, and maybe even on whether or not the sky stays overcast. We'll go on for as long as we can after sunset, then settle down in the best defensive position we can find, just in case."

A few minutes later, Captain Orlis relayed news that the colonel had ordered a few shuttle flights toward the rebel homeland—not quite a pointing finger in the sky, but a help. "Even if the rebels can't *see* the shuttles, they'll hear them well enough," Taiters said. "It should look as if we're reconnoitering toward Fremont."

"Why not just radio the rebels and say, 'Unless you give up now, we'll destroy your homes and farms'?" Lon said. Arlan did not bother to answer.

The overcast thickened and the cloud deck settled lower in the last hours of daylight, bringing an early twilight to the forest. A light mist started to fall just before sunset.

"I've told second squad to look for a place for us to camp," Taiters told Nolan. "There's no point to stumbling on in this if we can find some ground we can hold."

"If it hampers our militia, it hampers the rebels as well," Lon pointed out. "They won't be able to see any better, and they don't have guides with night-vision gear."

"If they want to move, they'll move, no matter the difficulties," Arlan said. "Never underestimate your enemy."

We seem to have done a lot of that here. Lon kept that thought to himself.

Fifteen minutes later, Tebba radioed that they had found a good location to stop, a broad hill crest with something of a swayback, a shallow depression that would give them high ground and ways to cover every possible approach. "There's no trees or water," Tebba added, " 'cept the water that's falling from the sky, but it has everything else we could want."

"Stay there," Taiters told him. "We'll join you." He lifted his faceplate to tell Captain Molroney about the place.

Molroney nodded. "That'd be Jeffrey Bald," he said. "If I'd knowed what you were looking for, I'd have mentioned it. Only place like it for miles around."

"Any problem with using that as a defensive position?" Taiters asked. "Any blind avenues up, anything like that?"

Molroney considered the questions before he shook his head. "I never looked at it as a military place before, but I'd say it's about the best natural site you could find within twenty miles. As long as the ammunition and water last, no way the rebels could drive us off, or get to us, 'less they were prepared to sacrifice a lot of men to do it."

"We're not interested in staging a 'last stand,' " Taiters said dryly. "All we want is a safe place to spend the night, and maybe part of tomorrow. If the rebels don't hit us by shortly after dawn, we'll move on." Molroney nodded.

"Maybe it's time to start thinking about other places we can use tomorrow," Taiters said. "Once we get situated, you and I can check out the mapboard and see if we can keep a good defensive position within reach during the march."

"Sure thing," Molroney said, nodding. "But I'll tell you up front, won't any of them be half as good as Jeffrey Bald."

22

Holing up in this place would be suicide if the rebels had any ground-support aircraft, Lon Nolan thought as he surveyed the top of Jeffrey Bald. There was no cover at all from air attack, and the rocks would set off ricochets that would double the effectiveness of aerial strafing. But against an enemy that was strictly infantry, it was still the *high ground.* It should do very well indeed, Lon decided. The only real danger would come from grenades, and the rebels appeared to have only hand grenades rather than grenade launchers, which could reach farther and more accurately.

As long as they haven't been holding anything back, Lon worried. It was possible that the rebels had not yet shown everything they had. They had changed tactics, started to show increased discipline in the time that the Dirigenters had been on their world. There might be additional weapons—grenade launchers if not fighter aircraft.

Lieutenant Taiters spaced his four squads around the banana-shaped perimeter of the crest and had Captain Molroney fill in with his men. "No matter which direction the rebels come from, there'll always be a core of my professionals with night-vision gear and years of experience close enough to face them," the lieutenant explained. "And your men to provide raw firepower. Between us, I think we can hold off anything the rebels are likely to throw our way."

Molroney's grin had been rather grim. "I'm certain of it, Lieutenant," he said. "Like I said before, this is the best spot for this sort of show anywhere in the area. We could hold out a long time here, no matter how many people they send.''

The first order of business was to improve what nature had provided, maximizing the defensive capabilities of the site. Then the men were given a chance to eat before being put on half-and-half watches—mercenaries and militiamen alike.

''Whenever you get a chance,'' Arlan told Lon while they were alone for a moment, ''talk with Molroney. See what you can find out about the situation here. He's more likely to open up to you than to me.''

''You mean because I'm just an apprentice whose opinion doesn't matter?'' Lon asked with a grin, which Arlan returned.

''Because of that. I've told him that I'm going to leave you with him tonight to provide liaison. That way he and I can stay well apart. I explained the military advisability of that—little chance of both of us being taken out at the same time.''

''I'll do what I can. I want to know more about this fight myself. Some of it just doesn't make sense to me.''

Finding opportunities to talk with the militia captain was not simple. Molroney had a hands-on approach to leadership. If he was not eating or trying to rest, he was talking with his platoon leaders and sergeants, even chatting with men who held no rank at all.

''Now what was that you were asking before?'' Molroney asked when the two of them finally settled in. ''I'm too keyed to sleep anyway.''

''I was just wondering what it is that drives these rebels,'' Lon said. ''The other night, when they fought almost to the last man. That seems extreme just because of political differences.''

Molroney snorted. ''Some politics is more important than others,'' he said. ''And, well, I guess it's maybe a little more basic than that. I don't know how much you know about us here. . . .'' He looked toward Nolan.

"Not much at all,'' he said, which was true enough. "All they told us was that there were two main waves of colonization, that your people arrived thirty years before this other group, and that they haven't been very . . . cooperative from the start.''

"True enough,'' Molroney said. "Says a lot, but nothing at all, really.'' He stopped and looked directly at Lon—though it was too dark for him to see more than a vague silhouette. "Your lieutenant tells me you come from Earth. That true?''

"Left Earth less than a year ago,'' Lon said.

"Then maybe our story will make sense to you,'' Molroney said, "more'n it would to the number-punchers who seem to run your outfit. You see, we, the original settlers, came directly from Earth. The colony was funded and organized by the Charles and Emily Norbank Resettlement Foundation, and—one way or another—about a fifth of the original colonists were either Norbanks or related to them: kids, cousins, aunts and uncles, you name it. Charles and Emily didn't come, not the ones with the foundation, even though it had been their lifelong ambition to escape from Earth. Charles died six months before the ship left Earth, and Emily stayed behind because she felt she was too old to make the trip out and start from scratch on a colony world, especially without her husband.''

Molroney lay back. "The Norbanks wanted to get away from all the overcrowding, the crime, and too much government, too many rules. I guess they was really fed up with it all, enough to spend a lifetime saving money and making plans. They also set up a charter for us—just the absolute minimum number of rules to let us survive and prosper, that was the plan. Everybody free to do pretty much whatever he wants, unless it interfered with somebody else's freedom. At the top of the charter there's a quote from somebody named Jefferson, back on Earth. It reads, 'My freedom to wave my fist ends where your nose begins.' "

"And the rebels?" Lon asked when Molroney went silent for more than a minute. "They don't accept your charter?"

"Never have. They're Divinists."

Lon whistled softly.

"I see you've heard about them," Molroney said.

"Of course I have. We studied the Divinist Uprising at The Springs, the North American Military Academy. I didn't know that any large groups of them survived, though, or got off Earth."

"Sure wasn't because we *wanted* them here. Didn't know they was coming till they arrived; didn't know who they were or what they was about till later than that. The Confederation of Human Planets dumped them on us. I guess we were still small enough and unimportant enough that they didn't much care what we thought. Well, the Divinists set up their own colony, up the river from us, and stayed to themselves—I mean, with a *vengeance.* They wouldn't have nothing to do with us in Norbank City, wouldn't let our people visit, wouldn't do no trade or anything. All we ever got from them was religious propaganda."

"What made the situation change?"

"They decided that it wasn't enough for us to live on the same world and stay apart, and they weren't about to accept our rules. They demanded that we acknowledge they had all the right of it and that they were meant to rule us all. No way we could accept that. Well, then the troubles started. It wasn't no big thing at first, but it kept getting worse and worse, and then—finally—it went to all-out fighting."

"Back on Earth, even their women and children fought," Lon said, speaking as much to himself as to his companion. "But we haven't come across any women or children casualties here."

"Nope, ain't seen that here, leastwise, not yet," Molroney said. "But I expect we will, before it's done."

A few minutes later, Lon made excuses that he had to try to get some sleep and rolled over, away from the militia captain. He lay silently, listening to Molroney roll and squirm. Eventually the captain stopped moving and Lon called Lieutenant Taiters, speaking subvocally so that Molroney would not overhear.

Taiters had never heard of Divinists. "Religious fanatics from Earth," Lon explained. "Some seventy-five years ago they tried to secede from the authority of the world government, said that they had their own ways and laws and that no one else had any right to govern them. They tried to fight off the whole world, and it took more than two years to put the rebellion down. There aren't any official numbers, but I guess that more than a hundred thousand of them died rather than surrender—men, women, and children. Apparently the Confederation of Human Planets back home dumped the survivors here. And they're trying again."

Five minutes later, Taiters called Nolan back. "The colonel knew about Divinists, but not that they're what we're up against here. The Norbankers never mentioned that apparently. It doesn't change the plans, though. We're still to keep moving east until we draw the rebels into an attack, then we hold them until the colonel can bring in reinforcements."

Lon did not sleep the rest of the night. It was almost a relief when Molroney got up to roam the perimeter again, giving Lon an excuse to get up as well. The militia leader had lost some speed. The lack of sleep was beginning to tell on him.

"I don't mind a good fight," Molroney said, "but I wish they'd quit playing around and get on with it."

You might not think that once you get in it, Lon thought,

but there was no point in saying it. It would be a waste of energy, and energy was one thing he no longer had to spare.

At dawn, third platoon and the militia company prepared to break camp. "There's no call to hurry about it," Taiters told Molroney, "but we have to move on this morning. If we stay put, the rebels won't be in any hurry to head us off."

"I guess you're right, Lieutenant," Molroney said with obvious reluctance, "but I sure do hate to lose Jeffrey Bald."

Taiters sent the entire platoon of his men out first, to make certain that no booby traps had been placed across their presumed path during the night, and to look for any ambushes along the first mile. As soon as negative reports were back from the squad leaders, Taiters gave the word to move out.

"We'll pick up my men along the way," he told Molroney as they left the hilltop. "The point and flanker squads will be in position, and the rear guard will fall in behind us."

Molroney looked around while they were descending the slope, as if trying to spot the mercenaries.

Taiters chuckled. "If you can spot them from here, they're not doing the job I know they're capable of, Captain."

It was more show than reality, but through the first several hours of the morning, the mercenaries played a game of hurry up and wait, getting ahead of the militia, then settling down until the Norbankers drew close again. The idea was to create the impression of a pattern—a pattern that could be broken to good effect later if necessary. Lieutenant Taiters stayed in almost constant communication with Captain Orlis. The captain kept him informed not only of the movements of the remaining platoons of Alpha Company, but also those of the rest of the battalion and the other militia companies—and, when there was anything to report, aerial sightings of rebel movements.

There were few of those, most coming as the result of luck more than anything else. The rebels were showing that they had learned their lessons well. They knew they were vulnerable from the air and did all they could to conceal their movements.

"It looks like they are keeping close track of us," Taiters told Captain Molroney when the militia stopped for lunch. "They're staying well out, but seem to be paralleling us on both sides. And since two small groups have been seen more or less racing east, our Combat Information Center thinks they're setting up something for us, somewhere up ahead." Taiters had his mapboard out and was indicating where the sightings that morning had been. "We can't tell yet when they might hit us with sizable opposition. If they don't think they've got enough people in position to handle us, we might start running into ambushes designed to slow us down while they move more troops."

"You fellows got any guess on numbers?" Molroney asked. "How many of them are we like to run into?"

Taiters shook his head. "CIC won't even guess. The data are too fragmented, too inconclusive."

"What's the farthest east any of these sightings have been?"

Arlan hesitated for a second, then pointed to a blinking red spot on the mapboard. "Right there, about an hour ago."

"I don't have any fancy computers to digest questions and spit out answers, but I can make a good guess where they might hit us." Molroney dragged a finger along the screen of the monitor. "You see this water? That's Anderson Creek, named after the first family that settled along it. Heading toward the rebels' homeland, we've got to cross that creek. The last three quarters of a mile to First River, there's no way to ford the stream, too deep and too fast. But upstream from there, there are several good fords, this time of year, before the rainy season gets really cranked up." He pointed them out. "And if we wanted to take a big loop north, beyond this point''—he stabbed his finger at a spot three miles above the last fordable area before the river—''we could cross just about anywhere.''

''If we *were* making for the rebel homeland, which ford would we be most likely to take?'' Taiters asked.

''If we weren't worried about anyone trying to stop us, it'd be this one, the next-to-last one before the river. There's almost a good path there. It was made by the local wildlife, but it's been used by hunters off and on for about another twenty miles. If we were looking for a *safe* crossing, or safer, at least, and didn't want to go too far out of the way, we'd make for this place here.'' He tapped that location several times. ''This time of year, the water'd probably be a bit more than waist-deep, moderate current, but there's good cover on both sides of the water. 'Course, that cuts both ways.'' He shrugged.

''Either way, they'll have time to prepare,'' Taiters said. ''Assuming that they're watching us, they'll know which ford we're making for by the time we get to this point.'' The spot he indicated on the mapboard was about a mile and a quarter from either ford. ''Which end of this hill we head for.''

''What's that give them?'' Molroney asked. ''Fifteen, twenty minutes tops to switch if they're at the wrong place, or to bring their troops together if they're watching both.''

Taiters shook his head slowly. ''They could have a lot more time than that, Captain. All they'd need is a handful of hero types to get out and slow us down, sniping, throwing grenades, or just setting booby traps across our path. They might have both routes buggered for us already.''

''The idea *is* to have at them, isn't it, Lieutenant?'' Molroney asked. ''Make them fight us.''

''Without giving them a walkover, if we can, Captain. We do want to get home from this. If nothing else, making it too easy for them would be sure to make them suspicious.''

''Then this is the way to go,'' Molroney said, tapping

the location he had said would give them better cover. "The undergrowth is something else. Big vines like a maze all over the place, tangles sometimes as much as ten, twelve feet high, spreading from the shore back up onto the slopes on both sides along there. When the rainy season reaches its peak, the vines will stretch out over the water as well, but not now."

"Sounds like a real mess," Lon said.

Molroney chuckled. "It can be. Fellow can get lost as hell in those thickets. Now, you boys, with your night-vision stuff and all the electronic gear, it'd be no problem to you, even in the dark, but I sure as hell wouldn't want to get caught in one of them at night—not if I had to get out before morning."

"They dry enough to burn?" Taiters asked.

"Now, I haven't seen that patch at all this year, so I can't say for absolute sure, but I doubt it. Those berry thickets are just found near good water like Anderson's Creek. Sometimes I think their roots all run straight into the water. They stay green and grow even when everything else is parched."

"Edible berries?" Lon asked.

"Sure, but this time of the year it's second growth, and those aren't nearly as sweet as first growth. That comes at the end of the rainy season, about six months from now. Then the berries are bright red, and near the size of your thumb. Now they'll be a blackish purple, and only about half the size."

"How solid is the cover in this mess?" Taiters asked, frowning at the irrelevant distraction of the berries. "I mean, if we're in there, can they just sit up on the hills here and shoot down into us?"

"Now, they do much shooting, they'll get some break, but not at first. Those vines have leaves the size of your helmet, and a lot of 'em. But after a time, they'd be able to shoot up the cover so's they could see us. If we stay in there long enough."

"Where would we have to go?" Taiters demanded. "If we're coming across the creek here, through the thicket on one side and then into the thicket on the other, and the rebels are on the slopes in front of us, that doesn't give us many options."

"Well, this path sort of goes between two hills, into a more open area. Like I said, those vines stick close to water."

"Run a gauntlet?" Taiters asked. "Try to go between two enemy concentrations, with both of them able to shoot down at us from high ground? I don't think so."

"Anywhere we can cross Anderson's Creek, the rebels are going to have the high ground, Lieutenant," Molroney said. "We get through the thicket, there's trees and other sorts of stuff lower on the slopes. Give us a chance to fight our way up to high ground, or try to move past the rebels. The only other choice is to send just enough men across to draw the rebels' fire while the rest stay on the high ground west of the creek and have a long-distance duel. That more to your liking?"

"If we tried that, Lieutenant," Lon said, "what's to stop the rebels from just leaving enough guns on the next ridge to keep us pinned down? They could move the rest of their people off and we might have trouble finding them again."

Taiters stared at Nolan. "I think we're going to have to bite the bullet on this one, but Colonel Flowers is going to have to make the decision."

The choice seemed inevitable to Lon, but when Colonel Flowers made it official, it was still a shock. "Go in. We have to run the risk. But we'll get help to you as quickly as possible," Flowers had said after taking time to consult with his own staff and with CIC aboard *Long Snake*.

Additional air reconnaissance appeared to confirm that the rebels planned to contest any crossing of Anderson's Creek. Hard numbers were still lacking, but from the increased number of sightings, it seemed possible that the rebels might be moving the majority of their forces into position, either to contest this crossing or to meet additional advances.

Video and still photographs were taken of the creek and its banks near both of the primary fords, in both visible and infrared frequencies. Computer enhancements gave the mercenaries some idea of what to expect when they reached the extensive thicket—a child's playground maze gone absolutely mad.

A snake could tie itself in terminal knots in there, Lon told himself after studying the final product for several minutes. The only guide to direction would be a slight slope toward the water. That might not always be apparent. *I wouldn't want to try it without electronics.*

Just before three o'clock that afternoon, Lon lay atop a hill with Taiters and Molroney, looking down at the thickets and the creek that ran through the middle of them. The vine leaves were a brilliant, glossy, emerald green that seemed to reflect the sun almost as well as a mirror. Even with the full magnification of his visor, Lon could not pick out a route through the tangle, could not see ground beneath the vines.

"I caught a glint of sun on metal, on the next ridge," Molroney whispered after a couple of minutes. "Maybe just a degree or two off to my right, above that notched tree trunk. See where I mean?"

Lon and Arlan both looked. It was thirty seconds before both saw another glint. "I see," Taiters said. "Can't tell if it's one man or if they've got a company or more waiting for us."

"If it ain't a company or more right there, I'll bet they're not more'n a couple of feet below the ridge on the far side," Molroney said. "Waiting for the lookouts to give the word that we've moved out there. Hell, they may have people down below, waiting for us to come into the thicket."

Cheery thought, Lon thought with a grimace.

Lieutenant Taiters had one radio call to make before he gave the order. Colonel Flowers and Captain Orlis were both on the channel. "We're ready to move in," Taiters reported.

There was only a slight hesitation before Flowers said, "Go."

23

Platoon Sergeant Ivar Dendrow moved down the slope toward Anderson's Creek with his first two squads. They established a skirmish line that left a lot of room between men. Third and fourth squads would be the rear guard. They would remain on the ridge, far above the thicket, ready to give covering fire if necessary, until the rest of the troops, mercenaries and militia, had crossed the creek.

Captain Molroney split his militia company, sending two platoons behind each of the point squads. To minimize the time that the unit would be stretched out, the militia went in four columns, with the intervals the minimum that prudence dictated—in such heavy cover, the men were no more than six feet apart, following the sometimes twisted avenues available once they moved into the thicket about halfway down the slope.

Molroney, Taiters, and Nolan stayed in the center, near the front of the militia, thirty yards behind the mercenary skirmish line. Arlan and Lon maintained open channels with their noncoms, in front and behind.

At first Lon thought that it felt like descending into a green ocean. The huge vines completely dominated the lower slopes and the valley floor, choking out any competition. At the edge of the thicket, where the men started to sink into the green tangle, the footing was extremely tricky. Small runners and thin vine tips seemed to reach out and loop around feet and ankles, threatening to trip men and send them tumbling. As Lon reached that juncture, he found himself unconsciously holding his rifle higher, as if trying to keep it out of water—until he realized what he was doing and felt foolish about it . . . and looked around to see if anyone else had noticed, or was doing the same thing.

When the large leaves of the vines finally closed over Lon's head, he nearly started to hold his breath. He felt an instant of claustrophobic panic. The air under the leaves was humid, and felt twenty degrees warmer than it had above the thicket. There had been a light breeze "outside," but no air at all moved within the thicket. The air weighed heavily against Lon's chest, making breathing more difficult—psychologically if nothing else. *I want out of here!* he thought, but that was impossible. He had to go forward with the rest, could not show that it bothered him. After a few minutes, it no longer did. Only the slight additional effort breathing needed remained.

Even after the leaves closed overhead, it never got completely dark in the thicket. The upper layer of leaves seemed almost to glow, to radiate a diffuse emerald light.

Lon looked at the vines and the encapsulated universe they held. It was unlike anything he had ever seen—or dreamed about. Individual vines went on for dozens of yards, perhaps for hundreds, spiraling along like gigantic coils of living concertina wire—without the barbs. A dozen feet from the end of one strand, the woody vine was still as thick as Lon's upper arm, and covered with a knotty bark in a medium gray. Thin, wirelike roots extended from the lower reaches of each vine, anchoring it to the ground. The diameters of the spirals reached eight to ten feet and stayed remarkably constant, so there was no real difficulty in moving through the mess. The men simply had to be careful where they put their feet, and to remember to step clear each time they crossed a loop of vine. Different vine systems appeared to cross and recross each other, creating a tangle that could never be satisfactorily untangled. *Except like the Gordian knot,* Lon thought.

The berries that Molroney had spoken of hung from the higher levels of the vines, each growing near the stem of a leaf. Some had been partially eaten and left to rot by animals.

"We're at the creek and ready to cross."

Lon had become so fascinated by his surroundings that he was startled by Sergeant Dendrow's voice on the radio.

"Any sign of opposition yet?" Lieutenant Taiters asked.

"Not a thing. And we haven't seen any nasty surprises planted anywhere in this . . . whatever it is," Dendrow said.

"Take it easy crossing the creek. Do it four or five men at a time," Taiters said, although they had discussed that procedure earlier, before starting down the slope.

"Yes, sir, I know how to play it," Dendrow replied. "We're starting . . . now."

Again, Lon almost held his breath, as if he anticipated that the rebels would immediately take the point squads under fire as soon as they exposed themselves by stepping out into Anderson Creek. But he restrained himself. *Getting a good breath is hard enough in here, without doing something ridiculous,* he thought. *Next thing you know, you'll start closing your eyes so people can't see you.*

"Once you get all your men across the creek, move off twenty yards, establish a line, and take a breather," Taiters told Dendrow. "Give the reception committee a little longer to stew about just when and where we're going to come out of this mess."

"Will do, Lieutenant," Dendrow replied.

"If they don't show their hand by the time we get across the creek, I might send three or four men off to one side to set up a little distraction to make them think," Taiters said. "I doubt that it will come to that, though. I expect that once they see the main force hit the water they'll start shooting while they can see what they're shooting at."

"That's what we'd do," Dendrow commented. "Okay, sir, I'm going across with the last group now."

Lon imagined rather than heard the splash of water as

Dendrow and the last few others made their dash across the creek. Lon's hands tightened on his rifle's grips, another sign of tension, but there was no gunfire.

"We're all across, Lieutenant," Dendrow reported. "First squad is already on the line you indicated. The rest of us will be set up in three minutes. There's no sign of opposition."

"Okay, take ten," Taiters said. "Wait for my command to start moving again." He switched channels and spoke to Nolan. "The logical thing for them to expect is that we'd want to get out of this stuff as fast as we could, up on higher ground where we could see. When they don't see or hear anything, it's got to put them a little on edge."

"It would me," Lon replied. "I don't handle suspense all that well."

"I've noticed. That's why I'm telling you the why. Sometimes the best thing you can do is sit on your ass and wait. I think this is one of them."

"You're not worried that it gives them more time to get extra soldiers in position as well?" Lon asked.

"Of course I'm *worried* about it, but this still seems to offer us an edge. If we can force the rebels to commit to an all-out fight, without taking unacceptable losses ourselves, it has to bring the completion of the contract closer. We pick off one small group and let the rest get away again, it could take weeks, even months to get enough of them to make the rest quit."

"If they'd ever quit," Lon said. "On Earth, more than five out of six didn't, including kids and women."

"Let's just hope that they've mellowed a little since then."

Don't try to get a loan at the bank on that, Lon thought.

Taiters and Molroney kept the militia moving for another two minutes before calling a halt—narrowing the gap between the militia and the point squads. The men sat or squatted in place, those on the outside turned to cover the flanks. But there was no point in establishing a firm perimeter, not with soldiers who had only had a few hours of military training. It was enough that they remained generally silent, and alert.

For the first time, Lon gradually became aware of the sounds of birds and animals in the thicket. He was straining to hear more distant noise, especially gunfire, but what he heard was twitters and flutters, the scraping of tiny claws on wood, the sounds of chewing. He looked around but saw only a pair of birds twenty yards away, up in the top twist of one of the vines. The birds looked as if they must be of the same species, but one was predominantly colored green—the same green as the vines' leaves—while the other was a bright yellow, with red streaks on the bottom of its wings. *Female and male,* Lon guessed, assuming that birds on Norbank would follow the general pattern of birds on Earth, with the male more brightly adorned.

Lon took a sip of water from his canteen. It tasted salty. His face had been sweating in the thicket, and the perspiration had touched the corners of his mouth. He licked at his lips, then took another sip of water. The second was better than the first, though both seemed to be about body temperature.

"Why don't we have better insulation on the canteens?" he asked Taiters on the radio. "Even at The Springs we had chillers, and we didn't get much in the way of luxuries there."

Taiters glanced toward Lon—they were about eight feet apart—and frowned. That was masked by Taiters' tinted faceplate. He shook his head then, and held a finger up in front of his visor, about where his mouth was. Nolan took the hint and kept his mouth shut. He watched the timeline on his visor, while still trying to keep a good watch on the thicket in front of him. The wait might put off the rebels on top of the opposite hill, but it was doing a good job of doing the same thing to Lon. *And probably to our militiamen too,* he thought. *This is maddening.*

The ten minutes passed. Lon looked toward the lieutenant. He showed no hint of movement, no sign that he was ready to order the point squads and main body to start moving again.

Fifteen minutes. Taiters raised his right fist and made a pumping motion, up and down, a signal for Captain Molroney, who relayed it to his commanders. At the same time, Taiters told the point squads to start moving again. "Be ready to get down fast when the shooting starts," he added.

Lon's legs felt stiff when he got to his feet and took his first few steps forward, careful to stay as nearly even with Taiters and Molroney as possible. The militia companies were arrayed to either side of them, stretching out in front and behind. Molroney made several hand signals and his men started to put more distance between them, widening the front.

"Ivar, send your beamers and two riflemen on a loop to the left, like we talked about before," Taiters ordered the platoon sergeant. Each squad had one man with a beamer, an energy pulse weapon. "Tell them to find a good place without being spotted. Even when the shooting starts coming our way, I want them to keep out of it until I give the word. We'll save that surprise for when it'll do us the most good. The rest of you find good spots as near the eastern edge of this thicket as you can without losing your angle of fire on the ridge." Dendrow merely clicked his radio transmitter to acknowledge the orders.

There was one more stop for the militia, when they reached the creek, still under cover of the vines. Before anyone crossed the twenty yards of open water, Taiters and Molroney wanted to have plenty of firepower close to cover them.

When Molroney and Taiters moved closer to the front themselves, Nolan followed automatically. *A dangerous habit to get into. I could take a night job as a shadow,* he thought when he realized that he had moved without conscious decision. He was within twenty feet of the creek before he saw his first hint of water through the leaves. It appeared that some of the vines did go down into the water, but Lon could not tell if their main roots were there or if the coils just dipped out of sight.

"Okay, Captain," Taiters said eventually. "I think it's time to start sending your men across." Phrasing it as a suggestion was the politic way, since Molroney theoretically outranked him.

Molroney nodded jerkily, then signaled his men. A plan for the crossing had been agreed on earlier. The militia would cross the creek one platoon at a time, with the rest ready to provide covering fire if—when—the rebels started shooting.

Taiters warned his own men. They too had to be ready to cover the crossing. The men with the best chance of actually hurting the rebels were in the two squads that had been left behind. Although they would be shooting at long range, they would have the most visible targets when the rebels exposed themselves to fire at the men in the water.

Lon moved around until he found a small opening in the leaves overhead that gave him a minimal view of the eastern ridge. He brought his rifle up partway. The quiltlike pattern of large leaves would be shredded quickly once the shooting started. *More holes than I want, no doubt,* he thought. The better he could see out, the better the rebels would be able to see in, and the vines would not provide good cover, not like a tree trunk would—or a deep hole in the ground.

The first militiamen stepped out into Anderson's Creek and started wading across, moving as quickly as they could. There was a rocky bed under the water, which helped. Muck might have proved to be disastrous. As the first platoon moved out into the creek, the second platoon moved into position on the bank, rifles at the ready, anticipating trouble. Molroney, Taiters, and Nolan would cross with the second platoon—the captain and lieutenant at opposite ends of the formation, Lon staying with Molroney so the militia leader would not be out of radio contact with Taiters.

The first line of militiamen got five yards out from the bank, into water that reached the hips of the shortest men, before the shooting started. The rebels opened with a volley. Lon could only guess, but he thought that there had to be considerably more than a hundred rifles firing, perhaps two hundred or three hundred. Few bullets came into the thicket west of the creek. Clearly the barrage was aimed strictly at the visible men. It was not terribly accurate, but the volume was great enough that there were casualties.

Taiters and Molroney ordered their men to return fire. That quickly lessened the number of incoming rounds, as the rebels had to start thinking of their own cover. The second militia platoon moved forward. Lon stepped into the water, shooting at the eastern ridgeline as he moved, trying not to think of anything but walking and shooting. After the humid heat of the thicket, the water felt cold, but he only noticed the initial shock. The water was only an obstacle that slowed him down then.

Lon looked down just once, when his thigh bumped into something—a body. The red stain of blood was quickly diluted and washed away. The man was clearly dead. Lon pushed past, looking back to the eastern ridge and continuing to fire his short bursts toward it.

Crossing the twenty yards of Anderson's Creek took Lon an eternity squeezed into a minute of real time. The first militia platoon took the heaviest casualties, most suffered in the first fusillade. But once the last militiamen had crossed, the rebel fire followed them into the thicket on the eastern side of the creek.

Molroney's men moved away from the water, spreading out to either side, trying to hide from the metal hail. There was no time to total the casualties, scarcely time to give them first aid. Lon could see wounded men from where he lay, and he knew of at least one dead man, back in the creek. How many more there might be he could not even guess.

"Spring our surprise on them, Ivar!" Taiters shouted over the radio to his platoon sergeant. "As soon as that distracts them, we push forward. We've got to take this hill."

24

Sounds like something out of a bad vid, Lon thought as he started moving forward again with Captain Molroney and the Norbanker militia. *"We've got to take this hill."* He snorted. The addition to the battle on the flank was undetectable in the valley. Beamers' slight noise did not carry far, and two extra slug throwers could not make that much difference in the sound level. But once Sergeant Dendrow reported that the diversion had started, so did the advance out of the thicket and up the hill.

I just hope the rest of it is on schedule, Lon thought. Colonel Flowers had made one addition to Lieutenant Taiters' plan—close air support. It would not be much, no more than two of the battalion's attack shuttles, but it would help. They had been maintaining high surveillance most of the day, in relays.

Lon had not left the thicket yet when he heard the sonic scream of a shuttle stooping to the attack. The colonel still did not want to risk the craft *too* low, so the assault might not be as devastating as it could be if carried without regard to possible losses, but even though the aircraft never came below four thousand feet, their rockets and two or three seconds of gunfire could make a significant difference.

The distinctive stutter of a shuttle's Gatlings was audible over all the small-arms fire on the ground. Four rockets, accelerating from a supersonic launch platform, whined toward their targets and exploded, shattering rock and wood at the top of the hill into millions of shards of shrapnel.

Atop the ridge, the rebels had to abandon shooting at the approaching militia and seek cover. Some tried to take the attacking shuttle under fire, but their rifles were of no use, and neither of the rockets they launched came close enough to lock onto the shuttle—which had already pulled out of its dive and started to accelerate upward, out of reach. The mercenaries and militia made good use of the respite, racing up the slope. Even after the shuttle was gone, the rebels did not immediately return to their positions facing down the hill. By the time they did, Molroney's militiamen were halfway up the slope.

Then a second Dirigenter shuttle dove into its attack. The rebels were quicker to react this time, taking cover as soon as they heard the noise and getting their antiaircraft rockets ready. But the shuttle was scarcely visible before it unloaded its own munitions and pulled out of its dive, twisting away from the ridge, accelerating away from danger at the highest gee-forces its crew could withstand.

Even the militiamen below had to duck the rocky shrapnel blasted out of the hilltop by this attack. They were that close to the ridge. And before the rebels had recovered from the second air attack, the militiamen were over the top, moving in with bullets and bayonets.

Lon could not afford the luxury of looking around to see how many of the enemy there might be on the hilltop. The nearest were too close. He fired at the first rebel his rifle's muzzle tracked against and moved to the second with his bayonet. That man was just getting to his feet and never made it. Lon slashed across his throat and he fell to the side. But there was another enemy close then, coming in from Lon's right, swinging his rifle like a club. Lon ducked and threw a shoulder block into the man, knocking him backward. Before the rebel could recover, Lon shot him, then moved toward his next encounter.

The fight was over in less than ten minutes. There was no slaughter. The rebels did not attempt to fight to the last man. They withdrew under order, retreating down the eastern slope, supported by more troops who had been waiting beyond, on the other hills in the area. Only a few small groups of rebels were unable to escape the fight on the ridge. Those fought until they died or were too badly wounded to continue. Not one rebel surrendered.

"It wasn't as horrible as I thought," Lon told Arlan Taiters once the last close combat on the ridge had ended. He was still breathing hard, and his face remained flushed with excitement and effort. The two squads from third platoon had not suffered any deaths or serious wounds; only a few men had picked up even minor scratches. The men in the other two squads—still on the west side of Anderson's Creek—had suffered no casualties at all.

"Captain Molroney might disagree," Taiters said, gesturing at the militia leader who was going from one platoon to the next, trying to get a casualty count. "And it's not over. We're up here, but we're not going anywhere anytime soon. I don't think we faced a fourth of the enemy force getting this far."

"Any idea just how long we're going to have to hold here?"

"Well into the night, at least," Taiters said, looking up. Sunset was three hours away, but the sky was clouding up again. It looked as if there might actually be rain, even though Molroney had said it was too early for anything "really bothersome." The rainy season was still two months away. " 'Bout all we get this time of year," Molroney had told the Dirigenters, "is just about enough drizzle to steam the day up even more."

"I'm going to have third and fourth squads wait until dark before they try to join us," Taiters said. "There's a chance that the rebels will encircle us before then." He paused. "A damn good chance, I suppose, but even if they do, the squads should be able to infiltrate after dark. If the clouds don't break. If it doesn't look as if they can get through safely, I'll send them to meet the rest of the battalion."

I wish I could see all the pieces of the puzzle, Lon thought. *See where all the different forces are, which way they're moving.* If they had been fighting an enemy equipped with the same sophisticated electronics system the DMC had, that would have been possible—in theory at least.

"As long as they don't work themselves up to an all-out charge too soon," Taiters said, whispering now. "If they've got enough men out there willing to die to do it, they could run us over in no time flat."

If they're Divinists, they've got men willing to die, Lon thought. He closed his eyes for a moment, fighting the wave of fear that came over him. His paternal grandparents had lost relatives in the early stages of the Divinist Uprising on Earth, before the North American Union's army had a chance to mobilize to meet the threat.

The mercenaries and militiamen were forced to stay down. The rebels did not mount a full-scale offensive before sunset, but they did apply pressure, staging small raids partway up one section of the hill or another to test the defenses occasionally, and sniping from the neighboring summits constantly. Those were near enough the same height as the one Lon was on that there was danger to anyone who was at all incautious about staying low. Defenses were improved. Rocks were moved. Soil was scraped away for slit trenches, the dirt piled up in front, or packed in as mortar between stones.

Molroney and his men cared for their wounded as best they could without trauma tubes. Most could be stabilized, but two men died of their wounds before sunset. Their bodies were placed with the other militia dead on top of the hill. Those who had fallen in the creek or during the ascent had been left behind. The dead were relieved of ammunition and other supplies that might be useful to the living. Even the weapons and ammunition of the dead rebels had been collected for possible use.

As soon as darkness settled in, the amount of incoming fire decreased by two thirds. Only a fraction of the rebel rifles were equipped with nightscopes, and the night was unrelieved by any glint of starlight. The cloud cover was too thick, and lowering. Captain Molroney predicted fog during the night. "It can get so thick in these hills that you can hardly see your hand at arm's length," he told Taiters and Nolan. "And cap all the noise as well. Best damned sound insulation you ever saw. Them rebels could walk on up without us hearing or seeing them."

"Not a chance," Taiters replied. "We'll see them. Fog won't affect our night-vision gear. It would even make it a little easier to see anyone coming in. Greater temperature difference between the environment and the hot bodies. The one thing fog *would* do is make it easier for me to bring the rest of my men in from the other side of the creek."

Molroney nodded slowly. "You do bring 'em in, make sure my people know where and when. I'd hate for any of your men to get shot by us by mistake."

The two mercenary squads already on the hilltop were spread around the perimeter, two men together so that one could watch while the other slept—or tried to. Taiters and Nolan stood the same watches, as did the Norbanker militia.

It was ten minutes before midnight when the rebels staged their first serious assault. Fog had started to cling to the hillsides and flow into the valley, although the hilltop was still clear. The third and fourth squads from the mercenary platoon had just made it up the west slope at about eleven-thirty. They had moved into positions on the perimeter, giving the defenders more eyes—more night eyes.

The rebels came silently, more than two hundred of them, crawling up the slopes on the east and southeast. Behind them there was no change to the tempo of the sniping. A few rebels got within forty yards of the summit before one of the men in Girana's squad spotted them. A quick radio call alerted the rest of the mercenaries, and they alerted the militia, almost as silently as the men crawling toward the crest.

It took the mercenaries a couple of minutes to be certain that they had marked how far around on each side the rebels extended. By then the leaders were no more than fifteen yards below the crest, forty yards away laterally. One whole mercenary squad moved into position over the rebels. Lieutenant Taiters signaled Captain Molroney, gesturing, then raised his hand. When Taiters brought the hand back down, quickly, Molroney whistled softly. The militiamen over the rebels started firing down the slopes, unable to see targets until the rebels shot back, but knowing approximately where the enemy was. The mercenaries *could* see their targets, and fired more effectively. They made the difference. No rebels made it to the crest. Forty died. Most of the rest retreated down the slope, continuing to shoot at the summit as they did.

The second wave came from the north, more men than in the previous attack. This group started its climb while the first was still engaged. They were not spotted as quickly, and there were fewer mercenaries in position above them. As soon as the first shots were fired their way, these rebels got up and charged toward the top of the hill. A series of flares were fired into the air, illuminating everything in a harsh white light.

Molroney ran toward the new attack with a squad of his men. Lon Nolan stayed with them. By the time they reached the north end of the crest, there was hand-to-hand fighting. More than two dozen rebels had already made it to the top, and more were pressing up from below. The few mercenaries who were there found themselves targeted by groups of rebels. The uniforms and helmets of the Dirigenters set them apart.

It was difficult for Lon to tell friend from foe. He was not certain that he knew all of the militiamen by sight, not under these conditions. At first he concentrated on firing at men coming up onto the hilltop. Then he went to the aid of one of his comrades from third platoon. Anyone attacking a mercenary had to be one of the rebels.

Bayonets and rifle butts, feet and fists. The Norbankers, from both sides, were rough-and-tumble fighters, but few if any had any real training at unarmed combat. The Dirigenters were more than able to hold their own, and with the aid of the loyalist militiamen, eventually pushed the rebels off the crest.

They had to do it on their own, with just the few extra men that Molroney had brought along at the start of the attack, because another foray up the hill had begun, coming over the same ground the first attackers had climbed. And then another probe was launched up the western flank of the hill.

Each small battle was a chaotic realm, independent. The men in one fight could not worry about the others. For the most part they were not even aware of them. Even the Dirigenters with radio links were too hard-pressed to pay attention to anything but the most immediate warnings they heard. A fight fifty yards away might as well have been on a different planet.

Once into the melée, Lon discovered that he did not have to worry about being able to identify a Norbanker as friend or foe. Rebels attacked. Militiamen did not.

Hundreds of hours of drill in bayonet and unarmed combat techniques paid off for Lon. Reaction had to be automatic, reflexive, immediate. There was no time to consciously choose and choreograph movements and blows. The trap was that the Norbanker rebels did not have the same sort of training. They were as likely to come up with an unexpected sequence of moves as with one that cadets at The Springs or recruits in DMC training came up against regularly. But they were even more likely to come in with no thought of skilled bayonetplay at all, charging blindly toward a target, screaming, trying to skewer an enemy before he could react.

Lon faced two of those. They were easy to deal with and

impossible to forget. Block the rebel's rifle to the side, let the man's momentum carry him past, wheel, and either club him with a rifle butt or stick the bayonet into his rib cage. Then make sure that the man would not be able to get up again and resume the fight after your attention had turned elsewhere. And the only way to do that was to make certain that the man was dead.

As the fight continued at the north end of the hill, the Dirigenters gravitated toward each other. As a team they were more than the sum of their individual skills. Lon felt stronger, more confident, with men he knew at his side. The more of them got together, the better he felt. Together, the mercenaries pushed forward, trying to force the rebels off of the hilltop.

The rebels gave ground slowly, reluctantly. Many refused to retreat and fell as the attack lost its momentum. Finally, there were no more rebels left on their feet at the north end of the hill. Lon turned to scan the rest of the crest and spotted the other two areas where fighting was still going on.

"Lieutenant? Should we stay here or move to help?" Lon asked.

"Stay put," was all that Taiters said.

Tebba Girana touched Lon's arm, then pointed toward the northwest section of the hilltop. Several Norbanker militiamen were firing down the slope. "Looks like another batch of rebels coming," Girana said. He detailed three men to stay put and keep watch, then took the rest of the Dirigenters at the north end over to help repel the latest assault.

Eight mercenaries took up positions and fired down into the new rebel force, concentrating on the nearest men, sweeping the upper reaches clear. This time no rebels made it to the top. But there were others coming, in other sections. The rebels appeared to be increasing the frequency of their assaults.

It's not going to take much more to overwhelm us, Lon thought as he followed Girana and Captain Molroney toward the next location, on the east. *We're not going to last till morning. Where the hell is the rest of the battalion?*

25

Two o'clock in the morning. For the first time in more than two hours, the men defending the top of the hill east of Anderson's Creek had a chance to rest and catch their breath—for a few minutes. Nine separate assaults on the ridge had been repelled . . . or destroyed. At last the defenders had a chance to regroup, to take care of their wounded and count the dead. Three mercenaries had died; seven others had been wounded, but only two of those were incapacitated by their injuries; anyone who could still move and hold a weapon would have to fight if more attacks came. Ammunition was checked—and scavenged from the dead and those who were too badly wounded to use what they had.

"It's not good," Lieutenant Taiters said. Sergeant Dendrow, Captain Molroney, and Cadet Nolan were with him, near the center of the hilltop. "They hit us many more times and we're not going to have a bullet left." Some of the militiamen were down to fewer than a half dozen rounds; few had more than twenty. If it were not for captured rebel weapons and ammunition, some of the loyalists would already be without. Among the mercenaries, the situation was not quite so desperate, but no one had a full magazine of rifle ammunition left. And the men with the beamers were all on their last power packs—that meant no more than about fifteen seconds of use.

"Where are the rest of our people?" Molroney asked. "Mine and yours?"

"Off where that gunfire is coming from," Taiters said. That had been audible for the past twenty minutes, since the last fighting on the hill had ended. "A little more than a mile north of us. Half of our people are there. The rest are about the same distance away to the southwest. They plan to cross the creek at the lowest spot you said could be forded."

"At best, it'll take either group twenty minutes to get here, more likely a half hour or more, even without reckoning the opposition," Platoon Sergeant Dendrow said. "Be more realistic to figure that it's going to be an hour, minimum."

"Has that batch to the south of us hit any opposition yet?" Molroney asked.

"Not that I've heard," Taiters said. "Nothing more than a small patrol, anyhow. But the way the land lies, they'll need longer to get to us than the others, even if the fight to the north ends right now and the group on the south doesn't have to fight at all before they reach us."

"We've got a good chance yet," Dendrow said. "Anyway, maybe we've blunted the rebels' enthusiasm. We've had—what?—almost twenty-five minutes without any attacks now."

"They'll be back," Molroney said. "They've had a taste of blood tonight. And as soon as they find out that we've got reinforcements close, they'll want to finish us off before the odds go against them."

"They've got to be able to hear that shooting, even if they haven't had any messages get through," Lon said, his voice as dulled as the others. There was no longer any hint of enthusiasm or excitement left in him. He was even too exhausted for fear.

"I expect you're right, lad," Molroney said, glancing toward the sound of the gunfire. "And I expect they're getting into position for their next attack now. It won't be long."

• • •

Molroney and the others had scarcely returned to their positions along the perimeter when the first rebels of a new attack were spotted coming up the slope on the southeast. This time the rebels did not try to stagger their assaults, or overlap them as they had before. They came up both sides and ends of the hill at once.

Short on ammunition for their rifles, the mercenaries freely used their also-dwindling supply of grenades. Conditions were poor for grenade launchers. They were meant for longer range, not for firing downhill at men on a slope below them. The rocket-propelled grenades tended to go too far, or to ricochet away from their targets before exploding. But the Dirigenters used them for as long as possible, aiming them as close as practical. The few remaining hand grenades were husbanded, used when the attackers got to within twenty or twenty-five yards. It was against training to use them that close—the killing radius was nominally thirty yards—but the terrain made it possible.

Lon used his pistol first, saving what ammunition he had left for his rifle until the fight closed to bayonet range. Sometimes a blade would not come free and had to be blown loose with a bullet. He emptied the magazine in his pistol and reloaded—his last clip for the handgun. When that too was empty, Lon had no time to reholster the weapon. He merely dropped it in his hurry to get his right hand back on his rifle stock. The rebels were almost to the crest.

Lon's mind had attained a sort of numbness, insulation against the havoc around him, the killing and dying, the odor of gunpowder and fear, the sight of blood and gore. Conscious thought was virtually absent. His training carried him and his comrades—as it was meant to do.

At first he was not even aware of the slash he took across the left side of his body, a tear from the armpit to the bottom rib. A rebel had come at him with a bayonet, and Lon had been just a fraction of a second slow in his attempt to parry the thrust. Lon turned toward the man, bringing his rifle butt up and around, and clubbed him from behind as the rebel's momentum carried him by. Then Lon took a step closer and brought his own bayonet down into the middle of the fallen man's back, twisting the blade as it went in, then propping a foot on the man's back as he pulled the blade back out, slicing, snapping a rib.

Someone else bumped into Lon, staggering him. He turned as he fought to regain his balance, and almost fell. The man who had bumped into him was on the ground, dead. It was a Dirigenter. Lon knelt and opened the helmet visor—Raphael Macken, from Girana's squad.

Sorry, Mack, Lon thought. There was time for no more. He was already back on his feet, looking for the next man he would have to fight. Rebels were still coming up the slope.

It looks like this is it. Lon raised his rifle and fired at one man who was a clear target—ten feet away. That man tumbled backward, off of the crest. Lon saw movement to his left and turned, bringing his rifle around to parry another reckless bayonet charge.

But this rebel did not depend on the blade his rifle carried. Lon saw a muzzle flash and felt fiery pain in his shoulder as the bullet spun him halfway around. His return shot was a reflex. That it hit at all was absolute chance; that it destroyed the rebel's face was incredible serendipity. Lon watched the man he had just shot stagger backward before he fell, dead three steps before he fell, unaware that he himself was falling, settling to the ground almost in slow motion. It was not until his buttocks hit rock and he fell backward that Lon realized what had happened to him.

Lon tried to get back to his feet, but his body would not respond. He had trouble taking in a breath. Inhaling hurt. He looked at his shoulder. The wound did not appear to be all that serious, not nearly as bad as his injuries in the earlier fight. The bullet had merely carved a notch across the outside of his shoulder. It had not gone deep into the joint or broken bone.

Shock. Lon felt himself blink, slowly. *I've lost a lot of blood. I'm in shock.* That was not good. He squinted, focusing against the rising pain in his shoulder and side, concentrating, trying to force his mind to ignore the injury—injuries—and get back to work.

I can't just lie here. I've got to get up. The fight's not over. He felt a surge of fear. The image of a rebel coming along and sticking him with a bayonet had run through his mind. *Like squashing a bug. I don't want to die like that.*

He managed to turn half onto his side and brought his rifle around and used the weapon as a prop to help him get to his knees and then, after a rest, to his feet. Lon swayed unsteadily, looking for the nearest danger. His vision was blurred. Squinting seemed to help relieve that, but only minimally.

Someone ran at him, rifle and bayonet coming around into line. Lon got his rifle's muzzle lowered and pulled the trigger, not even certain whether he had a bullet left in the weapon. But it fired, and the rebel went down. The recoil made Lon stagger backward a step and nearly knocked him flat.

"Here, stick with me." A hand gripped Lon's arm. He turned his head, blinking again. Corporal Girana. "You're hurt."

"I'll manage," Lon said, though it was an effort.

"Not like that, you won't," Girana said. Lon did not see the foot that the corporal swung, knocking his legs out from under him. Tebba caught Lon on the way down, lowered him almost gently to the ground. "Just stay there," he said. "Use whatever ammo you've got left if you have to, but stay down."

Sure, Lon thought as a wave of dizziness broke over him and flowed past, dissipating. *Just sit here and let someone kill me. No way.* But neither could he get back up right away. It was not just that Tebba stayed close. When Lon *tried* to move, the dizziness returned and he had to stop.

I'll just rest for a minute. Then I'll be ready, he told

himself. He had to squeeze his eyes shut again. The pain in his arm and side was mounting, and the dizziness stayed longer each time it returned. *Am I going to faint?* That felt . . . ludicrous. Lon leaned forward, using his rifle as a prop again, bending his head forward, trying to stop the blood from draining away from his brain. *I've got to stay conscious. I've got to stay awake.*

The vomit came as a total surprise. Lon scarcely had time to lift his faceplate to let it out. Three wrenching spasms later, he felt weaker—but the last of his vertigo was gone. He spat several times to get the foul taste from his mouth, and thought about trying to get a drink of water to wash out his mouth more thoroughly.

First things first. He looked at his shoulder. It was still bleeding, but not at any great rate. Then he twisted around to look at his left side and saw the long gash there. His battledress shirt was split, and soaked with blood all along the side. *Where did that come from?* Lon wondered. He needed a moment to recall the encounter in which it had happened. He could not tell if the cut was still bleeding. Blood was certainly not *gushing,* so no arteries or major veins had been severed. He fumbled at his web belt for the first-aid pouch, uncertain whether the bandage he carried would be sufficient to cover the wound in his side. *Find the deepest spot and make sure at least that much is covered,* he told himself. *Cover as much of it as possible.* For the time being, the fighting going on around him completely escaped his notice. He had to concentrate to do anything, and seeing to his injuries was, momentarily, more important. He was scarcely aware of Tebba Girana hovering nearby, making certain that no rebels got to him. And he was certainly not aware that the pace of fighting had slowed—finally. He got the bandage out, unwrapped, and in position over the long cut on his side. The bandage was self-adhesive. Lon would have been unable to tie it in place.

There, that's done, he thought with relief. He rested for a moment, then started to look around again. He saw that

Tebba was still on his feet, then realized that there were no rebels close to them. There was still fighting on the bloody ridge, but it was farther off. From his position on the ground, Lon's field of view was restricted. He could see only a small portion of the crest. There was no way to tell what the fighting might be like farther away.

Not aware of how slowly he was moving, Lon levered himself up onto one knee and braced himself by leaning against his rifle, the side of his helmet against the forestock. To Lon it seemed to be just a few seconds that he rested that way, not the four minutes it really was. Although no longer dizzy, he still felt weak, unable to collect the energy to move any farther.

Finally stirring himself to the attempt, he used his hands to ''crawl'' up his rifle, relying on that support until he was—more or less—on his feet, bent over, his hands locked around the muzzle of his rifle, still dependent on that third ''leg.'' Tears were streaming down his face, unnoticed, at the effort it took to get to his feet and stay there.

Where is the rest of the battalion? Why aren't they here yet? he asked himself. Slowly he lifted his head, blinking to clear his vision. He wanted to know what was going on around him. For the first time, he had a second to marvel at the fact that he had been unmolested during the time when he had been unable to defend himself.

Two men in DMC battledress were walking toward him, slowly, each holding his rifle in one hand, casually. Lon tried to straighten up, wondering who they were. Behind tinted visors they were anonymous, and nothing about their posture or movement suggested familiarity to Lon.

''Is the fighting over?'' Lon asked, lifting his faceplate enough to talk freely. He looked around. Where had Tebba gotten to? Lon did not see him.

''Near enough, I expect.'' Lon recognized Sergeant Dendrow's voice, though he had never heard it sound quite so strained before. ''I hope.''

''Tebba was here just a minute ago,'' Lon said, looking

around again. "I don't know where he's gotten to."

"He's off tending to the rest of his squad, Nolan," Dendrow said. "You look like you need some help."

"I'm okay," Lon said, nodding very slowly. "I'm okay now."

"Lieutenant Taiters is dead," Dendrow said. "He was killed in the last big attack, maybe forty-five minutes ago."

"No!" Vertigo swirled closer to Lon, poised to reclaim him, threatening his stability.

"I'm afraid so," Dendrow said. "Captain Molroney too. And a lot of other good men, ours and militia."

"The battalion got here?" Lon asked, his mind distracted by the fact that the platoon sergeant had said that Taiters had been killed forty-five minutes earlier. It did not seem possible that the fight, and Lon's efforts to recover from his wounds, could have taken that much time. He sat down suddenly, as if standing had simply become too much of an effort.

"They're close," Dendrow said. "Close enough that the rebels attacking us pulled back to concentrate against the rest of our people and the rest of the Norbanker militia. There can't be more than a dozen or so rebels still up here, and they'll be accounted for soon."

Lon looked up, the dizziness gone again. He turned his head, listening to the fighting. "I hear it," he said, nodding. "Have you heard anything about how that's going yet?"

Dendrow and the other soldier—who still had not lifted his faceplate or spoken—squatted by Lon. "The colonel thinks that the rebels have put everything they've got into this one," Dendrow said. "It's a real donnybrook, but there doesn't look to be any doubt about the outcome."

"Then we can get on with the training?" Lon started to try to get to his feet again.

"Then we can get on with the training," Dendrow agreed, moving quickly to catch Nolan as he fell backward. Lon had finally passed out.

26

Inchoate nightmares chased each other through Lon's mind in such rapid succession that he could hold on to nothing of them. There was only a vague realization that they were present, a web from which he was powerless to escape. But neither was he able to grasp pain or discomfort, or sense the duration of his sojourn in limbo. Even when his mind started to climb back toward consciousness, he could hold nothing of what was transpiring inside his head or happening to his body. It was not until he was actually waking that he realized that the experience had not been like the other time. When he opened his eyes and saw that he was not in a trauma tube, he was not surprised. A tube would have prevented most of the mental nonsense.

"How do you feel?"

Lon blinked. It was daylight. The sun was out. He did not recognize the face that was looking down at him. The man was dressed in the work uniform of ship's crew, the insignia of a medical orderly on his chest. "I've felt better," Lon said, his voice cracking over the words. He tried to clear his throat.

"Here, have a sip of water." The orderly held Lon's head up and brought a canteen to his lips, but did not leave it in place long enough to begin to quench Lon's thirst.

"Not too much," the orderly said. "You've had a rough time. We didn't have enough trauma tubes to go around, and the ones who were hurt worst had to have priority. All we could do for you was pump in blood bugs and painkillers. You'll have to do four hours in a tube on the way home to get rid of the scars and patch up the damage." He smiled. "Like as not, they'll schedule you for a night in. That way you won't miss any duty at all."

"On the way home? What about the couple of months of training we were supposed to provide?"

"Don't know about that, mate. Word I had is that this battalion will be going home in a couple of days. Maybe they're going to have somebody else come in for the training. Or maybe that's been called off. They don't tell me everything. I'm lucky if they tell me when it's time for chow."

"When can I get back to my mates?"

"Soon as you feel fit enough to get up and walk. Don't be in any big hurry about it, though. Sit up, have something to eat—if you can stomach food yet—and have a drink or two of water. That'll go a long way toward making you feel fit. Just don't push it. Remember, you haven't had your gig in a tube."

Lon sat up. There was still a little pain in his left shoulder and side—another reminder that he had not been in a trauma tube—and he still felt short on energy, but there was no hint of dizziness or nausea.

"I guess I'm going to make it then," he said under his breath. *Not like some.* Lieutenant Taiters came to mind. *I wonder how it happened?*

"You'll make it, in my professional opinion," the medical orderly said with a short laugh. "I'll leave this canteen with you. Yours were empty. And I've left you a meal pack here as well, straight from ship's stores, not the battle rations you've been living on."

Lon nodded his thanks and reached for the water. The medical orderly got to his feet. "Take it slow with the water for a bit. You have any problems, there'll be one of us around. If not, good luck."

•   •   •

He ate slowly, savoring each bite as if it had come from a gourmet kitchen instead of ship's stores, and taking a lot of small sips of water. The water was actually cool, not tepid, like most of the water he had drunk since coming to Norbank.

While he ate, Lon looked around. He was in a valley with at least forty other wounded men. Most were still on their backs. A few were up and eating. All looked the worse for wear. Lon was not certain if the valley was one he had seen before, or just where it was.

The sun was high enough that it left no shadow on the slope to the east, but Lon had to pick up his helmet and look at the timeline to see that it was after ten o'clock in the morning. He put the helmet on after he finished eating and selected the channel that would connect him to Sergeant Dendrow.

"The medicos are turning me loose for now," Lon said when Dendrow answered his call. "Where do I find you?"

"Don't try," the platoon sergeant said. "Just stay put. We'll pick you up in about twenty minutes."

"I'm okay now, Sergeant, really. I can make it on my own."

"Maybe, but save the effort. We've just got orders to move back to the capital, and we've got to go right past where you're at to get there."

Lon chuckled. It was not so much returning humor as simple relief at the prospect of getting back to his unit, his friends. "Okay, I'll be here. I've got nowhere else to go." There was a temptation to stay on the line, to continue chatting, just for the sake of hearing a familiar voice, but Lon knew that it would not be proper. Nor did he call Corporal Girana or get on that squad's frequency. The reunion would come almost soon enough. He could wait.

Fortified as much by that as by the food and water he had consumed, Lon felt stronger, better. The pains in his shoulder and side seemed somehow to recede. He got to his feet carefully, testing, waiting for any increase in his discomfort, or a feeling of greater weakness, but neither came. *I guess I am going to make it,* he conceded.

A few cautious steps reinforced his optimism. *No one's going to have to carry me.* He looked around the open-air hospital with a little more attention. Some thirty yards away, one soldier stood guard over several dozen weapons. Lon looked at the ground near where he had been lying. His rifle was not there. The web belt with his pistol—the holster anyway, Lon recalled dropping the handgun on the ground during the battle and he had never had a chance to retrieve it—was also gone.

I guess I'd better see if my rifle got here, at least, Lon thought, starting toward the guard. The soldier looked up as Lon approached, then lifted his visor. Lon did not know his name but recognized the face. He thought the man was from Charlie Company.

"My weapons weren't with me," Lon said. Then he identified himself. "I still had a rifle when I was hit last night. The pistol might have been lost before."

"You remember the serial numbers?" the guard asked.

Lon recited his rifle's serial number first. The guard pulled his helmet down to scan the list he called up on his head-up display. Then he lifted his visor again and went almost directly to the rifle and pulled it free from the stack. Lon took the weapon, checked to make certain that the safety was on, then pulled the bolt back to see if there was a round in the chamber. There was not. The magazine was empty as well.

"What about the pistol?" the guard asked. "Just in case it was turned in."

The sidearm was also there, and back in its holster. "That's more than I expected," Lon said. "Thanks." There was no need for him to sign for the weapons. The camera in the guard's helmet would have recorded the transaction.

"That's what I'm here for," the guard said. "That and to make sure nobody comes in and steals them."

"One question. Just where are we? How far from the hill where we fought last night?"

"You were in the platoon up on the hill?"

Lon nodded. The guard pointed due north. "That's where you were, right there," he said. "Top of that hill."

Lon turned and looked. Nothing about the hill looked familiar from this angle. He could not even see the thicket to the west of it, or Anderson's Creek. "Looks different now," he said. "Thanks." Then he turned and walked away, looking for the rest of the platoon, wondering if it was just third platoon or the whole company—or perhaps the entire battalion—that was heading back to Norbank City.

Lon was sitting under a tree when Alpha Company arrived—walking in loose columns rather than marching. It was shocking to see how shorthanded the company appeared. *Maybe it's not all casualties,* Lon thought, trying to reassure himself. *Some of them could still be on duty, just not with the rest of the men.* But he was not comforted by that possibility.

The company took five minutes, resting while officers and noncoms checked to see if any of their other wounded were ready to return to duty. Lon felt guilty that he had not even looked around among the other casualties to see if he knew any of them. It had not even crossed his mind.

Third platoon—what was left of it—welcomed him back warmly. There were missing faces. Lieutenant Taiters had not been the only one killed on top of the nameless hill. And there were men who had been shipped back to *Long Snake* in trauma tubes. Of Lon's special friends in second squad, only Dean Ericks was missing—and Phip and Janno were both quick to tell Lon that Dean was only wounded, that he had been among the first casualties sent back up to the ship, and that he would be all right. "Probably in better shape than you are, right now," Phip said, pointing at Lon's torn and bloody battledress top.

"Is it true that we're going right back to Dirigent?" Lon asked. "That's what the medical orderly said he had been told."

"I guess," Phip said. "Tebba said we're all going back to the ship anyway, today or tomorrow. The old man must be calling in someone else to do the training part of the contract."

Girana came over. He welcomed Lon back, then said, "We're going home. Delta Company is staying over to handle the training. *Tyre* is going to stick around to ferry them back to Dirigent afterward." *Tyre* was the supply ship that had accompanied *Long Snake*. Earlier in its career, *Tyre* had served as a one-company transport. It would not be as comfortable as the larger and newer *Long Snake*, but it could handle the chore.

"So the rebellion is over?" Lon asked.

Tebba shrugged. "I guess they figure there aren't enough rebels left to be that big a threat. This is just rumor, but the word is that more than two thousand of them have been killed since we got here. I know for a fact that the militia collected more than twelve hundred rebel rifles this morning, from a like number of bodies."

Lon could not repress a slight shudder. "Bodies? No prisoners?"

"Not many," Tebba said. "I know of only five rebels who were taken alive and unwounded. There may be a hundred or more who were wounded too badly to keep on fighting. They're being cared for by our people right now. Guess the old man doesn't trust them to the government. Don't say as I blame him."

The walk back to Norbank City was taken in easy stages. The company stopped for five minutes each half hour. Even so, it took only two hours to make the trip. The people in the capital were in a festive mood, despite the fact that their militia companies had suffered 38 percent casualties—killed and wounded—in the previous night's battle. No one seemed to have any doubt that the danger of the Divinist rebellion was past, that they would be able to handle those who remained.

Twenty minutes after Alpha Company reached the city, Bravo arrived. They were guarding the few prisoners who were not wounded. Tebba Girana had missed the count. Bravo had eight rebels with them.

More than a hundred civilians came to stare at the prisoners, to jeer and curse. The soldiers of Bravo's first platoon kept the civilians away, forming a ring around the prisoners, rifles at port arms. The rest of the company remained nearby, but not overtly part of the protection. Alpha Company was also close, in case things got out of hand.

I don't give much for the odds of them surviving long after we leave, Lon thought. *Somebody gave this mob the idea, they might try to stone the prisoners to death right now.*

It took fifteen minutes before a platoon of Norbanker militia arrived, escorting Colonel Alfred Norbank, the commander of the militia. Colonel Norbank went straight to Captain Wallis Ames, Bravo Company's commander.

"We'll take these men off your hands now, Captain," Colonel Norbank said. "I've brought sufficient guards."

"Glad to have your men here to help, Colonel," Captain Ames said, "but I can't turn them over to you yet. Sorry. My colonel told me to see them safely into town, but I don't have orders to turn them over to local authorities. And until Colonel Flowers does issue those orders, these men are still my responsibility."

Colonel Norbank hesitated, as if ready to argue the point. Lon Nolan watched closely. He was only twenty yards from the confrontation. He could see how tense the colonel was, and he saw when he made his decision. Colonel Norbank's posture relaxed, just slightly.

"I understand orders, Captain," he said, nodding. "I think it is a waste, but we will wait for your colonel to release these traitors." He turned to the militia lieutenant with him and gave orders for his platoon to take up positions around the prisoners, with the Dirigenters. Once they were in place, Colonel Norbank went closer to the captured rebels himself. He started around the group, moving clockwise, just inside the circle of soldiers and militiamen who were guarding them.

"They don't seem so fierce now," he said, turning toward Captain Ames, who had remained outside the circle.

What happened next came too quickly for anyone to stop it, or even give warning, but at the same time, Lon thought it seemed to be happening in slow motion.

He caught a movement among the prisoners out of the corner of an eye. One of them seemed to reach into the front of his trousers, as if he were going to scratch himself. The hand seemed to reach deep into his crotch. When the hand came back out, the other hand went to meet it. Lon blinked as the realization hit him that the man had managed to hide a hand grenade, and had it out now.

By the time Lon realized what was happening and opened his mouth to shout a warning, it was too late. The prisoner lunged toward Colonel Norbank, extending the grenade in front of him—holding it, not throwing it. Colonel Norbank turned toward the rebel. His mouth dropped open. Surprise blossomed on his face.

Then the grenade exploded, erasing not just the look of surprise but the face as well.

Lon was on his way down to the ground when the blast sounded, his warning cut off. There were screams from civilians, farther off, and cries of pain from wounded closer in—Dirigenters and Norbanker militiamen . . . and from a few of the other prisoners as well.

As soon as the shock wave passed him, Lon was back on his feet, rifle up and moving forward, even though he still had no ammunition for the weapon. Scores of other mercenaries were also moving in, rifles covering the remaining prisoners, hurrying to see to their comrades as well.

• • •

It took time to sort through the confusion. The prisoner who had set off the grenade was dead, as were two of his comrades. So was Colonel Norbank. Two other militiamen and one Dirigenter also had died. A dozen people had wounds, most fairly minor; the dead had absorbed most of the shrapnel. The remaining prisoners were stripped to make certain that no one else had any lethal surprises. The civilians were ordered away. They went, most of them quiet.

The wounded were separated from the dead and treated. The surviving prisoners were marched off toward the edge of town. They had not been permitted to put their clothing back on.

Lon went toward where the man who had exploded the grenade lay, uncovered, his head, arms, and the upper part of his torso horribly mutilated. His hands had simply vanished.

Lon shook his head as he looked at the body. "How can anyone hate that hard?" he asked himself, unaware that he had spoken the question, or that anyone was near enough to hear.

"Some people don't know any other way," Tebba Girana said. "For guys like this, dying is the only way to stop."

Epilogue

Autumn had settled in on Dirigent City by the time Second Battalion of Seventh Regiment returned from Norbank. Shuttles landed the men at the public spaceport late on a Tuesday morning. Buses were waiting to carry the returnees through the capital to the main entrance to the DMC's home base.

Lon looked out the window of the coach, watching the people they passed. Few of the civilians gave the military vehicles more than a passing glance. Lon assumed that the men out there who did stop walking to stare were in the Corps themselves, or had been. Some brought themselves to attention.

When the caravan reached base, the Corps was waiting to welcome them. It took three buses to carry the dead of Second Battalion. Those passed in review first, followed by the rest of the battalion. The men of the Corps stood at attention. The officers saluted. Regimental flags were dipped to honor the men coming home.

Tomorrow would see another formation, this time just Seventh Regiment. Lon would stand before the entire regiment while Colonel Arnold Gaffney pinned the red enamel and gold pips of a lieutenant on his shoulders.

But first—tonight—Lon was going to town. He planned to drink until he could no longer remember the blood rite that had earned those diamond-shaped pips for him.